when stars collide

USA TODAY BESTSELLING AUTHOR
MICALEA SMELTZER

when stars collide

© Copyright 2016 Micalea Smeltzer

All rights reserved. This book or any portion thereof may not be reproduced or used in any manner whatsoever without the express written permission of the publisher.

This is a work of fiction. Names, characters, businesses, places, events and incidents are either the products of the author's imagination or used in a fictitious manner. Any resemblance to actual persons, living or dead, or actual events is purely coincidental.

Cover design: Emily Wittig Designs
Photos: Regina Wamba
Models: Anthony Kemper and Hannah Peltier
Edited by Wendi Temporado of Ready, Set, Edit

one
...

thea

HOLY MOTHER OF ALL HANGOVERS.

I'd succumbed to the lure of Vegas and gotten completely wasted. Granted, that's what everyone did in Las Vegas but I like to think I *usually* have more sense than the social norm.

I rub my eyes and blink them open. The hotel room comes into formation around me. The walls are a warm golden color and the flat screen on the wall plays some home improvement show. I can see the bathroom from the bed, the tiled walls and large soaking tub.

I roll over onto my side, hoping I can sleep off the hangover, and reel back.

"Oh my *God*," I cry, flailing in bed.

My legs kick the sleeping guy beside me.

Not just *any* sleeping guy.

Oh no.

Xander Kincaid, my brother's *best friend*, lays in the bed beside me.

His dark hair tumbles over his forehead and his cheeks are covered with several days worth of scruff. His chest is bare and...holy shit. He's naked.

I look down.

Oh God, I'm naked too.

"What's wrong?" He asks, reaching his left hand out to pull me closer to him. That's when I see it.

"Is that a wedding band?" I scream shrilly.

His eyes narrow. "You don't fucking remember?"

I shake my head and look at my own hand. A thin silver band rests on my finger. "What did we *do?*"

He sits up in bed and I try to ignore how adorably rumpled he looks with his hair sticking up.

Everything begins flooding back to me in quick bursts.

Drinks.

Kissing.

Laughter.

Confessions of love and desire.

A wedding chapel.

Vows.

Rings.

A contract.

"We're married," I whisper. "Holy shit." It's all I've ever wanted—to be with Xander, but not like this. Never like this. "My brother is going to kill us."

Xander's face contorts with...is that irritation?

"Why does it matter what your brother thinks?"

I scoff. "Because he's my brother and *your* best friend."

Xander clenches his jaw and looks away.

I tumble from the bed and scour the floor for my clothes. I can feel his eyes on me but I don't dare look at him for fear of turning into a tomato. I find my dress and slip it over my head. Fuck a bra, I just need some clothes on.

I hold my hands out in front of me in a gesture of *I have this under control* when I definitely *don't* have this under control.

"I'm sure we can just go back to the chapel and undo this. I mean, this is Vegas. If you can get married in a drive-thru you can get divorced too, right?"

"*Divorced?*" He looks appalled that I'd suggest such a thing.

I laugh, but there's no humor in the tone. "We can't stay married."

He shakes his head roughly and bunches the sheets in his hands. I nearly groan. His hands...his hands had felt like the best kind of sin when he touched me last night.

"Why not?" He asks, and I know him well enough to see that he's straining to stay calm.

"Because it would be wrong." *Doesn't he know that?* "My brother—"

"Dammit, Thea," he snaps and anger pulses in his dark gaze. "Leave your brother out of it. I'm talking about you and me." He flicks a finger between the two of us and his wedding band reflects the light pouring in from the open window. I can't believe this is happening. This is the kind of thing you read about celebrities doing, not normal people like Xander and me, but shit happens. His voice softens and he looks at me tenderly. My stomach flips. It's the same one he's given me for years, the one that makes me yearn and ache for more, and now that I have it I'm trying to throw it away. "There's always been something between us. Don't deny it."

I swallow thickly, my pulse racing. "I know," I sigh heavily. "But it's not like you asked me on a date to see where things might go—we got *married*. Marriage is a big deal."

"Don't you think I know that?" He stands and I avert my gaze to the ceiling, even though I want nothing more than to check out his perfectly toned body from years of playing football. I can remember running my hands over his abs and grabbing his ass, crying out— "Thea?"

Suddenly he's right in front of me and I can see every amber fleck in his brown eyes.

He takes my face between his hands and I know I shouldn't let him touch me—my brain turns to mush any time he does—but I'm frozen to the ground. His intense gaze alone is enough to hold me captive.

"Why are you fighting this?" His breath is a tender caress against my face. He touches his lips tenderly to mine and my traitorous body curves into his. His chest is still bare and his skin is warm beneath my fingers. It's soft like silk and I stroke my fingers against the dents in his stomach like I'm playing an instrument. He rests his forehead against mine and I fight to keep my composure. Xander's kisses set my world afire and bring color to everything. "Why?" He asks again.

"This is a big deal, how can you not see that?" I defend and shove him away slightly. I can't think straight with him so close. All my brain can focus on is his slightly woodsy scent and the feel of his lips against mine.

His dark brows knit together. "I know it's a big deal—I don't take marriage lightly, but..." He lifts his hands in a gesture of *I don't know*. "You and I...there's always been something between us. Some spark that we've both fought for so fucking long and Thea?" His shoulders sag. "I'm tired of fighting. Maybe this is fate's way of finally bringing us together."

"Fate?" I repeat in a whisper. "I didn't know you believed in such a thing."

He shrugs and lifts his hand to reach for me but lets it drop like he's scared I'll reject his touch. "I have to believe there's some bigger reason for this," he admits and looks down at the ring on his finger and then on mine. "Don't you think?"

I look away. I can't stand seeing the hope and yearning in his eyes. It's killing me because I want him. I want this. I want an *us*. I've known Xander since I was in diapers. We grew up together and even though he's my brother's *best* friend, he's always been my friend too. He stars in almost every memory of my childhood and as we've gotten older he's always been there too. I've dated here and there and *always* compared the guy to him—which meant my relationships never lasted long because no one was ever as good as Xander.

Before I can reply there's a knock on the door and then the nob rattles. "Thea, get up. We have to get breakfast and leave. I can't get Xander up. He probably found some hooker and is passed out in his bed. I'm going down to the lobby to see if they'll give me a key to his room. You better be ready in thirty minutes," my brother, Cade, says through the closed door.

My eyes, widened with horror, dart to Xander who stands there with an amused smile. I glare at him and mouth, "Hooker? Really?"

He knocks on the door again and says, "Are you up?"

"Yeah," I call back with a shaky voice. "I'm up."

Xander bites his lip to hold in his chuckle. I'm glad *someone* finds this amusing.

"Good," he says through the door. "Thirty minutes."

I hold my breath and listen to the sounds of his feet against the floor heading away. I sag in relief and Xander busts out laughing. My arm snaps out and I smack my hand against his stomach, which only makes him roar with more laughter.

"You better grab your clothes and get back to your room before my brother discovers you're not in there."

He shrugs. "Let him."

I throw my hands up. "How can you be so blasé about this? I *know* my brother has threatened you numerous times about coming anywhere near me."

He picks his shirt up off the floor and tugs it on. "I'm not going to let your brother keep me from what I want and I want you," he says huskily, his eyes lingering on my lips.

The way he stares at me makes me feel like a small frightened animal backed into a corner by the big bad wolf.

"We have to ditch him on the way to the airport," I say suddenly. "We have to find the church we got married in and see if they can undo this." I wave my hands through the air like I can bibbidi-bobbidi-boo this away.

Where's my fairy godmother when I need her?

Xander's jaw clenches and he looks away. I know I've made him mad because I'm not willing to accept this is our fate. I'm not going to lie, I've dreamed of marrying Xander on more than one occasion. It was all I hoped for as a little girl when he was the dark-haired boy across the street who shared his animal crackers with me and carried me home when I fell off my bike. But I *never* imagined it would be like this—that I would barely even remember it.

"Whatever you want," he mumbles, not meeting my gaze.

I stand frozen and watch as he grabs his phone and slips his jeans on over his boxer-briefs. He pauses at the door and I expect him to look back and say something, *anything*, but he leaves. I can't say I blame him.

I take a quick shower, washing the scent of Xander's body from mine in case Cade can sniff it out like a bloodhound. I feel sick to my stomach that Xander walked out of my room with things still unresolved between us but I can't see why he doesn't see the issue. I'm *nineteen*. I only have one year at college under my belt and beyond that I have no clue what I want to do with my life. A marriage makes things even more complicated.

I dress comfortably in a pair of black leggings and a loose

gray tank top. I twist my long hair back into a sloppy ponytail and swipe some gloss on my lips. I pack my bags hastily and I'm almost done when Cade reappears at my door, knocking loudly.

"I swear to God, Thea, if you've fallen back asleep—"

I groan and run to open the door. "I'm awake and ready. I'll meet you in the lobby in five minutes." I purposely position my body so that he can't see in the room. It's still a mess with evidence left behind that I don't need him to see.

"Fine," he groans. "I'll be downstairs getting breakfast."

I watch him retreat and then close the door.

Before I can make it back to my suitcase there's another knock on the door.

"Cade, I'm going to punch you in the face," I seethe and swing the door open, ready to maim my big brother. "Oh, thank God. It's you." I step aside and let Xander back in the room.

"Do you need help with your bag?" He asks.

"I'm almost done packing."

I hate the awkward tension hanging in the air between us. It's *never* awkward with us, not like this at least, and I hate it. When things get bad I'm used to running to Xander and having him wrap his arms around me and tell me it's going to be okay, but not this time.

"I'll wait." He gives me a slight smile and I know he feels the tension too.

I finish packing and Xander paces around the room, looking to make sure he hasn't left anything behind in here. There are a few condoms scattered on the floor—let's just say we were making up for a heck of a lot of lost time last night—and he picks them up to throw them away.

"Shit," he curses and I look up from the blouse I was packing away.

"What?" I ask and his silence scares me. "Xander?" I prompt.

"This one's broken," he mumbles, nodding at the condom he holds.

"What?" I say again. "No."

"Thea—"

"I'm going to be sick," I cry, and run for the toilet. I collapse in front of it and heave up everything in my stomach—which isn't much.

Xander's hand touches my back and I flinch. His hand falls away and I can hear him running water in the sink.

I can barely handle the thought of us being *married*, but if I'm pregnant too? There's no hiding a baby.

I sit on the cold tile floor and lean my back against the wall. Xander kneels in front of me and wipes my mouth with a washcloth. His dark eyes are full of worry but he doesn't say anything. There's nothing he *can* say.

He helps me up and I brush my teeth, thankful I hadn't packed my bathroom stuff yet. He disappears into the bedroom and when I emerge from the bathroom I see that he's finished packing my bag for me and waits by the door.

We're both silent as we head next door to his room so he can grab his suitcase. I wait in the hall, fighting tears.

When he comes back into the hall, wheeling his black suitcase behind him, my chin wobbles.

"Thea," he says my name softly, almost pained sounding. "Please don't cry."

"I'm scared," I confess, my voice barely a whisper.

He lets go of his suitcase and pulls me into his arms.

His arms.

My safe place.

I only let myself linger in his arms for a few seconds before I force myself away and wipe the tear from my cheek. I won't let this get to me.

"When we go to leave, follow my lead," he tells me. "Okay?"

I nod.

Xander will take care of this. He'll fix it. That's what he's good at.

The walk down the hall to the elevator seems endless. He reaches out to push the button to call it to our floor and my hand flies out, grabbing his wrist. "The *rings*," I hiss. I completely forgot about them. I hastily rip off mine and go to stuff it in my bag but Xander swipes it from my hand. "Hey," I protest.

"I can't trust you with this," he whispers gruffly. "You might throw it away."

"I wouldn't—"

"I'll hold onto it, for now." He takes his off and shoves both deep into his pocket. I should be relieved to be rid of the ring, to not even have it in my possession, but I feel slightly empty inside.

The shiny elevator doors slide open and we step inside. My heart is beating so loud in my ears that I can pick out each individual beat. I look to Xander and I can't read his emotions. His face is a mask of steely calm, like he can take on the world and not bat an eye. It's what makes him such a good football player. The other team never knows what he's thinking.

The doors open to the lobby and we wheel our bags out.

I'm glad to be going home. The past week—last night especially—has worn me out. I never imagined when the three of us joined Xander's dad for a business trip—to learn more about the architecture business—that it would lead to this. I guess that's what we get for extending our trip into the weekend so we could have a break.

And somehow, in all the chaos of this morning, I've forgotten the fact that once I get home there will be no avoiding Xander. We live in the same house, our rooms side by side, and I'm his assistant at his dad's firm for the summer. My eyes dart to his profile—the elegant slope of his nose, and slight pout of his lips—and swallow thickly. Even if we get this taken care of today, I'm going to have to endure his presence every second of every day. It's already been a struggle, fighting my feelings, and after this? I don't know if I can do it.

Xander and I meet Cade in the dining area and leave our bags at the table he secured before going over to grab our food. Xander piles a stack of steaming pancakes on his plate and my stomach rolls. I don't think I can eat. I grab an orange juice and a straw and start back to the table.

"You need to eat, Thea," Xander calls after me.

I look at him over my shoulder and worry knits his

brows. "I'm not hungry."

He starts to say something else but I don't stay to listen. I slide into the chair across from Cade and he eyes my orange juice. "Hung over?" He asks.

"Yep," I lie. I might've woken up that way, but the whole *We got married* thing sobered me up real fast.

I sip my orange juice as Xander pulls out the chair between Cade and me and sits down. I expect him to protest on the not eating thing some more but instead he hands me a granola bar and says, "Just in case you get hungry on the flight."

Always worrying about me. "Thanks." I tuck the bar in my purse and thankfully Cade pulls him into conversation and I'm left with my thoughts.

I have no idea what Xander has planned for us to ditch Cade but I hope it's good. Cade's not stupid and he'll figured it out if it's not a believable lie.

I begin to worry that Xander's not going to say anything as we throw away our trash and head outside to the waiting taxi line. We start for the first taxi and the driver hops out to help with the luggage.

"Shoot," Xander says, patting his pockets. "I left my phone."

"You left your phone?" I repeat, like *really? That's the best you could come up with?*

Cade looks over at Xander in disbelief. "Seriously, dude?"

Xander's shoulders sag. "You got me, that was a lie." I gasp. He has to be kidding me. He can't tell— "Thea told me she wanted to go to the observation deck at the Stratosphere before we left and I promised I'd take her. You know I don't like to break promises."

"Our flight leaves in two hours," Cade warns. "Couldn't you have done this yesterday?"

Xander shrugs. "There wasn't any time."

You know, because we were too busy getting drunk, married, and fucking like rabbits. Logistics, though.

Cade sighs. "I suppose we can go."

Xander shakes his head. "Maybe you should go on ahead? That way—on the off chance we'd miss the flight, you don't. I'm sure Rae would be upset if she didn't get to see you soon."

Cade purses his lips and his eyes narrow in thought. I expect him to argue but instead he shrugs. "You're right," Cade agrees. "Keep an eye on her." He points a warning finger at Xander.

Despite the fact that I'm nineteen—almost twenty—Cade still treats me like I'm a little girl. He's always been the protective type and while it can be annoying, I know he does it from the best place in his heart.

"And *try*," he pleads, "to not miss the flight."

Xander salutes him. "I'll do my best."

The two of us wheel our bags to the sidewalk and watch as Cade gets in the taxi and leaves.

"Stage one, complete," Xander chimes.

"What's stage two?" I ask.

His dark eyes squint from the bright Vegas sun and he looks toward all the buildings on the strip. "Finding the church."

two

...

thea

WE LEAVE our bags at the front desk, much to the irritation of the receptionist. She only agreed because Xander sweet-talked her while I stood off to the side trying not to roll my eyes.

Xander and I grab one of the waiting taxis and ask to be taken to the nearest church. It seems to be the best place to start considering neither of us knows the exact one where the deed was done. After talking about it, we were able to piece together enough about the interior that we'll know when we find it.

The taxi parks in front of a tan-stoned building with a huge sign out front that says: **Viva Las Vegas. Themed weddings. Themed rooms.**

Xander and I exchange a look before sliding out of the car and into the heat.

"Wait here," Xander orders the driver. When he huffs in irritation, Xander adds, "Keep the meter running."

It doesn't take long for Xander and me to run in and determine that this isn't the chapel we got married in. It also only took the Elvis impersonator a few seconds to openly hit on me. It was gross, but the warning growl from Xander for the man to stay away made it worth it.

We stop at three more places and none of them are the one.

But the fourth looks promising. The outside is white, and it's built more like a traditional church with a steeple. It looks nothing like the gaudy and gimmicky places we've already checked.

Xander glances at me, and I know he feels it too—this place is where it happened.

I slide out of the back of the car and Xander takes my hand. I don't know if it's because he thinks I need the support or *he* needs it. Either way, I don't let go.

We head for the small white chapel and bits and pieces of last night flash through my memory.

Our laughter trickled into the air, and I reached up, wrapping my arms around his neck, and kissed him. There was no fear or hesitation. I kissed him like I'd been doing it forever.

"Are you sure you want to do this?" he asked, sweeping his lips over mine.

"Yes," I breathed, my mind foggy from him more than the alcohol.

His hands slithered to my waist and his thumbs rested on my bare skin at the space where my tank top had ridden up.

"You want to call me your husband?" he asked. His eyes were clear, happy, and wondering—like he couldn't believe this was happening any more than I could.

"More than anything."

He kissed me deeply, stealing my breath, and then we hurried into the chapel.

I glance up at Xander and wonder if he remembers too. His eyes betray nothing, though.

We enter into a foyer with white walls, tile floors, and beams crossing the ceiling. It has a Mediterranean feel to it that seems at odds with the gimmicky glamour of most places in Vegas.

Xander and I stroll further into the building and through an archway that opens up into a room with simple white chairs facing an altar. The building seems to be vacant but there's a door to our right and Xander starts for it. Before we make it, it swings open, and a white-haired man appears. He removes his glasses and grins at us.

"Ah, the young lovers. I'm surprised to see you. I figured you two would be locked away for the next week." I blush at what he implies. "It's rare to see such young, true love in Sin City." I nearly choke at that last bit.

Pain flashes across Xander's face as he looks at me and my stomach takes a tumble out of my body. I don't understand why he wants to stay married to me. It makes no sense. He just graduated from college and has his whole life ahead of him. I don't know why he'd want to be tied down with a wife. With *me*.

The man smiles, waiting for one of us to say something.

Since Xander has paled and looks like he's about to choke on his own tongue, I let go of his hand and step in front of him so I now stand closest to the man.

"We came to see if there's any way we can undo what we did." The man's lips quirk like he's fighting not to laugh. "We can't stay married," I say, hating the way my hands shake and clasping them together so hopefully neither of them notices. "This was a mistake." Even though I can't see Xander, I know that word hurt him, and I instantly regret saying it.

The man frowns. "I'm sorry. I can't help you. Everything was done according to guidelines. According to the law, you're married."

I gulp. "Sir—"

He holds up a hand to stop me. "I understand the lure Las Vegas can have on people. Believe me, I see everything and it's why I usually refuse to perform impromptu weddings. I don't marry people to make money like these other fools." He flicks a finger to encompass the strip. "People come *here* to get married for real. I don't believe it's a coincidence that out of all the chapels on the strip you were drawn here. I promise you this, I wouldn't have performed the ceremony if I hadn't seen something in the two of you. Something special. Hold onto that and don't let go. It's rare."

He starts to move around me, and I grab his arm. I open my mouth to say ... I don't know what I want to say—my mind is completely blank once I absorb his last words.

He pats my hand. "What's done is done."

And then he's gone.

I look to Xander—expecting to see a smug smile—but he looks nearly as confused as I am.

"Well—" I toss my hands in the air "—what do we do now?"

Forget Cade, the thought of telling my parents that I went to Vegas and ended up married ... I might as well dig my own grave in the backyard and save them the trouble.

Xander shakes his head, like he's clearing away his thoughts. "Would it really be so bad?" he asks softly, looking at me from beneath his thick, dark lashes. "Being married to me, I mean?"

I swallow thickly. "No," I admit, and don't miss the flare of desire in his eyes. "But we can't—"

He holds up a hand, urging me to be quiet. "Make me a deal."

"What kind of deal?" I hedge, looking at him skeptically.

"Give me the summer," he pleads. "Give me the summer to prove that this is more than some stupid *mistake*," he grates on the word, "and if at the end of the summer you still want a divorce then I'll sign whatever you want me to."

"And if I don't want a divorce?"

He grins. "Then we'll tell everyone that we're together and married."

"What if *you* decide you want a divorce? What if you decide I'm not right for you?"

His eyes narrow. "Trust me, that isn't happening."

"How do you know?"

He looks away and a muscle in his jaw twitches. "I just

know." I let out a sigh, knowing that's all the answer I'm going to get from him. "Do we have a deal?"

I bite my lip. Three months. It feels like forever right now, but in reality, three months isn't that much time. I know I can hold out for three months. It doesn't matter how sinfully good-looking he is, or ridiculously sweet; at the end of three months I will get that divorce.

"Deal," I say. Before I can blink he takes my face between his mammoth hands and kisses me. I'm breathless when he releases me. "What was that for?" I gasp.

He grins. "Most people shake hands to seal a deal. I figure since you're my wife, we should seal ours with a kiss."

I give him the finger and turn sharply, leaving him behind as I exit the chapel. His laughter echoes behind me, and despite my anger, I smile.

Something tells me the next three months are going to be interesting.

three
...

thea

WE MAKE it to the airport and through security just in time. Cade already stands in line to board the plane and gives us an incredulous look, like he can't believe we cut it that close.

Xander and I step into the back of the line and slowly make our way toward the lady to hand her our boarding passes. She smiles and says a few words and then we're on the ramp to board the plane.

Xander takes my carry-on bag from me and places it into the overhead compartment. I give him a grateful smile before taking my seat. I'm going to be stuck on the plane, sitting between Xander and Cade. Lovely. Thank God it's only a two-hour flight from Las Vegas to Denver. Then, we have a forty-five-minute drive home, but Rae will be picking us up so at least Cade will be distracted.

Xander pulls out his phone and puts his earbuds in, effectively cutting off any sort of conversation I might have with him. Granted, there's not much I can say with my brother right beside us. It's weird, how one day has completely shattered our dynamic. I've known him forever, and never had a shortage of normal things to talk about, but now everything in my head comes back to *us*.

I can't believe I agreed to give him the summer to convince me to stay married to him. There's no way in hell that I will, but I'll have to endure the whole three months as his *wife*. Working with him, coming home to the same house, and all the while keeping this a secret from the ones we love. Knowing Xander, he'd probably be fine with telling everyone what happened, but me ...? I can't. I don't want my family knowing that the first time I was granted any real amount of freedom I ended up married.

Beside me, Cade rubs his hands over his face.

"Tired?" I ask.

"Yes," he answers, swiveling his head toward me. His brown hair falls over his forehead, shielding his blue eyes. "I shouldn't have gone out last night."

I shrug. "You headed back to the hotel before Xander and me." *And thank God for that*.

"What time did you guys head back? Xander did make sure you got back safe, right?" His eyes flare with anger, and I know he'd go off if he thought Xander had left me alone in the middle of Vegas. With an overprotective big brother, and his equally overprotective best friend, it's safe to say I'd never gotten into too much trouble. Except for, you know, when said best friend and I ran off and got married.

"Don't worry, he took me back to my room and tucked me in safe and sound."

More like fucked me into the bed all night long.

"Good." He nods. "I worry about you."

"I know you do." I pat his hand. "But you don't need to. I can take care of myself. I'm tougher than you give me credit for."

He chuckles. "You and Rae both."

He settles into the seat again and I know he's done talking.

The plane goes to take off and Xander ever-so-slightly grazes his fingers against the side of my knee. He knows I hate take-off and landing. He's so incredibly in tune with me. He always has been.

I jolt awake as the plane touches down on the runway.

Xander flashes me a worried look.

"I'm okay," I pant, out of breath like I've been running.

He raises a brow in disbelief and winds the earbud wires around his phone. Beside me, Cade looks ready to jump out of the damn plane. I know he's missed Rae and can't wait to see her. I love that he has that and with someone I call my friend. They both deserve all the happiness in the world.

And don't you?

My eyes flicker to Xander with the thought. I swallow past the lump in my throat as the plane taxis in.

When it finally stops, we let the cabin empty out before grabbing our overhead bags and heading out.

We're all silent as we make our way through the airport and to baggage claim. Cade leads the way, and Xander and I fall in behind him. That's the way it's always been. Cade leading the way, forging ahead.

I glance at Xander, and his dark brows are drawn together as if he's deep in thought. He's always been that way. A thinker. He's smarter than a lot of people give him credit for.

We grab our bags and head for the exit. All the while, Cade types furiously on his phone, most likely letting Rae know we're on our way out.

I nearly jump out of my skin at the feel of Xander's hand on my arm, stopping me. Cade continues on, oblivious.

I look up at Xander, and his eyes flick from Cade's retreating figure down to me.

"What?" I prompt when he doesn't say anything.

He clears his throat. "I want you to know this doesn't change anything." I raise a brow, confused as to where he's going with this. He blows out a heavy breath. "You and me," he elaborates. "Us being married, it doesn't change who we are. We've always been friends. I don't want you to think you can't talk to me."

I nod and admit, "I don't want to lose you."

And I'm terrified that in three months when I tell you I still want the divorce you'll leave me for good.

He nods. "That's all I wanted to say."

Somehow, I doubt that, but I let him off the hook. Cade waits for us by the sliding glass doors.

"Jesus Christ, you guys are slow," he groans when we finally get there. "Rae's outside."

"You could've gone on out," I tell him as we step out into the sunlight. Thankfully, it's not as hot here as Vegas, but the humidity is a killer.

"Yeah, and then have you guys get lost?" He shakes his head.

I glance at Xander, both of us suppressing a laugh. "Yeah," Xander chortles, "because we don't know what your Jeep or girlfriend or *you* looks like."

Cade flips us off while we laugh.

When we spot the Jeep with Rae waiting outside of it, my big, burly, bear of a brother grins like a kid on Christmas and flat-out *sprints* for her. He scoops her up into his arms and spins her around while her giggles carry through the wind to us. It's nice to hear her laugh. Last August, when we were first assigned as roommates, she was so moody and quiet. She recently filled me in on what happened to her a year before coming to college and I completely understand why she was so closed off and cold. I would be too if I'd gone through something like that.

But now that girl is merely a shadow. The Rae she is now smiles, laughs, and cracks jokes. She's practically a whole new person, but I know this is the *real* Rae.

While Cade and Rae are lost in each other, Xander and I sidle up to the car and load our bags into the back. By the time we're done, they've managed to break apart, but they're both sporting the lusty eyes that make me gag.

"How was your trip?" Rae asks.

"Exciting," Xander answers.

Cade snorts. "If you call sitting in a room all day listening to a guy drone on and on about blueprints then, yeah, exciting."

Rae laughs, her hand pressing against his chest as she smiles at him. "But you guys stayed the weekend. Surely that part was fun?"

Cade shrugs. "It would've been better if you were there."

I mock-gag. "Stop," I whine. "I can't take it."

Cade chuckles, his hand sliding to Rae's waist, and nuzzles her neck. "Let's go home."

Those three words are the best thing I've heard all day, and I can't get in the car fast enough. Xander gets in beside me and we're silent the whole drive home, but Rae and Cade don't notice since they never shut up. But I notice the silence, and there's been too much of it between us today, and despite what Xander said about not wanting this marriage to change things between us, I can't help but feel, and know in my gut, that it's changed everything.

We get home, and almost immediately, Cade and Rae leave. After a week apart, they want alone time and they can't really get that with two roommates, which leaves me alone in the house with my *husband*. How fucking weird is that?

Xander and I part ways in the hallway, but immediately bump into each other considering we share a Jack and Jill bathroom. We each unpack our bags in silence, and I swear I can feel each second ticking off in my head.

I put my toothbrush in the holder, right next to his, and look up at him. He's so incredibly tall that I have to tilt my head back to really look at him and I'm by no means short.

Crossing my arms over my chest, I say, "This is ridiculous."

"Glad you agree." He sets his aftershave on the counter.

"I don't know what to say." My hands fall to my sides, shoulders sagging in defeat. "And you know that's unusual for me." I laugh but it sounds forced. "We said this wouldn't change things, but look at us. It already has." I frown.

He crosses his arms over his chest and leans his hip against the counter. He looks me over, trying to read what I'm thinking from my posture, and presses his lips together. "Is it the marriage that has changed things?" he asks. "Or the sex."

I nearly choke on my own tongue. When I sober, I admit, "Both, I guess. It's ... weird." I bite my lip, staring hard at his chest, remembering the way it felt pressed against me. "We crossed a line, and I don't think we can uncross it."

"So why try?" he asks as his arms fall. In one swift move, he's in front of me, cornering me against the wall beside the door leading into my room. His eyes fall to my lips and slowly make their way back up, connecting with mine. "We can still be friends and acknowledge the fact that there's more between us." His fingers ghost against my chin—they touch there and gone in a second, so fast I'm not sure it really happened.

My heartbeat flutters like a frightened bird, trapped behind my ribcage and desperate to break free. I lean my head against the wall, looking up into his dark eyes. They've always looked at me with such ... sweetness and maybe the occasional hint of lust or desire, but right now, he looks at me like I'm the answer to every question he's ever had.

When I don't speak, he adds, "You've already agreed to stay married to me for the summer, I think that implies that we see where things go." He grasps my hips, digging his own into my center and I can feel his hard length. I moan, holding onto his sides so I don't collapse onto the floor. "I want you to know you can talk to me, though. You always have. Your fears, your desires, whatever it is, I'm here to listen."

"Even when it's about you," I breathe.

He chuckles, tipping my chin up. "Even then."

I lay my head against his chest and wrap my arms around his body. He hugs me back, resting his head on top of mine. I feel him exhale a deep breath and his thumbs rub soothing circles on my back.

I step out of his embrace, and he looks me over with uncertainty shimmering in his eyes. "I'm okay," I tell him, knowing he needs to hear it. "Promise."

He nods once and disappears into his room.

I head into my room, smiling at the familiarity. It's good to be home. My room is an explosion of pink and cream. Rae has never been able to get over my love for the color pink. I wouldn't even say that I'm *that* much of a girly girl—I just like the color.

I take a quick shower, only rinsing off my body since I showered at the hotel but felt the need to get the airplane ick off of me.

I change into a pair of cotton pants and a loose t-shirt that slips over my shoulder.

I grab my phone off the dresser and pad downstairs and into the kitchen. It's a little late for lunch, but since we missed out on it from being on the flight and then the drive home, I'm *starving*.

I rustle around in the kitchen and procure everything I need to make a homemade pizza. I already have the dough laid out and am in the process of spreading the sauce when Xander saunters into the kitchen. He's changed into a pair of sweatpants and a thin muscle shirt that I swear he's had since high school.

"Whatcha doin'?" he asks, sliding onto one of the metal barstools that line the kitchen bar.

"I'm hungry, figured you were too. Is pizza okay?" It's a bit late now to ask him, but whatever.

His lips quirk up on one side. "Pizza's great—as long as there's pepperoni."

I hold up the plastic pack with the individually cut slices and shake it. "I'd never forget."

He grins, clasping his hands together and laying them on the counter.

I finish fixing the pizza and stick it in the oven. When I

stand back up, I can't help but notice that his eyes are glued to my ass. "Eyes up here, bud." I point to my eyes.

He chuckles, not at all caring that I caught him looking.

I set the timer and place my hands on the counter in front of me so that he hopefully won't see them shaking. I don't want him to realize he makes me nervous. He always has. Well, maybe not *him* but what I feel for him. A part of me itches to play the part of his wife. To go to him, and stand between his legs, where he'd put his hands on my waist, and I'd kiss him. I'm sure I've daydreamed about that exact scenario at some point in my life, but now that I have him, it feels wrong. Not wrong in the sense of not right with him, but wrong because it feels like I'm taking advantage of our situation. I guess that's exactly what we're supposed to do these next few months, but I'm scared. I need him to set the pace, so I can follow his lead, but he's probably waiting for me to do the same. It's a tricky situation.

"A penny for your thoughts?" he asks, noting my seriousness.

I mock-gasp. "I should be offended. My thoughts are worth much more than a penny."

He chuckles. "A quarter?"

I wince. "Still not high enough."

He laughs, the sound rich and melodic.

Changing the subject, I say, "I bet Rae and Cade will be gone all day."

He nods in agreement. "I'm sure."

"You know what that means?" I waggle my brows.

He grins cockily. "Baby, if you wanted sex you didn't need to be coy about it."

I grab a dishtowel off the counter and swat him with it. He laughs even as the cloth slaps his skin. "*No*. It means we can watch a movie. We never get the TV to ourselves."

He grins. "I liked my idea better."

"Of course you did." I fight the urge to roll my eyes. I hate him for bringing up the topic of sex, because now all I can think about is the smooth feel of his skin beneath my hands and our bodies moving together. I bite my lip, suppressing a moan at my naughty thoughts.

Xander says huskily, "If you keep standing there with that look on your face, I'm going to have to fuck you on the kitchen counter."

My breath catches and his eyes flick to my lips. The gesture is like a bomb going off. I don't know which of us moves first, but suddenly, I'm in his arms, and his lips press to mine, kissing me like I'm the air he desperately needs. My body is pressed flush to his, my soft to his hard, and I grasp his arms, holding on so that I don't fall.

He tips my chin back, and my butt presses into the counter as he pushes against me. He grasps my hips and lifts me up, standing in the open space between my legs. My fingers delve into his silky hair, drawing him closer to me. More, I need more.

I can't think, can't seem to do anything other than focus on the feel of his lips against mine.

His fingers dig into my hips, but I don't mind. The pressure keeps me grounded.

"Xander," I moan his name into his mouth, and he nips my bottom lip.

My arms wind around his neck and I arch my body, pressing my breasts into his chest.

His hands ghost up my sides, leaving a trail of fire in their wake.

He kisses his way down my neck and my head falls to the side, welcoming the press of his lips. My breaths come out as short pants, because he's effectively stolen all the air in my lungs.

He cups my face, staring into my lust-filled eyes.

Xander has always been the one guy to make me weak in the knees. No one has ever measured up to him, and now that I've had a taste, I know no one ever will.

He kisses me once, just a brief press of his lips, but even still it feels as powerful as the passionate kiss we shared moments before. My body shakes, but it's not with nerves like before; no, this is something more powerful, something I'm scared to even understand.

He tilts my chin up with a press of his finger, and my eyes meet his.

"Don't be afraid," he whispers. "Of me. Of us."

I swallow thickly. "I don't know where we go from here," I admit.

My feelings are all over the place. I feel conflicted because who *really* wants to be married at nineteen, but this is Xander—the boy I've lusted after my whole life. There's no one I love or trust more, so maybe this is some twist of fate bringing us together or something, but I always come back to the marriage thing.

Marriage is a big deal—at least to me, anyway—and not something to be taken lightly. And as much as I love Xander, as much as I always have, I don't know if I'm really *in* love with him. It's not like I know him enough in the romantic sense to feel that way.

But damn it, I *want* to get to know him that way.

I want to go on dates, and get flowers, and fall into bed together at night.

I just don't know if I want it like *this*.

I feel like it's fate's way of mocking me—give me the guy I've always wanted but with one big ass string attached.

"Hey, hey, hey," Xander chants, breaking into my thoughts. "Where'd you go? Down the rabbit hole, I presume?"

My lips twitch with the threat of a smile. "Something like that."

Luckily, the timer goes off and saves me from further inquisition.

I know I can't avoid talking to him about my thoughts forever, but right now, I need more time to think through things on my own.

four
...

xander

THEA and I eat our pizza in relative silence. A silence I'm not used to. She's always been chatty, and it's something I've never minded. It feels weird to sit in the open kitchen and not have her tell me about *something*—a book she's read, some football stat, or how cute she thinks the neighbor's dog is.

I don't try to get her to speak. I'm smart enough to know not to push her, and after the day we've had, she deserves the time to think. I know we've both already been doing a lot of it today.

We finish eating, and I volunteer to clean the plates. She smiles gratefully and leans her hip against the counter, watching me. I think about the night we shared, and the kiss not long ago, and I'm desperate to have her in my arms again. I feel like I've waited long enough to call her mine, and now that I have her, I still don't *really* have her, and it sucks.

I wasn't that drunk last night when we decided to get married, and she wasn't either. I *know*, because I would've never gone through with it if for a single second if I thought it wasn't something she really wanted.

We've been skirting around our feelings for years; last night, something imploded, and it couldn't be ignored anymore.

"What movie do you want to watch?" I ask her, rinsing off one of the plates. When she doesn't answer, I glance behind my shoulder and see that her eyes are glazed over and she's lost in her thoughts, so I repeat my question.

She jumps slightly and bangs her elbow on the countertop. "Ow," she cries, grabbing her elbow and rubbing the spot.

"You okay?" I ask, not asking about her elbow but how she's feeling.

She nods, but I know she's not. I've always had a sixth sense when it comes to Thea. When we were little, our parents used to joke about it, but I don't think they had any idea how true it was. I remember once, when we were much younger—she was probably only about three and I was six—she tripped in her yard and skinned up her knee on a bunch of twigs and started crying. Even though I wasn't the one hurt, I cried too, because even then her pain was mine, her joy was mine, and every other emotion in-between was mine too.

I finish with the dishes and dry my hands on a rag. Thea

still stands there, never having answered my first question about the movie. I cross the few feet separating us and place my hands on her hips. She jolts at my touch and goosebumps prickle her skin. I can't resist the upturn quirk of my lips when I see it.

The words are on the tip of my tongue, to ask her if she's okay again, to prod into her inner thoughts and figure out what the fuck she's thinking so I can fix it, but I *know* I can't, and I have to let her figure it out on her own. I can't understand why she's so against this, against *us*. We're right together, we always have been, and we've always fought what we wanted because Cade would never approve. But fuck Cade, he has no right to tell us that we can't be together—and believe me, he's warned me away from his sister too many times to count—but I'm sick and tired of trying to feel something with someone else when I only want Thea. I *can't* do it anymore. I hope she sees that soon, that we're good together—but I think she knows, and maybe that's what's scaring her, the reality that this could really be our forever.

I rub my hands up her arms and she shivers at my touch. Her hazel eyes look golden from the illumination of the sun shining through the window.

I cup her cheek and lean my forehead against hers. I don't say anything. I don't need to. I just want her to know that I'm here.

After a moment, she steps out of my embrace. "Jaws," she says softly after a moment. "I want to watch Jaws."

I smile widely. "Our favorite." She nods. "You go put it on and I'll pop the popcorn."

She smiles, and her eyes light up with humor. "Don't add so much butter this time. You nearly made me sick the last time you made it."

"The more butter, the more delicious," I reason.

She shakes her head, but she's smiling nevertheless. She disappears into the family room, and I shamelessly ogle her ass—she has a nice ass, okay?

I pop the popcorn and pour it into a large orange mixing bowl before adding the butter. I do use less than I did the last time but it's probably still too much for Thea.

Thea already sits on the large, black leather couch, covered in her favorite flannel blanket. She hits play when I sit down and I lift the bowl so she can stretch her legs out in my lap. We watch a lot of movies and TV shows together—Netflix is our kryptonite—so we have our routine down. I set the popcorn bowl on her knees so we can each reach for it with ease.

I'm glad that she's willing to do something normal with me—that she's not locking herself in her room and thinking of a million and one reasons why this won't work.

An ache builds in my chest. One full of worry.

What if I can't convince her that this is real? What if in three months she still wants a divorce?

I swallow thickly and my eyes bounce to her where she lays on the couch.

I don't want to lose her, but I also know I'll never break my promise, because I'll do anything to make that girl happy even if it kills me in the process.

five

thea

I LIE awake in the dark, my thoughts going round and round in a circle. I can feel panic rising in my chest like a suffocating wave. I know there's no chance of sleep finding me when I'm like this.

I throw back the covers and shove my feet into my slippers, stalking from my room and downstairs.

I jolt when I get to the bottom of the stairs and turn into the family room.

Xander sits on the couch, reading a book by the glow of one low light.

He hears me and looks up. His dark hair is a wild mess around his head, like he'd been tossing and turning in his bed before coming down here to find solace like I'd planned to do.

"Hi," I say softly.

He looks me up and down, noting my loose t-shirt, shorts, and ratty slippers.

"Nice slippers."

I shake my head. "Hey, they're cute," I growl.

He chuckles. "They're falling apart."

This is true, but I refuse to part with the shark-shaped slippers—ones Xander got me for my sixteenth birthday. It might seem like a stupid gift to some, but I'd cherished the nod to our love of *Jaws*.

When I don't say anything, he adds, "I'm glad you still have them, though."

I look down at them, falling apart and barely held together, the shark on my left foot missing a tooth so that it has an awkward smile. "They're my favorite." I shrug. "I can't abandon them." He puts a bookmark in his book and closes it. "What are you reading?" I ask.

He chuckles. "*The Great Gatsby*."

"Again?" I laugh and creep closer to him. "Haven't you read that like a million times now?"

He shrugs. "I guess I love it the same way you love those damn slippers."

I laugh and take a seat on the couch, drawing my legs up and sitting sideways so I can face him. "Why are you up?" I ask him.

He sighs and pinches the bridge of his nose. "Couldn't sleep. I take it the same is true for you."

I nod reluctantly. "'Lot on my mind."

"Yeah, me too." He looks away.

My heart lurches with fear that he's having second

thoughts about us, which is stupid because I'm the one that's spent the whole day fighting this. If he *is* having second thoughts, I should be jumping for joy, not feeling so glum. I'm beginning to realize that the next three months are going to be harder than I thought. I mean, for instance, take the incident in the kitchen this afternoon—he kissed me and I just *melted* into him instead of pushing him away like I should have.

I clearly am a glutton for punishment.

I don't know how I'm going to go to work tomorrow and act completely normal—like something monumental hasn't happened.

Even though I've spent the day trying to ignore what's happened, I can't.

This man sitting beside me is my husband.

"Come here," he says and opens his arms. I dive into them gladly, resting my head on his chest.

This right here feels like home, and I know I could get all too used to it.

He brushes his lips softly against the top of my head and whispers one low word.

"Please."

I know what he's saying without him even speaking the words.

He wants me to give him a real chance. He knows that I only agreed half-heartedly this morning. I don't answer him, but I lean closer, and he sighs in relief.

Nothing more is said, and we both drift off to sleep.

six
...

xander

I WAKE UP EARLY, thankfully, and carry Thea up to her bed. She's so out of it that she doesn't even stir as I lay her in her bed and pull the frilly pink blankets up to her chest.

I can't help but stand there and look at her a few seconds longer.

She's so beautiful and completely unaware of the effect she has on me.

I tiptoe across her room and into the bathroom that joins with my room.

It's only four in the morning, and I don't have to be up to get ready for work for another two hours, but I know I'm never going to be able to fall back asleep. I only managed to get a few hours in because Thea was with me.

I walk over to my closet and grab a blue button-down shirt and a pair of navy pants and a tie.

It was all a lie as I put on the clothes, playing the part of the good son and friend, following in the steps of what everyone else wanted for me. This life isn't for me—working in an office five days a week, nine to five. Don't get me wrong, architecture isn't *bad*, and my dad is cool, but it isn't what I love.

I love football.

I love the rush, the adrenaline, the high of screaming fans. I love the sounds of our cleats tearing into the turf and how the power seems to build inside you, making you feel invincible. Football has been my life since I could walk.

I'd had agents interested in me and stupidly turned away all offers because I deluded myself into thinking they were only interested in me because of Cade.

Cade is one of the best football players I know, and the guy could have gone pro, but he didn't want it. Not like I did.

I entered in the draft, unbeknownst to my friends and family, hoping I got picked. I didn't tell my parents, or Cade, or even Thea. No one knew. They all thought I was content to head into my career in architecture. But I wasn't. And then I got picked for my hometown team, the Colorado Rebels; that was two months ago, and I still haven't told anyone. I don't know why. My parents have always been supportive of my love for football, but my dad was so happy when I went to work for him during my senior year of college, and I guess I'm afraid that maybe he'll be disappointed if I don't follow in his footsteps. As for my friends, I know Thea, Rae, and Jace would be happy for me, but Cade? I don't fucking know. We've done practically everything together since we were little and it only seemed natural that we'd both become architects and work for my dad too. But then this last year, I realized that's not what *I* wanted. I want to play ball, so I kept it from them. I lucked out that apparently no one close to me watched the draft on TV. Sure, my teammates and coach knew, but it was easy to keep it a secret from Cade. After the football season ended, he hasn't wanted to have anything to do with the sport—I've always gotten the impression that he never really loved it all that much. Since I don't want Cade to know, I've kept it a secret from everyone else too—it's not their burden to bear—but I know my time's running out and it ticks down incessantly in my mind.

I set my clothes on the chair in the corner and go to shower. It doesn't take me long, and when I finish, I dry my hair with a towel and put on a pair of basketball shorts and head downstairs to cook breakfast.

The four of us take turns making breakfast, but since the three of us have been gone for the last week, I have no idea whose turn it is. Luckily, we're all easygoing so it doesn't really matter.

I pull out the ingredients for pancakes and start making the batter.

When that's done, I set the bowl aside and pull out bacon and eggs from the refrigerator. I fry the bacon first, then finish the pancakes, before finally making the eggs.

I'm sliding the eggs onto one large plate when Rae comes into the kitchen.

"Hey," she greets with a yawn.

"Hi," I say. "Hungry?" She nods.

"I have to leave soon. Nova and I are driving a few hours away to take photos in some park she knows about." She grabs a plate and begins piling the food onto it. "How was Vegas?" she asks, an innocent enough question but I tense anyway.

"Good," I say.

She raises a brow before pulling a chair out at the kitchen table. "You guys were gone for a week, and all you have to say is *good*?"

I laugh, but it sounds forced. "We spent most of the week in seminars, so boring would be a more apt word." I shrug and pile food onto my plate. My plate is overflowing compared to Rae's.

She opens her mouth to say more, but Cade comes in then and bends to kiss her cheek. "Morning," he says in a sleepy voice.

Rae smiles up at him, and for a moment, I feel envious. It's not an emotion I feel often, but I envy their easy and open relationship. I still don't know where Thea and I stand —if she even wants to really *try* to be with me—but what I do know is, no matter what, she wants to keep this a secret. And that hurts. I understand where she's coming from, I really do; if we try this, and it doesn't work out, it would hurt the people around us and make things awkward, but dammit, I want to be able to kiss her and touch her openly without worrying about everyone else. I've already spent enough time hiding how I feel.

Cade gets his food and sits down beside Rae, completely oblivious to the sudden dark cloud hanging over my head.

I shovel a big bite of pancake into my mouth while they chat. Eventually, I can't take a second more of them looking at each other lovingly, so I clean my plate and head back upstairs, bumping into Thea in the hall.

"Whoa," she cries, colliding with my body. I steady her with my hands on her arms. She looks up at me with a sheepish smile. "I suppose I have you to thank for carrying me to bed?"

I shrug. "I wasn't going to leave you on the couch."

"Do I smell your pancakes?" She points down the stairs. I nod and she moans. "*Yes*, you make the best pancakes."

I want to tell her what else I'm best at, but I keep my mouth shut.

We part ways and I close myself in my room to change into my work clothes.

The button-down shirt feels constricting—like a damn straight jacket around my body.

I tuck the bottom of it into my pants and smooth down the front. My reflection stares back at me with an irritated expression. I shake my head and smooth my fingers through my hair, doing my best to make the longer strands look somewhat tamed. When I look halfway decent, I grab my motorcycle jacket and shrug it on.

I shove my wallet into my back pocket and grab my backpack—it makes bringing stuff on a motorcycle much easier.

My feet thump on the stairs as I head down, not bothering to be quiet now that everyone is awake.

I'm heading for the side door into the garage when Thea calls out my name.

I want to keep going, to pretend I didn't hear her, but I couldn't ignore that girl if my life depended on it.

"Yeah?" I call back, hand on the doorknob.

Her head pokes around the corner and she lifts a brow when she sees me by the door. "You're leaving?"

I nod. "Wanted to get an early start."

A lie, but believable.

She nods, accepting it as answer enough. "Breakfast was delicious. I'll see you later."

She disappears back into the kitchen and I swallow thickly.

The words are on the tip of my tongue to ask her if she wants to ride with me, but she never has before and it would raise suspicions, so I don't.

I grab my helmet from the garage and start my bike. It's new, a graduation gift from my parents. I've wanted one forever but never had the funds for one. I was shocked when they surprised me with it. Best damn gift ever—aside from waking up to Thea as my wife, but who the fuck knows how that's going to turn out?

I beat the early morning traffic and make it to the downtown building without incident.

Kincaid Architecture takes up the whole top floor of one of the largest buildings in Denver. My dad's business started small, as most do, and grew into one of the most revered architecture firms on the west coast.

I park my bike in the garage and hop off, removing my

helmet. I run my fingers through my flattened hair, hoping it doesn't look like a complete mess. My dad might be cool, but this *is* his business, and we're all expected to dress and look decent.

I store my helmet before heading for the elevator, pushing the button; the doors slide right open. It's still early enough that not many people are in the garage or building.

I step inside and press the number for the floor then lean against the side of the elevator.

I wish I had just one more day at home before coming to work. I want to be able to *think* and talk to Thea without my focus being on work.

She agreed to give me three months to change her mind, but I'm still terrified she's going to go running before then, and I don't want that to happen.

I need to show her how good we are together, but I know I need to take things slow—in other words, what I said in the kitchen yesterday, and the kiss, were a bad idea. But I can't take it back now, and I don't want to, I'm going to have to be more careful, though.

I head into my office—yeah, office and not cubicle—Thea's assistant desk sits inside the room near mine. It had originally been outside but after only a few days of working together, we realized I was shit at giving her anything to do unless she was in here.

I drop my backpack behind my desk, shuck off my jacket, and collapse in the chair. My collar bites into my neck, and I pull on it, trying to loosen it like it's a vice cinching around me.

Papers sit on my desk, important documents I need to go over for builds, and I just don't want to.

I pinch the bridge of my nose.

Being here day in and day out is a brutal reminder that I'm lying to everyone I care about.

Fuck, I'm lying to my own *wife* now.

I tug on the ends of my hair. I keep digging myself a deeper hole and I don't know how the fuck to get out of it.

A shadow falls across the doorway, and I look up to find my dad standing there.

To most, Cooper Kincaid is an intimidating sight. Even though he's nearing fifty he's still fit, and tall—easily two inches taller than my six-foot-three—his hair is graying at the temples, and he almost always wears a smile that says he knows what you're going to say before you even say it. I've never been intimidated by him, though. Growing up he was nothing but a big softy when it came to my older sister, little brother, and me.

He taps his finger on the doorframe. "You're here early," he comments.

I shrug. "I was up—figured I'd go ahead and get started."

He nods. "I need your proposal for the Hammel account by this afternoon."

"I'll have it done," I assure him. In fact, it's already done, but I don't feel like going over it right now. My mind is too all over the place to focus on work.

He presses his lips together, and I know he's contemplating saying more, but after a moment, he leaves and heads down the hall to his much bigger office.

I sigh and lean back in my chair, crossing my hands behind my head.

"Get your shit together," I mutter to myself, and let out a disgusted breath.

I rub my eyes and reach for the stack of papers on my desk.

Time to get to work.

"I thought you might want this." Thea holds out a cup of coffee from one of our favorite places across the street. "You left so early I figured you forgot to get any." She shrugs like it's no big deal.

I smile and take it from her. "Thanks—and you're right, I did forget."

She laughs and the twinkling sound washes over me. "Is there anything you need me to do?"

I set the coffee aside and finally look at her—and fuck me, she's wearing this tight black skirt thing and a loose pink blouse. Her light-brown hair hangs in waves past her shoulders and I remember distinctly wrapping my fingers in it that night and tugging and—

"Xander?" she prompts with a raised brow, and I nearly choke when I realize I was basically having a full on fantasy while she stared at me.

Only, it wasn't a fantasy. It was real. And I wanted it to happen again.

I clear my throat. "Um, yeah, here—I need you to run these down to Sherry." I thrust a stack of papers that were lying on the side of my desk into her waiting hands.

She looks from the papers to me. "Are you okay?"

"Yeah." And of course, my fucking voice cracks. *Traitor*.

She eyes me for a moment longer in disbelief before turning and leaving the room, her high heels clacking on the floor.

I let out a pent-up breath.

Day one of working together post-marriage so far is not a success.

seven
...

thea

TODAY MIGHT GO DOWN in the record books as the most awkward of my entire life.

Xander and I barely spoke, and when we did, it was stilted and not at all like us. I can't for the life of me figure out what's going on in his head. It was only this morning that he whispered that one word—*please*. I thought he meant to *please* give him a chance, but maybe he meant *please* can we forget this ever happened? I can't imagine him changing his mind like that, since he's been pro-marriage since we woke up yesterday morning, but who knows?

"Do you want to go get dinner?" I ask, closing out my computer and shutting it down.

Xander lifts his gaze away from the computer and looks at the clock. His head immediately whips back, and he jumps from his seat.

"Fuck, I'm late," he curses, bustling around to grab his backpack, knocking the chair over in the process.

I stand. "Xander?"

"I can't talk right now, Thea," he says roughly and starts for the door. He must realize how his tone was because he halts his steps and looks at me with an apologetic expression. "I'm sorry," he whispers. "I'll see you tonight. We can start *Charmed*."

Before I can respond, he's out the door and gone.

His behavior is so off-putting that I can't even be excited that he said he'd finally watch *Charmed* with me. I've been begging him for months to start that one.

Since Xander left in such a hurry, I pick up the fallen chair, turn off the lights, and lock up.

He's been running off a lot like that lately—so I know at least *that* has nothing to do with me and I take comfort in it.

I head down the hall to Cade's office and knock on the door before poking my head inside. "Hey, loser." I crack a grin as he looks up from a paper. "Time to go."

He glances at the clock. "I didn't realize the time."

"Want to pick up a pizza on the way home?" I ask hopefully. I'm starving.

He shakes his head. "No can do. Rae and I are going out."

Why am I not surprised?

"Oh, okay then. More pizza for me."

More pizza is never a bad thing.

Cade packs up and we head out to the parking garage. The drive home is quiet, and for that, I'm thankful. If I had to force conversation with my brother for forty-five minutes I might gouge out my eye with my finger.

When we arrive home, Cade heads straight up to shower.

Me? I go to order my damn pizza. Who cares if I made one yesterday? Pizza never hurt anyone.

Oh, hell no. Is this a craving? Like a pregnancy craving? I laugh at my own thoughts. It's absurd considering said possible pregnancy sex happened two nights ago. Yeah, no baby here. Yet.

Oh, God, now I can feel the panic building inside me.

I'd dismissed the broken condom from my mind, but now I can't seem to stop thinking about it.

I touch my stomach like there's already a bump there, a little baby growing inside me.

I can't be a mom. I'm not ready. I don't even know how to change a diaper.

"Are you okay?" Rae asks, breezing out of the laundry room with a basket of clothes under her arm.

"Fine," I squeak, when I'm anything but fine.

She raises a brow doubtfully. "Want to talk about it?"

"No," I say too quickly.

She shakes her head and looks at me quizzically. "You're being weird. Weirder than normal," she adds with a soft laugh. She tilts her head to the side. "If you need someone to talk to you know where to find me."

She brushes past me and the stairs squeak as she goes up.

I let out a breath. There's no point in freaking out about the possibility of a baby. I won't know anything for a few weeks, until either my period shows up—in which case I will do a dance—or I'm forced to take a pregnancy test.

I close my eyes at the thought. If I have to pee on that stupid little stick I'm making Xander go to the store to buy it. No way in hell am I buying one of those. Nope. If loverboy's super sperm fertilized one of these precious eggs, the least he can do is buy the damn test.

Ugh, I'm not even hungry anymore.

I kick off my shoes and grab a bottle of water from the refrigerator. I busy myself with cleaning the kitchen—wiping down the counters and vacuuming the floor. After a little while, Rae and Cade come downstairs to leave for their date. They're both dressed up and look nice.

"Have fun, you two," I tell them. "Don't do anything I wouldn't do."

Like get married in Vegas and possibly get pregnant.

"Are you okay here by yourself?" Cade asks worriedly.

I roll my eyes and point at him with the rag waving weakly in my hand. "I'm almost twenty, so I'm *pretty sure* I can handle being home by myself." Rae presses a hand to her mouth to hold in her laughter. "I don't know why you like my brother." I shake my head. "He's not the brightest Crayola in the package, if you know what I mean. *One too many hits to the head from football if you ask me*," I hiss under my breath, even though I know Cade can still hear me.

Cade groans and presses his hand to her waist. "We're leaving now."

I salute him. "See ya later."

He shakes his head, both of them laughing, and then they're gone.

It's rare to have a moment alone in this house. Living with three other people makes for some chaotic surroundings.

I abandon my cleaning endeavor and decide to take a bubble bath since it's not something I get to do often. Running the water, I add bubbles and some scented salts, then light candles and dim the lights.

This is exactly what I need after the last two days.

I clip my hair up and remove my clothes before sinking down into the hot water with a sigh escaping my lips.

My eyes close and I lean my head back, the water sloshing around my breasts with bubbles up to my chin.

I do my best to empty my mind of all my worries and relax, but it's hard when the events of the last forty-eight hours plague my mind.

I probably should've brought a book in here with me to occupy my mind but it's too late now.

The door from Xander's room opens, and I let out a scream, covering my body even though it's pretty pointless.

Xander pauses in the doorway, staring at me like a starved man seeing food for the first time. He licks his lips and his Adam's apple bobs. His hair is a wild and untamed mess like he's been running his fingers constantly through it in agitation.

He shakes his head suddenly as if he's shaking away the fog that has come over him.

"Sorry. I didn't know you were in here. I didn't think anyone was home."

He starts to ease the door closed, but in a small voice, I call out, "Stay." I don't know what makes me say the words, but I know I want him to.

He hesitates for a moment before coming in and sitting down on the floor beside me. He looks tired, wary even.

"Are you okay?" I ask him.

"Fine," he replies, his eyes not meeting mine.

"That's bullshit," I say, a bite to my tone. His eyes flick up to mine. "You should know by now you can't lie to me."

He lowers his head and rubs his hands over his face. "I just have a lot going on, that's all."

"Is this about work? Or us?" I ask softly. If he's having second thoughts about continuing our marriage I should be dancing a jig, but instead, I feel saddened. "Do you regret wanting to see if this will work?"

His head whips up and he looks at me with fire in his dark eyes. "This has nothing to do with us," he assures me. "I'm still going to do everything I can to make you see that this isn't a bad thing." My heart beats faster at his words and the passion in them. He digs into his front pocket and pulls out our wedding bands. "I kept these with me all day, thinking about how fucking much I want us to be able to wear them and not hide this, hide *us*. I know why you don't want to tell anyone, I get it, I do, but it doesn't mean I like it—because what I feel for you is real and it's not going to go away."

I swallow thickly. "I'm scared," I tell him.

He raises a single dark brow as he stuffs the rings in his pocket. "And you think I'm not? We're both young and this was unexpected, but sometimes the surprises in life are the best things, and I definitely think this is one of the best so far."

The water sloshes as I move, leaning over so I can hold my hand out to him. He grasps it and draws my palm to his heart, pressing my hand flat against the cotton of his shirt. It doesn't take long for me to feel the fast-paced thumping.

"Do you feel that?" His voice is no more than a whisper in the darkened bathroom. "My heart beats out of control every time I'm in the same room with you. I think you think this is sudden, but it's not. I've wanted more from you for a long time and I was too much of a damn wimp to do anything about it—and I think you've wanted more too. I see the way you look at me."

My hand shakes, and for once, I don't want to do what I *think* I'm supposed to and instead follow my heart—and my heart leads me straight to him. It always has. It's hard to overcome my mind shouting about how wrong this is, how we're doing everything backwards. After all, it's not *first come marriage, then comes love*, but neither Xander nor I have ever played by the rules, so why start now?

"Get in," I say.

He startles. "What?"

"Get in," I repeat and move forward in the bathtub so there's room behind me.

He jumps up and kicks off his shoes before unbuttoning

his work shirt. I swallow thickly as his sculpted chest and arms appear before me.

He unbuckles his belt and reaches for the button on his jeans. A chuckle rumbles deep in his chest. "Like what you see?"

I smile widely. "You're my husband now. I can look all I want."

His chuckle turns into a booming laugh that shakes my insides. God, I love his laugh—the rich, deep, timbre of it.

His pants and boxer-briefs pool onto the floor and I slide forward so he can slip into the tub behind me. The water sloshes over the sides and onto the floor but I can't bring myself to care.

He settles behind me and I rest my back against his chest. I let out an embarrassing contented sigh and his chest shakes with barely contained laughter.

I lean my head to the side and look back at him. "Laughing at me, Kincaid?"

His lips quirk into a crooked smile. "I'd never laugh at you, *Kincaid*."

I can almost feel the blood draining from my face as my eyes widen.

Somehow in all the madness I forgot I wasn't a Montgomery anymore. I mean, technically I still am since I haven't had it changed, but ...

"Stop freaking out." He kisses the end of my nose. "You think too much."

"True," I concede, and wiggle, the movement splashing more water on the floor that we'll have to clean up later. I take a deep breath and say, "I might be scared, but I'm in. I'm going to give us a serious shot."

His smile blinds me. I don't think I've ever seen him smile this big, and that's saying something because Xander is a guy that smiles—he's not one of those broody types that glares at you for no apparent reason.

He touches my cheek with a feather-light caress of his fingers, like he's afraid his touch will send me running. "You'll see," he whispers into the darkened room, the shadows from the candle flame flickering over his face. "You'll see how good we are together. I'll show you." He presses his lips to my cheek in the same spot his fingers were only moments before.

My heart beats faster with fear? Excitement? Maybe a mixture of both.

He must take my silence for another one of my freak-outs because he adds, "I'll still give you an out—the three months will still be our ... trial period." He chuckles. "But we're in this together. No half-assing it."

I nod. "I still don't want to tell anyone," I whisper.

He stiffens but nods. "That's probably best. We won't have to worry about someone's opinion interfering that way."

I notice the way he says *someone* and not *anyone* but choose not to comment on it.

"So—" I laugh lightly "—we're back to where we started then?"

He laughs too and nips my earlobe. "Nah, not exactly,

because this time, you're actually in too. I knew you were only trying to humor me before."

I bite my lip. "I was that obvious?"

He shrugs and the water ripples. "Yeah." He grins.

"You really have faith in us, don't you?" I ask softly.

"I do," he says vehemently with a nod and then rests his chin on top of my head.

I close my eyes and a smile touches my lips. My mind is still warring with my heart, but for the moment, I'm content to just let us *be*.

eight

thea

I WAKE up to Xander in my bed—we fell asleep watching *Charmed* and stuffing our faces with Chinese food and not the pizza I'd planned to order. His chest rises and falls with each soft breath and his eyes roam behind his closed lids with the promise of sweet dreams.

I feel better after our talk last night, and I think we're finally on the same page. Don't get me wrong, this whole marriage thing still scares me, but I don't feel so confused as to where we stand. I know everything that was said last night is basically what we'd already agreed to, but it felt different—it felt real. Before, I had been too freaked out to think clearly and had agreed without a clear mind, but now that I've had time to think, I want to give this a real shot—make the most of the situation, so to speak. I'm still not sure that staying married is the best thing for us. I mean, I can't even commit to a major, so what's the likelihood that I can commit to a marriage? I'm pretty clueless when it comes to what I want from life.

I ease from the bed so I don't disturb him and pad across the room and into the bathroom to brush my teeth.

I brush my hair and pull it back into a sloppy ponytail. Since Xander made breakfast yesterday, today's my turn.

The house is quiet when I leave my room, and I close the door behind me so there's no chance of Rae or Cade seeing Xander in my bed.

I know Cade sounds like the biggest jerk of a brother, but he's not. He's one of the best, he's just protective of me—he always has been, and I think that stems from what a nasty asshole my father is. He hits Cade. He always has, and I'm sure he'll continue to do so until Cade actually stands up to him. Cade doesn't know that I know—I found out by accident once when I came home early from a friend's house and saw my dad punch him in the face. I know Cade keeps quiet about it in some convoluted way to keep my mom and me safe and happy, but he shouldn't protect that monster. I think our mom knows too—she'd have to, or at least she suspects—but I know she's afraid of our dad; most people are. You'd think my dad would stop walloping on him now that Cade's a man, but I don't think it has stopped. I haven't actually seen him hit him again since that one time I saw by accident when I was in high school, but I've seen the bruises—bruises that definitely couldn't have come from football, so I don't believe for a second that it was a one-time thing.

What sucks the most about no one knowing that I know

is that I have to play the part of the loving daughter who adores her father when I can't even stand the sight of him. All I hope is that one day it'll all be over and I won't have to play pretend anymore.

I dismiss the less than pleasant thoughts from my mind and tread softly on the steps so as not to wake anyone.

I flick on lights as I go, illuminating the house, and enter the kitchen.

I open the refrigerator and pull out everything I'll need to make egg sandwiches. It's just about the only breakfast thing I can make that's any good.

By the time I'm done, the other three have crept downstairs.

I put everything on plates and pass them out before sitting down myself.

"I feel like I need to get a job," Rae announces.

Cade's brows pull together. "I thought you wanted to focus on your photography this summer?"

She shrugs. "It's not like it's making me any money ..." she trails off.

"Why don't you advertise on Facebook?" I ask. "You could offer to do senior photos, or weddings—I know those aren't really your thing, but you could make some money doing what you love and maybe learn a thing or two along the way," I suggest.

She nods, but the way her lips twist, I don't think she likes my idea. "Maybe."

Cade takes a bite of his egg sandwich and says around a

mouthful, "You should ride with us into the city—take some photos of the buildings, we could get lunch."

Rae brightens at this idea. "That sounds fun."

Xander's lips twitch with the threat of laughter and he shakes his head.

Cade and Rae finish up and leave, piling their dirty dishes in the sink.

I raise a brow and eye Xander. "I am *not* playing third wheel to the lovebirds. You better let me hitch a ride on your bike."

He chuckles. "You aren't scared?"

"No," I say vehemently. "Motorcycles aren't scary."

"So—" he leans forward, his lips twisting with a calculated smile "—if I go fast, that'll be fine with you? You won't mind having to squeeze your legs tighter around my waist?" His eyes flick to my lips where my tongue has slid out, moistening them. I shake my head, and he grins. "Good—I'm thoroughly going to enjoy having you wrapped around me. Just be careful where you put your hands." He winks and stands with his plate in his hand.

I'm too stunned to move.

Something tells me Xander's just made the first move in a calculated chess match, and I have no idea how to play chess.

I'm screwed.

This was a bad idea.

Xander looks hot as fuck straddling the bike with his leather jacket—the epitome of the bad boy, only he's about as far from bad as they come which makes him all the more tempting.

He holds out an extra helmet to me. "Are you getting on or are you going to stare at me all day?"

I snatch the helmet from his hands. "I'm sorry. I haven't been formally introduced to this version of you, and it's a bit surprising." I wave my free hand at him.

He throws his head back and laughs. "Introduced to *this* version? This is the normal version. Now get on."

I straddle the bike behind him, wiggling around to get my balance, before I put the helmet on. I secure the strap and say, "Ready." The word comes out muffled thanks to the visor.

He kicks the bike on and then we're gone.

I don't find it scary like he thought I might. Instead, I find it to be one of the most exhilarating things I've ever done.

We race down the highway, and everything blurs around us.

All too soon, it ends as we arrive in the parking garage. My legs are stiff, but I don't let it show. We hop off and Xander secures the helmets.

"Why haven't you ever let me do that before?"

He laughs. "One, because I haven't had it long. Two, because you didn't ask."

"I want to do that all the time now," I tell him, smoothing my fingers through my hair. I'm sure it's a knotted mess but I already have to stop off at the restroom to change from jeans into my skirt for work—since Xander insisted that I cover my legs on the off-chance we got in an accident.

Xander smiles at my words. "Really?" He seems pleased, excited even, by the possibility.

I nod eagerly. "Oh, yeah."

We head to the elevator together and then separate when we reach our floor since he heads to the office and I go straight to the bathroom.

It doesn't take me long to change, but fixing my hair—that takes a bit more time. I finally get it looking semi-decent and head to the office I share with Xander.

I think some of the people working in the building think it's weird that Xander moved me into his office—the assistants usually have a desk or cubicle outside them—but they just don't understand our dynamic. We work well together, and when we were separated, he ended up taking on too much instead of delegating things to me. This suits us much better.

I slide into my chair and Xander looks up from a blueprint. "I need you to call Debra with Synchrony Homes."

"I'm on it," I say and salute him.

He cracks a grin and returns to studying the blueprint.

I make phone call after phone call until *finally* it's time for lunch.

"Let's go somewhere for lunch," Xander says, standing from behind his desk and loosening his tie a bit. Damn, forget the leather jacket, *this* version of Xander leaves my mouth watering. Button-down shirts and dress pants fit his physique like nothing else can.

"Where?" I ask.

He shrugs. "Maybe that little deli sandwich shop around the corner. It wouldn't be far for us to get back." I look around uncomfortably, and he adds, "Cade's already gone to meet Rae if that's what you're worried about."

"It wasn't—" I start to lie but he gives me an understanding smile.

"Should we go?" He points to the door.

"Yeah." I smile. Lunch with Xander isn't out of the norm, and I'm beginning to realize that we already do a lot of stuff normal couples do, minus the sex part ... until the other night when we added that too.

I thought that a lot would have to change for us to be a couple but I'm startled with the realization that basically nothing changes—we just get *more*. We get *real*.

I stand and smooth my skirt down, and when I look up, Xander is looking at me with a heated expression in his eyes. I'd be lying if I said I didn't feel zings of pleasure course through my body.

Xander and I head to the elevator and then to the ground floor.

We pass through the large glass doors and onto the street when he says, "Can I hold your hand?"

I look up at him, startled. "Why?"

"Because I want to."

People bustle by us on the streets and yet it still feels like it's him and me alone in the world.

I nod—actually, it's barely even a nod, more of a little jerk, but he takes it as one anyway. He takes my hand, entwining our fingers together. I expect him to say something else, but he instead starts walking. We don't say anything as we make our way down to the little corner deli. It's a small building, with a drab dirty brick exterior except for a cheery red door. It's not the nicest place to look at, but the food certainly makes up for the aesthetics.

He lets go of my hand to hold the door for me and I step inside. There are a few other people already placing orders so I step into line and Xander falls in behind me. His large body seems to draw mine in like a magnet and I find myself leaning back into him. He touches my elbow, my waist, just fleeting little brushes of his fingers but my heart rate accelerates regardless. I try not to show how much I'm affected by those things because it'll only give him more ammunition against me.

The line moves quickly and I place my order. Before I can tell them that I want to pay for my own, Xander steps forward and says, "I've got it."

I'd like to make a big deal out of it and say he's only doing it since we're married now, but it would be a lie; Xander always insists on paying for my meal when we go out to lunch.

Xander pays for our food and we move off to the side to wait. When our number is called, he steps up, grabs the paper bag, and we head back out onto the streets since there aren't any tables free.

"Where would you like to go?" he asks.

"The park isn't too far." I shrug. "It's a nice day so I vote we eat outside."

He nods. "Good idea." He moves the paper bag to his other hand and takes mine with his free one, smiling down at me. His brown eyes are light and carefree. I love seeing him this happy but it's strange to realize that he's this way because of *me*.

A five-minute walk later, we reach the park and find a spot in the grass beneath a tree, the shade providing a much-needed cover from the blazing summer sun.

We sit and Xander stretches out his long legs. It's a little more awkward for me in my skirt, but I manage.

He opens the bag and hands me my sandwich and water bottle.

"It's a nice day," he comments, pulling out his own sandwich. "Don't you think so?"

I fight a smile. "Are you seriously talking about the weather right now?"

He cracks a half smile and a bubble of laughter bursts forth. "Yeah, sorry."

I smile and unwrap my sandwich. "Talk to me about anything *but* the weather. Please," I beg, brushing an invisible crumb from my skirt.

He plays with the paper wrapping his sandwich. "If you were one of the Halliwell sisters, which one would you want to be?" He asks. "Is that better?"

I laugh. "Yes, and I'd want to be Piper. She seems like the most level-headed one—plus, who wouldn't want to freeze time? What about you?" I take a bite of my sandwich.

He ponders it for a moment before finally saying, "Prue. She can move shit, and that's pretty awesome."

"Poor Phoebe," I comment. "She only gets to see the future—and call me crazy, but I wouldn't want to know that."

He nods in agreement and takes a bite of his sandwich. "I think our futures are always changing."

"You do?"

He chews and swallows. "Well, yeah—think about it. A decision you make today might affect something down the road and so on and so forth—just like we're always changing as people. Nothing stays the same so who's to say that the future will stay the same too? It has to be like the ocean, always moving like a current."

"Wow," I say, a tone of laughter to my voice. "You've given that a lot of thought."

He shrugs. "I've had to."

"What does that mean?"

He sighs and stares toward the sun, his eyes narrowed into slits. He turns to look at me and I can't quite decipher his expression. "A story for another time."

I'd normally pry to get information out of him, but something tells me not to press my luck.

We eat in silence for a little bit until he says, "Have you figured out your major yet?"

I sigh. "No." I pull up a blade of grass and rip it between my fingers like it's personally offended me in some way. "I have no idea what makes me happy. I just ... I don't want to be a teacher, I don't want to be a lawyer, or an accountant. There's *nothing* I want to do."

He presses his lips together and his tongue sticks out slightly—a telltale sign that he's thinking deeply. "What about something with sports? You love football. You should do something that makes you happy."

"Well, I can't play sports, for starters."

He laughs. "I was thinking something more along the lines of physical therapy."

"I failed health class my sophomore year—I don't think I possess the smarts to do that."

His laughter booms around me. "I forgot about that."

"I was so embarrassed," I mumble. "Who fails *health* class? Me. That's who." I point to myself, and we both laugh.

"Just think about it," he tells me. "Maybe something will come to you."

I narrow my eyes on him. "The fact that you think I haven't thought about it at all is mildly offensive."

He sobers. "No, I know that you have, but sometimes we get caught in the everyday and forget to think about the tomorrows. The tomorrows become the forevers so don't ignore them."

"You know, you're pretty smart for a jock."

He throws his head back and laughs. "Thanks, I think."

Music begins to play from somewhere in the park and I grin. I jump to a standing position and hold my hand out to him. "Come on, let's go."

He takes my hand and gathers up our trash to throw away in the other.

Together, we make our way toward the sound of the music and find a girl, maybe sixteen years old, playing her guitar and singing in front of the fountain that marks the center of the park. Her hair is a rainbow of colors and she sings with all the love and passion I wish I had for something. Her eyes are closed and she's so absorbed in the music she doesn't even know that a crowd has gathered around her.

I smile as I watch an older couple nearby. The gray-haired man reaches for his wife's hand and places his other at her waist. She beams up at him, clearly still as in love with him today as she was many years ago, and they dance to the music.

I look away and back to the girl, swaying slightly to the beat of the music.

Finally, I can't take the itch beneath my skin a second longer.

I step out of my heels and hand them to Xander. "Hold these."

"What are you up to?" He narrows his eyes on me.

I don't tell him. I show him.

I run for the fountain and cry out with joy as I step into the cold water. Someone will probably come and yell at me to get out, but for the moment, all I want to do is be crazy.

"Thea!" Xander calls out and I find him in the crowd. He's shaking his head but sporting the biggest grin. "You're crazy!"

I lift my arms above my head and spin around. "Better crazy than boring!" I call back.

His answering laugh echoes through my ears.

I close my eyes and a smile graces my lips as I dance

through the water, spinning in circles. If I'm not careful, I might fall, but I can't bring myself to care—and heck, if I did fall it would make for an even better memory.

When I open my eyes, Xander stands in front of me at the edge of the fountain. I run into his arms, giggling like a little girl, and dive into his arms.

He grasps my legs and swings me up into his arms. "Are you Prince Charming?" I ask with a laugh.

He grunts. "I'd rather be Peter Pan."

"Why?" I ask, curiosity leeching into my voice as he carries me to a bench.

"Because Peter Pan never had to grow up."

"You never want to grow up?"

He nods. "No." He bends down and grabs my foot, putting one shoe on. "But *you* must be Cinderella since it appears you've lost your shoes."

"Well, you put it on—so like I said, Prince Charming. Besides, I think it's a little late to be Peter Pan." I lower my voice to a hushed whisper. "In case you didn't notice, you're all grown up."

He laughs as he puts the other shoe on me. "Unfortunately, I noticed." He stands up straight and extends his hand to me. "All right, Cinderella, we better get back to the ball—and by ball, I mean work."

I pout. "The ball sounds more fun."

"For once I'd have to agree with that. The Hallman account is kicking my ass."

I frown. "I'm sorry."

We start back through the park, and after a few minutes of silence I ask, "Are you happy?"

"Yeah," he answers immediately, looking at me like I'm crazy for thinking he's not.

"I don't mean in general," I clarify as we walk, waving my hands wildly like that will help drive home my point. "But working there—architecture, does it make you happy?"

A shadow passes over his face. "Yes," he answers, but it sounds robotic, and I don't believe him for a second.

It was only minutes ago that he told me I should do something that makes me happy, yet I can tell this doesn't make him happy.

Are we all fools to think there really is such a thing as true happiness in this world?

Or are we all destined to live a lie spun of our own delusions?

nine
...

xander

I WALK OFF THE FIELD, sweat beading on my face. I'm exhausted. I thought college ball was bad but it has nothing on the pros. It's absolutely grueling and yet, I love it.

My practice schedule makes working for my dad difficult but not impossible. I know my life would be a hell of a lot easier if I would tell him and quit so I could focus on football completely, but for right now I want to keep this to myself for as long as I can. It's difficult, considering there's a lot of people out there who know I'm on the team—and this is my home state, which increases the odds of someone recognizing me. My college coach and teammates all know—all except Cade. I know Cade won't understand when I tell him—which I will, I'll tell them all—but I hope he'll be able to forgive me since we've been friends since we were in diapers. Although, I conveniently forget that I married his sister—

yeah, after he finds out about that and coupled with this ... I might lose my best friend.

A sharp pang pierces my chest as I head for the showers.

I remind myself that even if he gets pissed—which he will—he's a pretty chill guy and he'll eventually come around. Unfortunately, I'll probably have to let him punch me before he feels better.

I finish my shower, change my clothes, say my goodbyes to a few of the guys, and head out. I'm exhausted and my body aches all over. All I want to do is get home and tumble face first into bed.

I yawn as I head to my bike with my gym bag slung over my shoulder.

Bed.

I am going home and going to bed.

Forget dinner. All I need is sleep.

Unfortunately, I'm going to hit peak traffic time, which means the normal forty-five-minute ride home will be closer to an hour and a half.

I fix my bag onto the bike, slip on my jacket and helmet, and get out of there.

An hour into my drive, I watch, stunned as the fluffiest dog I've ever seen darts out into the road and into traffic. I slam on my brakes and the car behind me honks its horn. The car in the lane beside me doesn't see the dog in time and hits it.

Time seems to stop.

My bike passes the dog, lying there on the ground, and I see the blood matting its fur, and something inside me breaks. I can't leave this dog here to die alone. I veer off the road and park on the side. People honk at me as I run across traffic to get to the dog but I don't give a fuck; I'm not leaving it there.

I pick the dog up in my arms and carry her over to the side by my bike. She looks up at me with big, pleading, brown eyes and her breath is labored. "I'm going to help you," I tell her, and she blinks like she understands.

I fish around in my bag for my phone and call the most recent contact.

"Hello?" Thea picks up.

"Thea," my voice cracks.

"Xander?" She sounds worried. "Where are you? Are you okay? Oh, God, please tell me you haven't been in an accident."

"I'm fine," I assure her. "But there's this dog, it got hit by a car and-and I can't leave her here to die, I need to get her to a vet. I can't take her on my bike, though. I need you to come to me."

"I don't have a car," she reminds me.

"You can borrow my truck."

"Oh, right. I guess so. Text me where you are. I'll be there as quick as I can."

"Thank you." I breathe out a sigh of relief.

"And Xander?"

"Yeah?"

"Don't do anything stupid."

I chuckle. "Never."

She hangs up and I text her my location before I put my phone away.

I look down at the helpless dog in my arms as the traffic passes us by.

"It's going to be okay," I tell her, searching for the spot where the blood is coming from. I lay her down and remove my jacket and then my shirt so I can use my shirt to help stop the bleeding. I'm not sure if that's what you're supposed to do, but it seems like the logical thing to do, so I'm going with it.

Her tongue lolls out of her mouth but her eyes stay firmly fixed to my face.

Since I have the best fucking luck in the world, it begins to rain. It doesn't take long for me and the dog to be drenched, but I don't care. I'm not leaving her.

When my Nissan Titan finally pulls up, I breathe out a sigh of relief.

Thea hops out and shrieks, "Where's your shirt?" while waving her hands wildly at me.

"I used it for the dog." I stand with the dog in my arms and head to the backseat of the truck to put her in. Thea gets the door for me and I lay the dog across the seat. Her breathing has grown more labored and a desperate ache has seized my chest. I don't want anything to happen to her.

When she's lying down and I don't feel like she's just going to roll off onto the floor, I step back. Thea's standing beside me, her t-shirt and jean shorts soaked through, with her hair plastered to her forehead but she's still the most beautiful girl I've ever seen. With one look she steals my breath and seals my fate. I'm hers.

I want to take her face between my hands and kiss her beneath the pouring rain.

But we have more pressing matters at hand than me wanting to kiss her.

"I need to get my bike in the back," I tell her.

Thunder cracks in the distance and she shivers, looking up at the dark and rolling sky.

"Get in the car," I tell her, but the stubborn woman refuses. I'm not the least bit surprised.

I start for the bike and Thea calls out, "Can you lift that on your own? Do you need help? Xander, please don't break your spleen." She winces as I pick up the bike.

"Are spleens even real things?" I ask as I roll my bike to the back of the truck and lift it onto the bed. My muscles scream in protest from the weight of the motorcycle but I refuse to leave it here to be potentially stolen.

"I don't know," she answers honestly. "I'd have to Google it." She shivers again as I pick up my jacket from the ground.

"I'll drive," I tell her, heading for the driver's side.

She doesn't object.

When we're seated in the car and I've pulled back onto the road she says, "I already Googled nearby emergency vet clinics. There's one about five miles away."

"Perfect. You tell me the way."

She gives me directions, and in no time, we're pulling into the circular drive of the clinic as lightning strikes in the distance.

"You can stay here," I start to say, but she's already hopping out of the car.

I get the dog from the back and my stomach gnaws with worry. She doesn't look good. Her breaths are feathering and barely there and her eyes are only open a slit.

When I get inside, Thea's already there telling them what's happened and in moments, a metal gurney is brought out and they instruct me to lay the dog on it.

She's wheeled away from us like we're in a real hospital and I watch helplessly, wondering if this is the last time I'm going to see her alive.

I mean, it's not like she's my dog, but she's an innocent creature that's been hurt and I care about her. I've always had a soft spot for animals, especially dogs.

The receptionist asks us a list of questions, ones I can't really answer since she was a stray.

I catch the words, "—more than likely she'll be euthanized—" and see red.

"No," I say over the woman speaking. I know she's only doing her job, reporting the facts but I don't want to hear them.

"Excuse me?" She tilts her head up at me from where she sits at the desk.

"I said, *no*."

"Sir." She gives me a sympathetic look. "We're a vet clinic, not a shelter. We can't afford the cost of performing surgery on strays—"

"I'll pay it," I say, slamming my palms on the counter. "Whatever it is, I'll pay it."

She gives me a hesitant look. "It could be several thousand dollars." Her cheeks flush, and I wonder why she's blushing but then I realize I'm still shirtless.

"Xander—" Thea touches my arm.

"I don't care. I can pay it. Do you need proof? Is that it?" I start pulling out my wallet.

"If you'd like to pay for the procedure we need a five-hundred-dollar deposit, and if it's more, we settle that at the end, and if it's less you'll be reimbursed." I hand her a card and she appraises me carefully. "I assume this means you'd also like to adopt her?"

I nod. "Yes, I would."

Our rental house allows pets and I really don't give a fuck if Rae and Cade agree. Probably the wrong mindset to have since they *are* my roommates, but there's no way I'm letting that dog go to someone else.

She nods. "I'll get the paperwork together for the deposit and adoption."

Thea looks at me and her lips quirk slightly. "So ... a dog?"

"Yeah, a dog." I run my fingers through my wet hair. "You like dogs, right?" I rack my brain for any memory of Thea not liking them.

"Yeah." She laughs, gathering her damp hair into a bun on top of her head. "I'm just surprised is all."

"Surprised? Why?" My brows knit together.

She shrugs her slender shoulders and the edge of her t-shirt slips over one. Before I even think about it I'm reaching out and righting the fabric. A small smile touches her lips at the gesture.

"I don't know. It seems like you have a lot going on right now." I tense, momentarily thinking she knows about me being on the team. "What with working for your dad and this whole ... marriage thing." She smiles shyly at me. "Don't you think adding a dog into the mix might be a bit much?"

I shake my head. "Never."

She nods once. "I figured you'd say that." She smiles, and it's a happy smile, not like she's tense and worried about this. "So, what are we going to name her?"

Fuck it if my heart doesn't beat a little faster when she says *we*. The last week we've been doing good—great, even. We've been more like our old selves and it's been nice. I still wish I could kiss her anytime I wanted and ... well, there's a lot of other things I'd like to do to her, but baby steps.

"I don't know," I admit. "We'll figure it out."

She pushes a wet strand of hair behind her ear and looks up at me through thick dark lashes. "I think we better go home—"

"I'm not leaving her," I declare.

She laughs lightly. "You didn't let me finish. I think we should go home and change and then come back. We're both soaking wet. And um ..." She waves a hand at my bare chest and then points over to the waiting area. "I'm pretty sure you're giving that old lady heart palpitations."

I look to where she's indicated and find a white-fluffy-haired lady of about eighty staring at me with an unhealthy grip on her Persian cat.

I chuckle as my gaze swings back to Thea. "Yeah, I guess you're right. But I'm coming back."

"And I'm coming with you," she warns, like she's afraid I might tell her to stay.

I smile and grip her hand in mine. I cherish these moments, where even for a second, it feels like we're a real couple. I crave the freedom to touch her without the fear of being judged for it.

Without a word, we head out to my truck and home.

Cade and Rae are in the family room when we come inside.

"Heard you ran over a dog." Cade chuckles, eyes glued to the TV.

"*I* didn't run over it," I snap with a bite to my voice.

He looks up and his brows scrunch together. "Where's your shirt?"

"With the dog." I sigh, heading for the stairs. "Thea and I are changing and then we're going back to the vet."

"Why?" Rae asks, peering over the couch at us. Thea's already started up the steps and I stand on the bottom one. Rae's eyes narrow on us, and I know she's thinking, piecing together what might be happening under their noses. Granted, I don't think she'd ever guess we're married, but she's no dummy. She'll figure something out eventually or get Thea to spill with as close as those two are.

"Because I adopted her."

"You got a dog?" Cade laughs.

"Yeah." I shrug. "I hope you guys don't mind." I smile sheepishly.

Rae smiles back. "I don't care."

"Me either." Cade turns back to the TV. "But if it shits in the house and I have to pick it up, I'm putting it in your bed."

I laugh. "Fair enough."

With Cade and Rae occupied by the show they're watching, Thea and I head upstairs to change.

I don't know how long we'll be at the vet so I dress comfortably in a pair of sweatpants and a sweatshirt. I meet Thea in her room just as she's pulling a loose sweater on. I hiss between my teeth as she tugs it down and her black bra disappears. She tilts her head, looking at me over her shoulder, and smiles shyly.

"Do you have any idea how much I want to kiss you right now?"

She turns fully and pulls on a pair of cotton shorts. "Why would you want to kiss me? You could kiss anyone you wanted—so why me?"

I swallow thickly. "Because you're the only girl I ever see."

Her eyes flick from mine to my lips and back again.

Just like that day in the kitchen, it's like a switch is flipped. I cross the room to her, take her face in my hands, and kiss her. I kiss her like she's the sun, and moon, and stars all wrapped in one. She's everything in this world that dreams are built upon. A quiet moan builds in her throat and it spurs me on. My hands leave her face, ghosting down her sides, where I grasp her legs and lift her up, sitting her on top of the dresser. Her fingers wind into my hair, tugging on the strands near my neck. I know we're playing with fire, but I don't give a fuck if we get burned.

Her hands move down to my neck and over my shoulders and then she starts pulling and tugging on my sweatshirt, trying to get it off. I break the kiss long enough to pull it over my head and then I'm back, taking her lips in mine. She tastes sweet, like coconut and I wonder if maybe she'd just put Chapstick on. Her hands roam down my chest settle on my waist.

I yearn for more, so much more, but I know now isn't the time. We're still on rocky ground and I don't want to push her too far, too fast, to the point that I lose her before I have her.

She gasps for air when we part, and I hover there, my nose brushing hers. I'm scared if I move that Thea will go back into her freak-out-zone and I don't want the shutters to come back down on everything we feel. I want, just once, to not feel guilty for what I feel—for what *we* feel.

She raises her eyes to mine. "You're going to be the end of me."

I chuckle and wrap a piece of her damp hair around my finger. "Funny, I was going to say the same about you. I guess we'll just do each other in."

She smiles widely and her eyes squint at me. That's something I've always loved about Thea; when she's truly happy and gives you a genuine smile her eyes all but disappear. "I guess we'll go together then." One arm wraps around my neck and her other hand lies palm flat against my chest over my heart.

My hands settle on her hips and I lift her off the dresser, setting her on the floor. She blinks up at me with wide eyes and says, "You make me happy. You should already know that, but in case you don't, I'm telling you."

I do know I make her happy, it's evident from all the time we spend together talking and laughing, but regardless, it feels good to hear her say it.

I don't know how to respond so I simply nod and smile and bend down to pick my sweatshirt off the floor. I slip it on over my head and tug it down.

"Maybe we should bring your laptop," I suggest. "If we're there for a while we can watch more *Charmed*."

She laughs and goes to grab her laptop off her nightstand, putting it in her backpack. "You really like that show, don't you? And you were so reluctant to watch it," she tsks.

"Yeah, yeah." I shrug like it's no big deal. "You were right, and I was wrong. It's a good fucking show and I'm addicted, okay? I need to know what happens next."

I follow her to her door and when she swings it open, Rae is standing on the other side. Thea jolts back and into my chest. I grab her elbow to steady her and she quickly jerks away. I know I shouldn't be offended, but I am. I don't let it show, though.

"Interesting," is all Rae says before heading down the hall to the room she shares with Cade.

Thea looks up at me with worried eyes and I shrug.

There's nothing we can do about it now.

ten
...

xander

WE FALL asleep in the waiting room of the vet's office watching *Charmed*, and when I wake up, my body is stiff and hurting. It doesn't help that I had one hell of a practice yesterday, but I blame most of the pain on sleeping on the wooden bench sitting up. Thea's stretched out with her head on my lap, sleeping peacefully. I run my fingers through her hair, rubbing the soft strands against my thumb and forefinger.

"Sir?" A hushed whisper sounds somewhere behind me and I turn my head. "Oh, good, you're awake." A different woman from yesterday comes over and sits down in the chair in front of me. Instantly, my heart seizes with worry that she's going to tell me the dog didn't make it. "I wanted to let you know that the surgery was successful and your dog will be fine. She's going to need to rest for a while, and be watched carefully, but she's doing well."

I breathe out a sigh of relief. "Thank you."

Thea stirs in my lap and sits up, rubbing at her eyes. "What's going on?"

"She came to tell me the dog's going to be okay."

"Oh." Thea brightens. "That's great."

The woman nods. "Does she have a name yet? I'm aware you only put in the adoption papers last night." She laughs lightly. "So if you haven't picked one yet, that's fine, but we'd prefer to call her by her name if you've decided."

I look at Thea and she looks at me. "Prue?"

I grin. "Prue," I repeat. "It's perfect."

The woman smiles and stands. "Prue it is. She won't be able to go home with you for at least a day—we typically monitor them for twenty-four hours following surgery. So I suggest you guys get on out of here and prepare for your new addition to come home with you."

"Thank you," I tell the woman. "And can you tell the vet and nurses thank you too?"

She nods with a warm smile. "Absolutely." She rounds the receptionist table. "We can finish your payment and then when you pick her up you won't have to do anything but get her."

"Perfect," I say, pulling my wallet out of the pocket of my sweatpants. I hand Thea the keys. "You wanna go on out to the car?"

She nods and takes them from my hands, heading for the

automatic glass doors. I can't help but stare at her slender legs and the way her shorts hug her curves just right.

I step up the desk and make the payment, sign the receipt, and hand it back.

"You look familiar," the woman says, staring up at me.

I shrug. "Must have one of those faces."

She shakes her head. "Do you play football?"

My shoulders tighten. "Yes," I admit reluctantly.

She smiles widely. "I knew it. You're new to the Rebels this year."

I nod once and grit my teeth. I don't want to say anything but I have to. I look out the doors and then to her. "If you don't mind, could you keep that information to yourself. Thea—my wife ... She doesn't know yet."

"Doesn't know?" She looks perplexed as another receipt prints out and she hands this one over for me to keep.

"It's complicated," I grind out.

"Yes, well, I won't say anything," she promises.

"Thanks." I nod. "You guys have my phone number and you'll call if anything happens to Prue, right?"

"Of course." I start to walk toward the doors when she calls me back. "Sir?"

"Yes?" I stop and turn around, crumbling the receipt in my fist.

"I know it's none of my business, but you should tell her. That's the kind of secret that you don't keep from your spouse."

I flinch. She's right. "Thanks," I mumble, and then I'm gone.

I slide into the driver's seat of my truck and glance at Thea. She's pulled her hair back in a sloppy ponytail and her face is free of makeup, but like always, she's the most beautiful girl I've ever seen.

"You hungry?" I ask.

She nods. "Starving."

I don't even ask her where she wants to go: I already know. That's the beauty of knowing someone better than you know yourself.

We arrive at the local restaurant a few minutes later. It's a favorite of all of ours and under normal circumstances, I would've called the whole gang to join us, Jace and Nova included, but I selfishly want Thea all to myself.

I park and we head inside, and when she smiles over her shoulder at me as we're guided to our table I feel like the luckiest guy in the world. I have my dream job and my dream girl, life can't get any better. Except for the fact that I'm keeping said dream job from my dream girl. I don't know how she'll react when I tell her, but I know now that it's not something I can keep a secret from her for much longer. She deserves to know more than anyone else. Not because she's my wife, but because she's always been there cheering me on, my biggest support system. I don't think she ever missed a game that we played. She was always there in the stands, rain or shine, screaming her lungs out.

We take our seats and both immediately slide our menus to the edge of the table.

Thea reaches up and pulls her hair from the ponytail, shaking out the longer strands.

"I need a nap," she declares, rolling her neck.

"Me too," I agree.

"But first we should pick up some things for Prue."

I nod in agreement. "Yeah, we're going to need a lot of stuff."

She props her elbows on the table and her head in her hands. Her eyes are tired but they shine with something I'd like to think is happiness—because selfishly I want to think that she's happy because she's with me, that *I* make her happy.

"What all do you think we'll need?" she asks, wrinkling her nose. "I know nothing about having a dog."

I laugh and tap my finger against the table. "Well, for starters, we'll need a collar and name tag. A leash. Toys. Food. Bowls."

She holds up a hand. "I get the idea."

I grin as the waitress comes by to take our order. Once she leaves, I clasp my hands together and look across the table at Thea. "You're beautiful." I don't know what makes me say it—in fact, the words seem to fall out of my mouth without me even thinking about them, but they're still true.

Thea looks at me in disbelief. "Are you kidding me? With my dirty hair and clothes I slept in I'm sure I'm the furthest thing from beautiful at the moment."

I shake my head. "That's where you're wrong. Beauty is in the chaos—in those little imperfect moments where we just *are*."

She purses her lips, fighting laughter, but after a moment, she can't hold it back anymore. "You sound like an infomercial or maybe like a poet. You really break the stereotype for jocks, and I kind of dig it." She winks at me.

I chuckle. "You dig it, huh?" I smile in thanks at the waitress when she sets our glasses in front of us. I'm more than grateful to have something to drink.

"Yeah, I do. Even if you are a pretty big dork at the end of the day." She shrugs, taking a sip of her water.

"A dork? What makes you say that?"

She gives me a look that says I've clearly lost my mind. "You read *The Great Gatsby* for fun the other day and before that you were reading *Hamlet*. You're a dork."

"Well, you've got me there," I agree.

She smiles and her laughter fills the air. Making her smile and laugh is one of my favorite things, and I'll never grow tired of it.

Our food is brought out and we grow quiet, too hungry to talk. I stuff my face with eggs and bacon, barely pausing to breathe. Apparently, sleeping in the vet's office makes you ravenous.

We finish eating, pay for our meal, and head down the road to the nearest pet store to get everything we need.

I push the cart and Thea strolls along beside me. "What about this?" She picks up some sort of purple rope toy.

"Put it in the cart."

She looks at me, fighting laughter, and twists the rope around her fingers. "You've said that about the last five toys I've asked you about."

I shrug. "I don't know what Prue will like so we have to get a bit of everything."

"All right." She drops the rope in the cart. It joins the pile of balls, a squeaky bone, some sort of Frisbee thing, and a Chewbacca chew toy. She picks up a few more random toys and adds them in before we start down the aisle with leashes and collars.

I pale. "Why are there so many choices?" I pick up the one nearest me, a plain black collar, and ask, "This works, right?"

She snatches the collar from my hands and puts it back on the display. "That's so boring, Xander. You can do better than that. She's a girl. Pick something *girly*."

"You pick then." I sweep my hand to encompass the aisle.

She shakes her head. "She's your dog. You should choose."

"She's *our* dog," I remind her.

She laughs. "Then we'll pick *together*."

She moves in front of me and scans the aisle before picking three collars. "I like these, which is your favorite?"

I appraise them. One is pink with a flower thing on it, another is purple polka dots, and the last one has daisies on it. I point to the last. "That one seems more like Prue."

Thea nods. "That was my favorite too." She puts the others back and grabs the matching leash, dropping both items in our quickly filling cart.

We move to the dog food aisle, and end up asking for help since I have no fucking idea what kind of dog food to get, and then we head to the checkout where we also pay for a nametag.

Once we have that, we load everything in the truck. I

know we should head home, but instead, I swing back by the vet. I feel bad for poor Prue there all by herself. It would have to be scary.

"They're going to think you're a psycho," Thea tells me when I park in the lot.

I shrug. "I don't care. Prue's more important than what people think of me. Besides, I want her to have one of her new toys."

I hop out of the truck and open the back door, rummaging through the bags to find what I want. I pull out the little brown bear toy and head inside with it.

"Hi," I say politely to the new lady manning the front desk. "I'm Prue's new owner. I just wanted to drop this off since they said she'd have to stay the night."

She takes the bear. "I'll make sure she gets this."

"Is she doing okay?" I ask.

She nods. "She's sleeping, but doing fine. You have nothing to worry about."

"Thanks." I tap my finger against the counter before heading back to the car. I know it might seem silly, since twenty-four hours ago I didn't even know this dog, but I already care about her.

I slide into the car and Thea smiles at me. For a moment, my heart stops because this girl ... this girl owns me. Heart, body, and soul, I'm hers and she doesn't even know it.

"Home?" she asks.

"Home," I echo.

I know she's talking about a place, but I'm talking about her.

eleven
...

thea

I COLLAPSE INTO BED, exhausted. I haven't done much today so there's no real explanation for my exhaustion. I'm still marveling at the fact that we have a dog now. I couldn't even keep my hamster alive when I was ten—poor Brownie, may he rest in peace—so I doubt I can do much better with a dog. Hopefully, Xander will be better at it than me.

I roll onto my side and smile at the moon shining through the window and the bright stars beyond.

When I was little, I was obsessed with stars. I thought if I grew tall enough I could reach up and grab them, but it didn't take long for me to learn that the stars would always be unattainable. Sometimes, the greatest things in life are only meant to be seen and not obtained because once you have something it's no longer as powerful to you.

The door to the adjoining bathroom cracks open and Xander steps into my room. My breath catches and I think *maybe* I was wrong, because right now I have Xander and he still holds just as much power over me as he did before.

"Scoot over," he whispers into the dark.

I slide to the other side of the bed and he dives under the covers. The bed bounces and I laugh softly as I roll closer to him and basically land on top of him. I start to pull away but he reaches up, touching his fingers to my cheek.

"I love it when you laugh," he murmurs. "I love it even more when you're laughing because of me."

Before I can blink, he closes the distance between us and presses his lips to mine. The kiss starts out soft, hardly the hottest kiss on the planet, but soon it's like a match has been struck and we become an inferno.

My palms press against his bare chest as I try to get closer—like I wish I could claw my way inside and sink down into him. One of his hands fists in my hair and the other settles on my waist, dangerously close to my butt. I move so I'm straddling him and he sits up, the movement pressing me more firmly against him and he growls lowly. My heart speeds up at the sound. I love that I unravel him in a way I've never seen him come undone before.

His hand on my waist tightens to a bruising pressure, but I don't mind. My hands move up his chest and wrap around his neck. He nips at my bottom lip and I moan.

We're playing with fire, straddling a dangerous line of getting caught before we figure our shit out, but I can't seem to stop this. I don't *want* to stop this. I've been denying myself what I want for years, trying to save other people's feelings, but I'm done with that because what *I* want is important too and I want Xander in a way I've never wanted another person before. It's always been him, and while getting married wasn't in my plans, it might not be the worst thing that's ever happened—not that I'm going to tell him that.

He moves suddenly so my back is pressed into the bed and he hovers above me. I arch up, missing the feel of his body pressed to mine, and he obliges by lowering so we're flush. I nearly sigh in relief and wrap my legs around his waist. He groans and his hands slide up my shirt, little by little, until he finds my breasts. I'm not wearing a bra and he makes a sound of approval, deepening the kiss. He cups my breasts, and even though they're not the largest in the world, he doesn't seem to mind.

He breaks the kiss long enough to tear my shirt off and then his lips are back. This kiss is unlike any other I've ever had. It's like we're dancing to a song that only the two of us know. His thumb rubs against my nipple and my hips buck.

"Xander," I moan into his mouth, but the word is barely distinguishable as English. "Please," I beg, but I don't really know what I'm begging for.

He kisses down my neck, between my breasts, and over my stomach.

When he reaches the area above my sleep shorts, he presses one last kiss and then looks at me with heated eyes.

My heart sounds like thunder in my ears, drowning out my thoughts.

I can see Xander warring with himself, with whether or not he should stop, and frankly, I don't know what I want him to do. The rational part of my brain screams that we shouldn't do this, but fuck it, I want to.

"Thea," he whispers and he sounds pained. I think maybe he wants me to stop him, but I can't. I can't find the words, because my throat is clogged with everything I want and don't want to say.

He moves back up my body and kisses me deeply, branding himself on my soul. My fingers wind into his hair and I tug on the dark strands.

His hand ghosts over my stomach and slips beneath my shorts. I gasp and then bite his lip as he slips a finger inside me. I clench around him and I'm pretty sure I whimper.

His touch is heaven and hell all in one.

His eyes find mine and they're shimmering with desire. I can't believe that he's looking at *me* like that.

I grasp his face between my hands and our lips hover near each other, barely touching, sharing breaths.

His eyes dart down, looking beneath the covers where his hand disappears. I whimper as he applies more pressure and my breath picks up.

Close. So close.

And then I fall off the ledge and he drowns out my cry of pleasure with a kiss.

He pulls his hand from my shorts and lays down, draping my body across his. I can barely breathe but I start to move, to give him the relief he just gave me, but he shakes his head and tightens his hold on me so I can't move.

"This was about you, not me."

I lay my head on his chest. "Has anyone ever told you that you're too nice?"

He chuckles. "Maybe once or twice."

"Your blue balls are going to hate you later," I warn him.

He chuckles and kisses the end of my nose. "Yeah, well, some sacrifices are worth it. Baby steps," he murmurs and kisses me again, this time on the lips, but it's simply a peck unlike the passionate one from moments before. Just the same, it leaves me weak in the knees.

It's in this moment that I realize I'm dangerously close to falling in love with Xander.

When you've already loved someone the way I've loved him for years, it's all too easy to fall over the edge into a new kind of love.

A better kind of love.

A forever kind of love.

Xander looks like a kid in a candy store as we stand in the little waiting room and Prue is carried in. I'm seriously expecting him to break out into song and dance at any second.

The nurse hands her to him and he looks like he's going to explode from happiness. He looks to me with a goofy grin on his face and I find myself smiling in response.

"She was good last night?" he asks.

"A perfect angel." The nurse nods. "I have some release paperwork for you to sign and then you're out of here."

"Excellent." He sways with Prue in his arms. She's a medium-sized dog but she looks pretty small in his arms. Her mop of hair falls down in her eyes, and I swear she flicks her head to disperse the hairs so she can see.

We take a seat and Xander holds her in his lap while the nurse goes to get the last of the paperwork.

"What do you think?" Xander asks her. "Are you ready to go home with us?"

Prue shakes her body and I laugh. "I hope that means yes."

"Of course it does. We're awesome."

"All right, guys," the nurse announces as she breezes back in, "here's the last of it."

Xander stands and hands Prue to me and I grunt under her weight. She gives me a look as if to say *I'm not that heavy, get over it.*

The nurse explains what he's signing for and he scribbles his signature on the papers.

When he's done, she hands him his copy and smiles at us.

"I think it's so nice what you've done for Prue. Saving her and giving her a home."

Xander glances over his shoulder at us and smiles. "Some things are meant to be and will find a way no matter the circumstances."

My body heats at his words because I know he's talking about more than just the dog.

We head out to Xander's truck since we obviously couldn't ride his bike here.

He opens the door for me and I sit down with Prue in my lap. When the door closes, she raises her paws to the sill and looks out. I ruffle the hair on her head. "You're going home, girl," I tell her. Even though I might not be the most animal obsessed person out there, I still like them, and I'm glad she won't be living on the streets anymore.

Xander gets behind the wheel and slips his sunglasses on. "We're going for ice cream," he announces.

"Oh, we are?" I laugh.

"Yep. We have to celebrate."

"Hey—" I shrug "—I'm not going to complain about ice cream."

He drives about ten minutes away to a local place. It's small, with a few seats inside and more outside. He goes inside to order—he doesn't even ask what I want, he already knows—while I snag one of the picnic tables and sit with Prue. She sits beside me, tail wagging, and leans over to lick my face. I giggle.

"You're pretty cute," I tell her, scratching behind her ear. Her tail thumps madly and she tilts her head, encouraging me to scratch her neck.

Xander joins us a few minutes later and hands me my chocolate brownie sundae with extra sprinkles on top.

"I will never understand your obsession with unicorn shit." He grins and sits across from me, taking a bite of his peanut butter sundae.

"They're sprinkles, not unicorn shit," I defend.

He eyes my sundae. "Pretty sure you're wrong."

I make a big show of licking my spoon. I mean it to be playful but his pupils dilate and I realize what it really looks like and I blush.

We grow quiet, enjoying our ice cream and each other's company. It's a nice day, with blue sky and fluffy white clouds. The temperature is warm, but not too hot.

Xander finishes his ice cream first and disappears for a few minutes before returning with a small vanilla ice cream cone.

"Please tell me you're not eating that." I laugh.

"Of course not." He holds the cone out to Prue and her tongue slides out to lick the ice cream. "I gotta feed my other girl."

Prue takes a few more licks before devouring the entire cone in one bite.

I look at Xander with wide eyes. "Was that safe? What if she chokes?"

Prue licks her mouth and I swear she smiles at us. "See, she's fine." He shrugs.

I finish my ice cream and toss it in the nearby trashcan. "We're so not good at this whole dog parent thing and it hasn't even been a full day yet," I tell him. "Heck, it hasn't even been an hour."

He picks up Prue and carries her back to the car. "Are you kidding me? We're great at this."

I pat his arm. "You keep telling yourself that."

"Prue, no!" Xander yells. "Bad girl."

I snicker from the corner. "I told you we weren't good at this."

Xander picks up Prue and continues to scold her against chewing on furniture. "You see this?" He picks up a toy. "You chew on *this*, not the table leg."

She looks at him with wide innocent eyes and his shoulders sag. "She's so cute I can't even be mad. Look at this face." He holds her out to me.

I shake my head. "You're such a pushover."

He sets her on the floor and she immediately runs right back to the table leg. I cross my arms over my chest and raise a brow. "Cade's going to kill you and I'm going to laugh."

"You mean, you're not going to save me?" He pouts and his eyes shimmer with humor.

"You made your bed, now lie in it."

"It won't be so bad," he defends. "She'll learn."

"I hope so." I sigh. "But if she chews up my shark slippers, I'm done." I raise my hands to emphasize my doneness.

Xander presses his lips together to hold in his laughter. "Your slippers are already falling apart.

"They're *sacred*," I defend.

"Do you even know the definition of sacred?" He smirks and strides forward. He's so tall that he only has to take two steps before he's right in front of me. He places his hands on my waist and bends down to kiss me. For a moment, my body seizes with fear at being caught, but then I remind myself that Cade's at the gym and Rae's grocery shopping.

"Yes, I know the definition," I breathe, slightly light-headed from his proximity. His dark eyes flit over my face and I see so many things reflected there. Things that scare me with their intensity. "Why are you looking at me like that?" I whisper the question in the shared air between us.

His tongue slips out, wetting his lips. "Because I see you."

A shiver runs down my spine. "That makes no sense." *Yes, it does.*

His lips turn up slightly but he says no more as he steps back and breaks the moment. I'm growing used to these short and powerful moments between us. It's like we're a rubber band pulled back and we can only go so far before we snap together.

Xander picks up Prue and heads for the kitchen.

I watch him disappear from the room, and wonder to myself how I ever thought I could resist him.

That boy is my kryptonite.

twelve

...

thea

IT'S BEEN two weeks since Vegas and my period is late.

I sit at the kitchen island, with my head in my hands, hating life. While Xander stands there oblivious with a spatula in one hand and a pan in the other. Under normal conditions, the sight of him about to make breakfast in only his sleep pants with the barest hint of his boxer-briefs peeking out the top would be enough to send me into cardiac arrest.

"How would you like your eggs?" he asks.

My face crumples. "Not fertilized." Xander looks at me blankly and then when he notes the tears in my eyes it clicks into place for him. "My period's late," I confirm, and my chest tightens with the words. *Is this what a panic attack feels like?*

He sets the pan and spatula down and braces his hands on the counter. He looks at me from beneath his thick lashes and I see the worry there. "Aren't periods late sometimes? It doesn't necessarily mean you're pregnant, right?"

I swallow past the lump in my throat. "My period hasn't been late in nearly a year, so ..." I hesitate and he clenches his jaw, looking away from me.

"Don't freak out," he tells me, leveling his dark gaze on me.

"Too late," I whisper. "I'm not ready to be a mom." My voice goes high with fright. "I may not know what I want to do with the rest of my life, but I do know I'm not ready for a baby. Poor Prue would probably starve to death without you." I wave a hand at him before burying my face in my hands. A sob racks my body. "Xander, I'm *scared*." I look up at him as a tear slides down my cheek.

He reaches out and swipes it away so fast that I'm not even sure he actually touched me. "Just breathe," he whispers, taking my chin in his hand and holding me captive. "I'm going to run to the store and get a test. You just ... sit here and try not to panic too much."

A humorless laugh bubbles out of my throat. "Easier said than done."

Xander swipes his car keys off the counter and uses them to point at me. "Don't do anything stupid."

Me? Do something stupid?

Never.

"What the fuck?" Xander pauses in the doorway, and I can feel his gaze on me. Prue sits beside me, licking ice cream out of the gallon container that sits on the floor beside me.

Me? I'm sprawled out on the floor in only my bra and underwear. I got so freaked out that I swear my temperature rose and if I didn't get out of my clothes then I was going to suffocate. So then, after I removed my clothes, I laid down on the cold hardwood floor in the kitchen. It seemed like the best idea in the world at the time, but I realize now from Xander's perspective I look like I've lost my mind. The ice cream drips on my bra and stomach probably don't help my case, either, but it's really freaking hard to eat ice cream while you're sobbing.

"I got hot," I mumble, spreading out my arms and legs like you would to make a snow angel. I end up bumping my arm against the ice cream carton and it goes sliding across the floor and Prue runs after it, lapping up more of the quickly melting ice cream.

He shakes his head and sets the plastic bag on the counter.

The plastic bag that holds my fate.

"Thank God your brother isn't here."

"Eh," I mumble. "He would've just shaken his head at me and left. *Rae* is the one that would ask questions."

"Where are they anyway?" he asks. "They're never here."

"He said something about going to see her parents yesterday. I think they're gone for the whole weekend."

Xander waggles his brows. "A whole weekend just the two of us?"

I hiss at him—like a cat, because I mean *seriously?* "Buddy, I think we should figure out if I'm pregnant first, because if I am you're losing your dick. Just sayin'."

"Buddy?" he mumbles to himself like he can't figure out why on Earth I would've called him that.

Still lying on the floor, I hold out a hand to him. "Help me up Mr. Betta-Not-Be-My-Baby-Daddy."

He suppresses a laugh and holds out a hand to me. Growing serious, he asks, "What are you going to do?" He sounds pained. "If it's positive," he clarifies.

I sigh. I know what he's thinking. "I wouldn't get an abortion," I tell him. "I don't think I could do that, but ..." I bite my lip. "I'm not ready for a baby, and how could you be, either? A baby's a big deal and we're already dealing with the whole uh-oh marriage thing. I don't want an uh-oh baby too."

"You don't think we could do it?" he asks. "Be parents."

"I'm sure we could." I shrug, reaching for my shorts that lie on the floor. "But I think we could be better parents down the road. Like ... when I'm thirty."

He chuckles. "So, you promise one day, if this is negative, you'll have my baby?" He grabs me by the waist and pulls me to him.

"Number one, it better be negative—no *if* about it—and number two, yes, if we're still together. I'd like kids one day ... far, far, into the future."

He lowers his head and nips my bottom lip. "Now there *you* go using the *if* word."

I shrug. "Hey, the summer isn't up yet. You might grow sick of me."

He chuckles. "I haven't in the last nineteen years so I think you're safe." He winks at me and steps back, grabbing up the plastic bag. "Shall we?"

"We?" I echo. "Last I checked you don't have to pee on the stick." I snatch the bag from his hand and head for the bathroom.

He follows, of course.

I try to push him out of the bathroom but he's too big. "Ugh," I groan. "Go away."

"Nuh-uh." He shakes his head. "You can't get rid of me that easily."

"Obviously," I mutter, letting my hands fall from his chest. The guy is as solid as a brick wall.

I take the box out of the bag and air whooshes out of my lungs. My hands shake and Xander notices. He doesn't say anything as he takes the box from my hands and opens it. He reads the directions out loud and hands me the slender white stick.

He takes my face between his hands, forcing me to look at him. "It'll be okay," he tells me. "No matter what, it's going to be okay."

I nod once and then go to pee.

I don't bother telling him to leave. I know he won't anyway, and besides, I kind of want him here. Without him there, I might make a mad dash for the window, and running away from my problems won't erase them.

I finish, lay the stick on the counter, and wash my hands.

Xander wraps his arms around my body, smoothing his long fingers through my hair. His lips press ever-so-softly against the top of my head and I wrap my arms around his body, pressing the side of my face against his hard chest. Wetness coats my face, soaking into his shirt. I hate that I'm crying again, but I can't help it. I'm scared to death.

"It's okay," he whispers. "I'm here. I'm right here."

He is and he always has been. He's my rock—the impenetrable force that holds me up when life gets rough.

Minutes pass and finally, he says, "We can look now."

I ease out of his hold and reach for the stick. My stomach drops. "What does this mean? I forgot what you said. Is it positive? Xander?" I ramble, seconds away from losing what's left of my mind.

He picks up the directions, reads them, and looks at the stick. "It's negative."

I exhale a heavy breath. "You're sure?" He nods and I break out in my happy dance. Raising my arms in the air, I chant, "Hallelujah, no bun in the oven here." I smack my stomach for emphasis.

His lips twitch with laughter and he leans his hip against the counter, crossing his arms over his chest as he watches me. I'm sure I'm putting on an entertaining show as I dance around.

When I finish my awkward dance, I look at him, fighting a smile. "Let's grab our furbaby and go for a walk to celebrate."

He shakes his head. "That's your idea of a celebration?"

"Well, that and an Oreo McFlurry." I wink.

"Of course." He steps away from the counter. "You better put on a shirt, though. You might give the old guy down the street a heart attack if he sees you like this." He nods his head at my black bra.

I shrug. "Then he shouldn't be looking. Not my fault these things are fucking great." I grab my boobs—which to be honest there isn't all that much there to grab—and Xander busts out laughing.

"You ..." He pauses, wagging his finger in the air. "You're something else."

"Eh." I shrug. "I try." I sashay out of the bathroom, floating on cloud nine, because even though Aunt Flo might be late, I'm not pregnant.

I jog up the stairs and Prue lifts her head from where she's lying outside Xander's door. When she sees it's only me, she promptly lies back down.

I grab a shirt and tug it on. My hair's a mess from lying on the floor so I run into the bathroom and brush it quickly before pulling it up into a messy bun. When I leave my room, Prue's no longer lying on the floor and I find her downstairs with Xander, already on her leash. Her tail wags giddily; Prue loves to go for walks.

The last few evenings, Cade and Rae accompanied us for her evening walk, so it's nice to go just us.

Xander bends down and rubs her head and makes the funniest face at her; I laugh but I probably shouldn't since I'm sure I've made the same face countless times. There's something about a dog that brings out the weird in you.

"Ready?" he asks.

I nod, shoving my feet into a pair of my flip-flops strewn on the floor. We head out through the garage and I stop to grab our sunglasses from his car. I hand him his and slip mine on before opening the door. It whirs up and then we wait for it to go back down before heading down the long driveway.

We're quiet as we walk and I marvel at the sunlight shining through the leaves of the trees. All too soon fall will be here and they'll shrivel up and die. I'm scared that what I have with Xander will shrivel up and die with them. I know I went into this completely against it, but I *love* Xander and I can already feel myself falling *in* love with him. I don't want to lose him, but I don't see how I can keep him. We went into things all wrong. Who gets married and then decides to stay together? I feel like we're destined to end in a fiery flame. I don't want that but I can't shake my feeling of foreboding.

As we walk, Xander eventually reaches over and entwines our fingers together. I smile and walk that much closer to him.

I guess, if this is meant to end, there's no harm in enjoying it while it lasts.

I look up at him and he smiles down at me. His dark hair tumbles over his forehead, and I swear he's the most handsome man I've ever seen. It's no wonder I've had no luck in the dating department the last few years. When you compare a guy to Xander, they're always going to fall flat. And what I really love about him is he's more than a pretty face—his heart is pure and kind, and he's the most caring person I know.

I lean my head against his shoulder and I know, rather than see, that he's smiling.

We walk another block before he speaks. "Let's go on a date tonight."

I lift my head from his shoulder. "Like a real, actual date?" I raise a brow.

He grins. "You *are* my wife, so a date seems appropriate, especially considering we haven't had one before."

I nod. "I'd like that."

He grins. "Good. Pick you up at six." Then he winks.

I laugh. "Lucky you, you won't have to go far to pick me up. Only the next bedroom."

He chuckles. "I promise to knock on your door like it's a real date."

"I'm going to hold you to that," I jest.

This, right here, feels good. It feels right. It feels *real*.

What does one wear on their first date with the man that's actually their husband?

A skintight sexy dress, that's what.

I put more effort into my makeup than usual and leave my hair down, the ends curling.

I slip my feet into a pair of strappy heels and admire my reflection in the floor-length mirror on my wall. I don't get dressed-up often, but damn I look good—if I do say so myself.

I grab my clutch off my dresser just before a knock sounds on my bedroom door.

It's six on the dot.

I swing the door open, and I can't stop the smile when I see Xander. His hair flops over his forehead and he reaches up, pushing the shaggy strands back. Someone else might think he needs a haircut, but I like the look on him, along with the stubble on his cheeks. He's dressed in a pair of gray pants with a blue button-down shirt tucked into them, and a black belt. He grins crookedly and pulls his hand from behind his back, revealing a single peony.

My favorite flower.

I gasp, shocked that he'd remember. I think it's something I've only mentioned once, twice at the most, that I liked the flower. But he remembered.

"Thank you." I take it from him. I inhale the fresh scent of the flower and try to hide the fact that I'm swooning. The boy is good. Too damn good.

"We better hurry," he says. "We have reservations at Blanco."

I gape. "That place is like crazy expensive."

He shrugs. "You deserve the best."

"I would've been happy with McDonald's."

He laughs and shakes his head. "That might be so, but we're not having our first date at McDonald's."

"Is McDonald's second date appropriate?" I ask as I step out into the hall and start down the steps.

His chuckle sounds beside me. "More like third date."

"You ruin all the fun. Happy meals are the best."

I head to the kitchen and find that the single peony I hold is actually a part of a much bigger bouquet that he already has in a vase. I turn around and smile at him.

"You're good," I say, slipping the flower into the vase with the others.

He shoves his hands in his pockets and lifts his shoulders. "I try."

Prue brushes against my leg and I look down to find her standing between us, tail wagging.

"Aw, look at her." I frown. "She wants to go with us."

Xander bends and pets her. "Sorry girl, not this time," he tells her. "We'll be back soon."

She looks at us sadly but pads over to her bed and lies down, like she knows exactly what he said.

"We should stop off on our way home and bring her some T-R-E-A-T-S." I spell out the word, because Prue already knows what that word means, and if I say it out loud she'll expect one right this second.

Xander smiles and swipes his keys from the kitchen counter. "We should," he agrees, taking my hand and leading me out through the garage and to the driveway.

He unlocks his truck and opens the passenger door for me. I slip inside and he closes the door, jogging around and sliding into the driver's seat a second later.

He grins over at me and says, "You know, I never actually thought we'd end up here."

"Married with a furbaby?" I ask, raising a brow.

He laughs and puts the car in reverse. "Well, that too, but I meant going on a date."

"Man, we do everything ass backwards." I laugh and bend down to adjust the strap of my heel.

"I wouldn't have it any other way."

When I look over at him, he's grinning from ear to ear, and I can't help but smile back. "Yeah, I wouldn't, either," I admit.

"You know—" he clears his throat "—I wanted to take you on a date long before this."

I lean my head against the headrest. "Really? And when was the first time you thought about it?"

He shrugs and keeps his eyes on the road as we exit the neighborhood and head for the highway.

"Come on," I plead. "Tell me. I won't be weirded out."

He wets his lips and glances at me quickly. "I was sixteen and you were thirteen and you were going out for pizza with that weird kid that only wore polo shirts. I have never been so jealous of a dorky-braces-wearing-*kid* in all my life. I felt like shit for feeling the way I did. You were practically just a kid and I was ... *not*."

I laugh lightly and glance out the window. "That's the summer you basically ignored me."

"Yeah, well, I was afraid I might do something stupid."

"I wouldn't have minded, you know? If you'd done something stupid."

He smiles crookedly. "That so?"

"Hey," I say defensively, "crushing on your brother's best friend is nothing new and you're hot, who could blame me?"

He shakes his head. "So you still think I'm hot?"

"I *did* marry you."

"So you married me because you think I'm hot?"

"No, I married you because I wanted to."

The words slip out so quickly and there's no way for me to take them back. It's the first time I've admitted the part I played in us getting married, and the fact that I remember more than I originally thought.

He chooses not to mock me for what I said—like I might him in this situation—and instead, reaches for my hand.

We arrive at the restaurant soon after, and I marvel at the niceness of it. I've never been here before, and I wasn't lying when I said I'd be happy with McDonald's but something tells me this is going to be much better.

Xander pulls up to the front and hops out, handing his key to the valet before turning to grab my door and help me out.

A restaurant with a valet? This place is even snazzier than I originally believed.

Xander guides me inside and straight to the hostess.

"Reservation for Kincaid," he tells her.

She looks at us questioningly, probably noting our young age, before her gaze drops to the list. "Ah, here you are." She turns sharply on her heel and expects us to follow.

My heels clack against the black marble floor and my eyes keep roaming over the white walls and chrome fixtures. It looks like something out of a Bond movie.

The restaurant is large, with many seating areas that are somehow designed so they seem relatively private, and the kitchen is viewable to the eating area through a thick glass wall.

She leads us to a table near the kitchen in a prime spot to watch all the action.

Xander pulls out my chair for me and I mumble a thank you.

"Enjoy your meal," she says, handing us our menus.

I take the menu from her and open it up, nearly falling out of my chair at the prices. "Xander," I hiss. "I'm going to have to sell a kidney to be able to afford this meal."

He chuckles. "Nah, I got it. Don't worry." And then he *winks*, fucking winks at me like it's no big deal, which I guess to him it's not. But I still don't want him spending his hard-earned money on a meal this expensive.

"Xander—" I start.

"Thea," he says my name the same way I said his. "Don't worry about it," he assures me. "I want us to enjoy tonight and not worry about the little things."

I press my lips together and say no more. A waiter comes and we both order water and Xander also requests a bottle of wine. I'm surprised when the waiter doesn't card either of us —Xander's legal, but I'm not—but I choose not to say anything.

By the time the waiter returns, I've picked out a pasta meal that I can't even pronounce and definitely can't spell, but it sounds good so that's what matters.

"Have you all decided?" he asks us, motioning to our menus sitting on the other side of the table.

I nod and point to what I want—no way am I butchering the Italian name for the pasta, and Xander orders a steak.

When the waiter leaves, I reach for my wine glass and hope Xander doesn't notice the slight shake to my hand. I don't know why I'm nervous. This is *Xander*—a guy I've known my whole life, and the last two weeks have been great, but this right here makes what we're doing real. This isn't us sneaking around the house behind our friends' backs, or secretive glances exchanged at the office, this is us out in the open exposing ourselves as a real couple. We're not *hiding* and that makes me nervous. I mean, I doubt anyone we know would see us here anyway, but it still feels slightly dangerous.

Xander toys with the napkin in his lap, and I wonder if he's as nervous as I am.

I sip a big gulp of wine and nearly choke.

That's enough wine for now, I think to myself and set the glass on the table.

Xander sips at his own glass, sets it down, and taps his fingers on the table.

Tap. Tap. Tap.

Just when I can't take the awkward silence between us anymore, he blurts, "I have to tell you something."

My heart momentarily stops with fear at what he might be about to say. Illogical thoughts run through my mind.

He's changed his mind and wants the divorce right now and he brought me to this nice restaurant to soften the blow.

He has a secret love child.

He hates cheese.

"I got drafted for the Rebels."

Wait? What? "Yeah," I say hesitantly. "I already know." His eyes widen in surprise. I think he was expecting me to scream and throw my wine at him or something. "*That's* what you wanted to tell me?" I ask for clarification and he nods.

"How did you know?" he asks.

I snort. "Xander, I'm a football-obsessed freak. Did you seriously think you could get drafted to our hometown team and I wouldn't know? Man, you don't give me enough credit." I take a sip of my wine.

"But," he starts hesitantly. "You never said anything."

I shrug. "Neither did you," I counter. "I figured it had something to do with Cade so I kept my mouth shut."

"So, he doesn't know?" Xander asks.

"I mean, I guess he doesn't. I don't think he's paid attention to anything football related since before the season ended. I always felt like football was more of an obligation for him than a passion." I cross my fingers together. "So, that being said, why didn't you think you could tell *me?*"

He sighs and rakes his fingers through his hair, his jaw ticking. "I don't know. It's stupid. For a while it didn't seem real, and then I felt like I was letting everyone down for pursuing football as my career."

"But it's what you love," I counter. "You're letting yourself down if you don't pursue it."

He shakes his head, a smile playing on his lips. "Has anyone ever told you that you're very wise?"

"No, but I'm glad you think so." I raise my glass to my lips and take a small sip.

"So," he says hesitantly, flicking his dark hair from his eyes with a swish of his head, "you're not mad at me?"

"Well, I think you're an idiot for keeping this a secret from everyone, but no, I'm not mad. We all have our secrets," I whisper, thinking of Cade and my father. "Have you told your parents? Who all knows?"

"Well," he says with a swoosh of his hand, "you're the only person I've told, but you already knew, so now I'm wondering how many other people know."

"You should tell your parents," I tell him. "Stop leading your dad on. I know he's thrilled you're supposedly following in his footsteps, but he'll also be thrilled for you to follow your dreams. Don't forget that."

He smiles at me and reaches across the table for my hand. "I'll tell them soon," he promises. "Will you go with me?"

"Sure," I say. Xander's family is practically mine.

"Mom's been begging all of us to get together for a family dinner—you and Cade included."

I fight a smile. "Does that mean you're inviting Cade to this dinner to tell him too?"

Xander lets go and sits back, exhaling a heavy sigh. "I suppose. Might as well tell everyone."

Before he can say any more, our meal is brought out. My stomach rumbles at the scent of my pasta meal, and I try not to act like a savage as I dig in, but I'm *starving*.

Apparently, thinking you're pregnant burns a lot of calories because I feel like I haven't eaten anything all day.

We're quiet for a few minutes as we eat and then he laughs, laying down his fork. "I seriously can't believe you knew and didn't say anything."

"Hey." I raise my hands in surrender. "Don't be mad at

me, you're the one that kept it a secret, I was just following your lead."

He shakes his head. "I feel so stupid for not telling you sooner."

I shrug and take another bite of my pasta. "It was stupid," I agree. "But I guess you felt like that's what was best for you at the time. Now tell me, how's practice been? Is it brutal? Can I watch? There's nothing quite like a bunch of sweaty guys piling on top of each other in those tight pants." I make a grabbing motion with my hands.

Xander chokes on a bite of food and beats at his chest with a closed fist. "Thea," he says my name in shock.

"What?" I shrug innocently. "I love the game, but you can't blame me for wanting to look at their butts. I mean, those pants ... yes. Just yes." He gives me a funny look and I raise my hands in a placating gesture. "Don't worry, I always look at your butt the most."

He snorts. "I have to say, you never cease to surprise me."

"Good." I grin. "It keeps things interesting."

"That's for sure," he agrees and takes a sip of his wine. I finish mine and ask for a water instead of having another glass of wine.

Xander moves the conversation away from butts—such a shame—and I listen intently as he answers my previous questions. He tells me about his practices and how grueling they are, especially with him pulling double duty and still working for his dad. My chest tightens with sympathy. It's had to be hard juggling all of this. I don't know why he's put himself through it. I guess most of us will sacrifice ourselves to please the ones we love. It's ingrained in our DNA to lessen the burden from others.

"As for you coming to a practice?" He pauses, leaving me at the edge of my seat. "I'll see what I can do." And then he winks.

I let out a groan. "You can't leave me hanging like that. That's like dangling a piece of chocolate in front of my face and expecting me not to bite."

Laughter shines in his dark eyes. "I have to okay it with my coach. Sorry." He tries to look innocent, but he's far from it.

"Mhm," I hum, finishing the last of my pasta. "I'm sure you're *real* sorry."

We finish our meal and skip dessert. Xander pays and I balk at the price. But it was a nice meal and I enjoyed myself so I don't comment. As we leave, he reaches for my hand and I find my body drawn to his side like we're magnets.

We wait for his truck and I tilt my head toward the sky. The sun has just set and there's *still* a smidge of color left in the sky, making it look more like a royal purple than inky blackness.

Xander's truck is pulled to the front and I find myself wishing it was the motorcycle even though there's no way I could safely get on it in this dress.

"I wasn't kidding about getting Prue some treats," I tell him. "She looked so sad when we left."

He chuckles. "There's a pet store down the street. We'll stop there."

It doesn't take us long to reach the store and we pick up a

few items—including one really large bone that I know she'll have a field day with.

Back in the car, Xander grins at me. "I do believe I owe you a celebratory McFlurry."

"Mmm." I lick my lips, and his eyes zero in on my tongue. "That sounds good."

He clears his throat and puts the truck in gear. "Good," he says, his voice slightly raspy. It's like he's seconds away from losing the control he's trying so hard to maintain. Even though it's dangerous for us, I secretly love that it doesn't take much on my part to unravel him.

He pulls into the McDonald's drive-thru a few minutes later and I bounce in my seat because I'm about to get a McFlurry, and who doesn't love those? He orders an Oreo one for me and an M&M one for himself.

"Are McFlurrys on the NFL practice diet?" I wag my brows. "Are you breaking the rules with me?"

He chuckles. "I burn enough calories to eat a McFlurry if I want to." He sits up and grabs his wallet from his back pocket.

"I can pay—" I reach for my wallet and he gives me a death glare.

"No," he says sternly. "I'm buying it."

I shrug. "I'd normally argue with you because I'm like that, but I did think I was pregnant with your giant spawn today so you kind of owe me." I sit back in the seat while he hands over a ten-dollar bill to the cashier.

He shakes his head. "Giant spawn?"

I wave my hands at him. "Have you not looked in a

mirror? You're like six-foot-five and built like a tank. Your child would break my vagina."

The cashier squeaks and throws the money at Xander. Apparently, she doesn't like the word vagina.

Xander shakes his head again, his laughter filling the car. "I'm six-foot-three."

I guffaw. "Oh, big whoop, like that makes such a difference. And I can't believe I mention the breaking of my vagina and you focus on your height."

"Well, my height is factual and our child is fictional." He grabs our McFlurrys and hands me mine before driving over to an empty space and parking his truck.

"Bleh," I gag. "Just hearing you say *our child* makes my ovaries shrivel up and die." I pull the spoon out and lick the ice cream and Oreo goodness from it.

He frowns. "Don't diss our fictional baby. He has feelings."

"What if our fictional baby is a girl?"

"What if it's a squirrel?" he counters.

I gasp and flick my ice cream at him, and it lands on the side of his face. "Our fictional baby isn't a *squirrel*."

His eyes widen. "Did you *flick* ice cream at my face?"

I smile sheepishly. "Sorry—heat of the moment and all that jazz."

He's not listening to my weak excuse, though. Instead, he slings ice cream at me and it lands in my hair. I look down at the blob of ice cream and lone blue M&M then back up at him.

"Oh, it's on."

And then we're slinging ice cream at each other. Our laughter fills the air and ice cream goes everywhere, but for the moment, we don't care about the mess, because the joy is in the now and the rest can wait until later.

Sticky ice cream sticks to my skin and I should probably be cringing at that fact, but I don't think I've ever had more fun than I am right now so it doesn't matter. Xander's just as much of a mess as me, with ice cream stuck in his hair, dirtying his clothes, and even some stuck in the scruff on his cheeks. We run out of ice cream and our cups fall to the floor. The only sound in the space of the truck is our breathing and we stare at each other as the temperature rises.

I think I move first, leaning my body over the center console and wrapping my hands around his neck, drawing him close to me.

I press my lips to his and he groans low in his throat. His hand finds my waist and he tries to get as close to me as possible. My hands move to his face and stick slightly from the drying ice cream. He angles my head back, sweeping his tongue into my mouth. My whole body ignites with desire and he pulls me onto his lap. The space is cramped, but neither of us seems to notice.

His fingers press into my hips with enough pressure that I won't be surprised to find bruises in those spots in the morning.

We're so lost in each other that we don't even realize someone's knocking on the window of the truck. It takes a loud smack of their hand and for them to yell, "Hey!" before we notice them.

The McDonald's employee glares at us like we're ruining her day. I wonder if it's the same one that was scared by my use of the word *vagina*.

Xander reluctantly rolls down the window.

"You guys need to go." She glares. "Or we're going to call the cops," she warns.

Xander nods. "We'll go."

She stands there, waiting for us to do just that, and Xander lifts me off his lap onto the other seat, looks pointedly at the McDonald's employee, and puts the truck in reverse.

Once we're out of the parking lot I dissolve into laughter. "That was *the* best. I thought she might throw a rock or something at us."

"Rock throwing amuses you?" He glances at me with a smile.

"Not actual rock throwing, just the figurative kind."

He chuckles. "Uh-huh," he says, tightening his hand on the wheel. I can't help but notice the vein running up his arm and the firm set of his jaw, and suddenly I'm completely turned on again.

"I want to kiss you again," I whisper. I want to do a lot more than kiss him, but I'm scared to say the words out loud —terrified of his reaction, which is stupid, I know.

He glances at me and the heat in his eyes is unmistakable. "I better drive faster then," he says, and his eyes flick quickly over my face, zeroing in on my lips, before he glances back at the road.

I wiggle uncomfortably in the seat, my bare legs sticking to the ice-cream-covered seats.

When we arrive home, we tumble from the car and into the house. I drop the bag with Prue's stuff on the counter and before I can turn around, I feel Xander's hand on my waist. He flips me around and his other hand delves into my hair

His lips latch onto mine and he kisses me slow, but deep. We're not in a mad rush like we were in the car and that turns me on even more.

He backs me up until my butt hits the counter and then he lifts me up and I sit on the edge of it. The added height puts me closer to his and he doesn't have to stretch down as far. I wrap my arms around his neck and my breasts push into his chest. A small moan leaves me when his hands edge slightly up my thighs where my dress has ridden up.

He moves his lips down my neck and my whole body arches, giving him further access. "Shower," I pant. "We should shower."

He stops what he's doing and pulls away, his body language suddenly cold. I'm surprised by the sudden change. "Oh," he says solemnly, and from that one word alone, I know he thinks I've used that as an excuse to stop things. He goes to step back but I grab ahold of his shirt and tug. He looks at me with a raised brow, waiting for me to explain.

"Together," I breathe, my eyes reluctantly meeting his. "I meant we should shower together."

Immediately, his eyes flood with relief and the coldness leaves his stance. "Fuck, yes," he growls, and kisses me quickly and slightly rough. He grabs the bone from the bag on the counter beside me and tosses it at Prue where she lies on the floor. "Have fun, girl."

And then he picks me up and tosses me over his shoulder caveman style, running up the stairs with me.

My laughter echoes around the stairwell and I swat at his butt. "Put me down!" I try in vain to get out of his arms.

"Not until you're wet." He chuckles, and I don't think he means it sound dirty but it does and I kind of love it.

He pushes open the door to my room and heads straight for the bathroom. Without putting me down, he turns on the shower and we end up inside, fully-clothed. The water beats against me, coursing down my bare legs.

"Now I can put you down." He lowers me from his shoulder but keeps his hands on my waist so I don't slip. I kick off my heels and reach down to toss them out of the tub. Next he gets rid of his shoes. He turns us so his back is to the water and I'm shielded from the spray. His eyes linger on mine as he reaches for the top button of his shirt and slowly slips it through the hole. He moves to the next one, and the next, and all the way down until his shirt is completely undone and the shirt hangs limply from his shoulders. The shower is small, and with the space his large body takes up I don't have to stretch my arms far to grab ahold of each side of his shirt and push it down his arms. It falls to the floor of the shower with a wet thump. His hair is plastered to his head and I watch the rivulets of water slide down his torso, getting lost in the fabric of his pants.

I know he's waiting for me to go next—he won't push

this, won't push *me*. He wants me to know the power is in my hands, and while I appreciate the gesture, he should know by now that I'm powerless when it comes to him.

I turn around and tug my hair to the side, exposing the zipper in the back of my dress. I look at him over my shoulder and take pleasure in the darkening in his eyes and the way he bites his lip. He reaches out a tentative hand to the zipper and slowly—oh so slowly—lowers it. My heart races in my chest and I crave his touch more than I ever have anything else. The dress begins to slip from my body and I let it fall, leaving me only in my lacy bra and underwear.

The dress pools on the floor along with his shirt, and before I can turn around to face him, he cages me in with his large body. The tile wall of the shower is right in front of me, and I brace my hands against it as he towers behind me. He rubs his hands up and down my sides before settling one hand on my stomach and pulling me more firmly against him. I gasp at the feel of him pressing against me and a moan leaves my throat.

God, I want this. I want him. This isn't like the frantic night we shared in Vegas. This is raw and real and us.

I reach my hands up behind me and wrap them around his neck, tugging on the strands of his hair. I tilt my head back and the look on his face nearly undoes me. He looks at me like I'm everything he's ever wanted in the world.

He moves his hands up my sides and cups my breast. I shiver against him.

"Please," I beg. His fingers find the strap of my bra and he undoes the hooks. It goes slack, and I let it fall down my arms. I move aside the shower curtain and toss it out and then do the same with my underwear.

I turn, facing him, and he eyes me up and down. Maybe I should feel shy beneath his gaze, but the only thing I feel at the moment is beautiful.

I move forward, pressing my hands to his solid chest and relishing in the slight twitch in his muscles. He's just as affected by this as I am.

"Please, tell me you want this," I breathe the words above the sounds of the water beating against the floor. A drop of water slides down my nose and onto my lip and I lick it away. Xander watches the movement and his Adam's apple bobs.

"You know I do," he whispers. "I want *you* so much."

Hearing those words … They feel surreal. For so long, I thought I was just another girl crushing on her brother's best friend, but to know that he's always felt the same feels pretty damn good.

"Good." I take his face between my hands and kiss him. The spray of the shower covers us both, the water coursing down our bodies.

Xander pushes me away slightly and removes the last of his clothes.

I stare at him, overwhelmed by the feelings coursing through me.

This is … *intense*. I never knew it was possible to feel so many things at once.

Fear.

Lust.

Worry.

Hope.

Love.

Yes, even love.

"Turn around," he says gruffly.

I do as he asks and then feel the water wet my hair more fully—since he'd been blocking most of the spray with his Viking-sized body.

When my hair is soaked, he steps in front of the spray once more and then I hear the sound of him squirting shampoo into his hands. He lathers the shampoo into my hair, working it into my scalp. I'm pretty sure having your hair washed—or brushed—by someone else is one of the best feelings in the world.

He moves aside and guides me back so he can rinse the soap from my hair. When it's out, he moves on to conditioner. I feel relaxed, but somehow excited at the same time.

When my hair is clean he moves on to washing my body. He doesn't try to use it to his advantage to tease me, but it works nevertheless. By the time the soap swirls down the drain, I'm a panting, wanton mess.

He washes his hair next—there's no way I could reach his head to do it—and the whole time his eyes are locked on mine. Even though he's not touching me and there's nothing sexual about what we're doing, I still think it's the most erotic moment of my life. There's something about the waiting and the *knowing* that this person is special.

It's not like I have the most colorful sexual history in the world—only a few random fumblings here and there—but somehow I *know* that this is different.

The bond we have is unique, and while I might try to play it off, I honestly can't deny its potency.

When we're both clean he turns off the water and neither of us move, locked in a silent stare down. I think he's still waiting for me to get scared and blurt an excuse to keep this from happening. But I can't. I'm tired of running. For years I've been running from this and in the last two weeks I've been flat out sprinting—and yet somehow, no matter how far or fast I run, I always end up back here with him. That has to tell me something.

He reaches for my cheek, his touch light and tentative, and I relax into him. "I'm scared I'm going to push you away," he whispers.

"You won't," I whisper back.

He brushes a wet piece of hair from my forehead and searches my eyes to see if my words are true.

"I don't know why my heart's beating so fast," he murmurs, and grabs my hand placing it over his heart. I can feel it thumping madly and I know mine echoes the same beat in my chest.

"Because," I whisper, "this is different than Vegas. This is ... This is ..."

He places a finger over my lips. "I know."

We climb out of the shower and he reaches for a towel and hands it to me. I quickly dry my body and he does the same.

We're not rushed, even though we both know what's coming. I think we both purposely want to take our time unlike the night in Vegas. I want to remember every second of this, and I never want to forget the way I feel.

I watch the steady rise and fall of his chest as he stares back at me.

I reach for him first and he picks me up, carrying me swiftly into his room. A moment later the soft feel of the cotton of his sheets presses against my back.

He releases me and looks down reverently. "We don't have to—"

I sit up and place my hands on his hips. "Just shut up already."

He chuckles huskily and lowers his head to kiss me. It starts out slow, just a gentle sweep of his lips, but it quickly grows in intensity. We're both desperate and aching for the touch of one another. I hold onto his broad shoulders and he angles his large body over mine like a protective shield.

He pulls his lips from mine with a gasp and presses his nose to my cheek, his lips a breath away from my neck, and whispers, "You have no fucking clue what you do to me."

I want to tell him that I think I do because he has the same effect on me, but I can't find the words.

I lie back on his soft sheets and he rubs his hands along my hips and down the sides of my thighs. My legs fall open and his eyes flash. His face is bathed mostly in shadow, but there's enough light in the room that I can't mistake the look on his face and it rocks me to my core. It's the kind of look you see a man give a woman in the movies—you know, the look where he's desperate for her and she's oblivious to the way he sees her, but I'm not oblivious, at least, not now.

But in the back of my mind, I recall flashes of this same look he's given me over the years—a look I've ignored or chalked up to something else—but there's no denying it now.

I want to yell at myself, and him, for being so stupid for so long—for delaying the inevitable.

Xander and I are like two stars colliding—I always thought we'd turn into a black hole, but right now, in this moment, I see that's not it at all. No, we've simply merged into one, making a larger, more magnificent star.

We've both listened to the voices of others for far too long—denying what we wanted, what we *needed* to not rock the boat.

Xander came to his senses sooner than I did, because if it was up to me, I would've gotten a divorce the morning we woke up in Vegas.

I'm selfishly glad now that he asked me to give him a chance, because what we have isn't something you find every day.

I know we still have the whole summer left, and things might change, but right now I'm happy and I think … I think I'm *in* love with him. When you already love someone so deeply it doesn't take long to take that plunge. It still scares me, though. Loving someone this much is only setting you up to be destroyed.

Xander's hands move back up my sides and he cups my breasts.

All thoughts leave my mind in that moment, and all that exists is him, me, and the emotion welling in my chest.

He lowers his body over mine and kisses me. The pressure of his lips is nearly bruising, but I love it.

His hands make a slow journey down my sides and one hand moves dangerously close to the point where I ache for his touch the most. He pulls back slightly, his eyes searching mine, and I beg silently for him to touch me.

His tongue slides out to moisten his lips and he swallows thickly, looking me over as I lie across his bed. I wonder if he's thinking the same thing I am—that I thought we'd never end up at this point. I know we had sex in Vegas but that was far different. Here, where we live, where the reminder will cling to the sheets not just in the morning but *always*, it means more.

My hips buck, seeking his fingers that are still *right there* but impossibly far away at the same time. My whole body is tight with the need for release. I haven't ever felt this worked up before, and he's not even touching me yet. I'm terrified that as soon as he does I might go off.

He bites his lip and the muscles in his stomach jump.

A moment later, he sinks to his knees and I'm about to ask him what he's doing when his mouth latches onto me.

Oh, that's what he's doing.

My eyes nearly roll back into my head from the sensation. My legs move restlessly and he places his hands on my knees, keeping me still.

My heart thunders in my ears as his tongue traces circles around my clit. I'm pretty sure it's about to beat right out of my chest. I wouldn't be surprised if it's flopping around on the floor right now, wondering how it got there.

His tongue moves in a rhythm that has my hips lifting from the mattress, begging and pleading for more. His name leaves my lips in a breathless whisper and my fingers delve into his damp hair. I need to hold onto something so I don't fall apart into a million pieces.

He sucks on my clit, the pressure just right, and then I do fall apart. My body shakes and he moves up, holding onto me. His breath is ragged, his lips pinker than normal.

I reach up, cupping his stubbled cheeks in my hands. With each breath I inhale, my breasts touch his chest. "I think you might kill me," I whisper.

His chuckle vibrates through his body. "You're tougher than that." He kisses me then, stealing the little breath I have left.

Even though I just found release, my body is begging for more. So much more.

"Please," I beg against his lips. "I need you inside me."

And that's exactly how I feel at this point. It's a need, not a want. I need it more than I need air to breathe. I need to feel him on me, in me, moving above me, branding himself on my heart and soul.

I reach between us and wrap my hand around the base of his cock, slowly stroking upward. He hisses between his teeth, ducking his head into the space where my neck meets my shoulders.

He pulls away roughly and fumbles with the drawer to his nightstand.

A moment later, I hear the sounds of foil ripping.

I watch as he rolls the condom on and flicks his head to

the side to keep his dark hair from falling in his eyes. He grabs my hips and slides me closer to him, positioning himself at my entrance. His eyes meet mine in the darkened room, and he's looking at me, not for confirmation that this is okay, but instead like he's taking a mental picture of this moment—like he too wants to remember every detail.

He guides himself inside me and I clench around him. I grab onto his back, my fingernails digging into his skin, but he doesn't protest.

He holds onto my hips and pulls out slowly, then slowly back in. I'm desperate for more, but I feel like we need to take it slow this time.

He lowers his head and his hair brushes against my forehead and his nose rubs against mine. His lips meet mine a moment later and I kiss him back with fervor. My skin is heated and it's not just from the friction. It's from the overwhelming feelings welling inside me.

His hands move to cup my breasts once more, his thumbs rubbing against my pebbled nipples. My hips move against his, our rhythm evenly matched.

He presses kisses down my neck and over my breasts. My head falls to the side and he quickly grasps my chin, forcing my gaze back to his. My breaths leave me in short pants and sweat slicks my skin. I press my hands to his chest, sliding them down his abs, and hooking them around his hips, pushing him more fully into me.

He bites my bottom lip and I moan. My fingers delve into his hair and my tongue tangles with his.

He wrenches his lips from mine and pants, "You have no idea. No fucking idea."

When my eyes connect with his I think to myself: *I know, Xander, because I feel the same.* But I don't say that—and even if I wanted to, I don't have the breath to spare.

His fingers dig into my hips once more, angling them up. The change forces him into me deeper and I grasp at the sheets so I don't fly away.

When I look up at him, I find that he's biting his lip, eyes closed, head thrown back.

I decide then and there that this is the hottest thing I've ever seen, watching him lose himself because of *me*.

As if he can sense me watching him, his eyes open and *fuck*. The force of the emotions in his eyes is enough to knock me down—you know, if I wasn't already on my back with my legs in the air for him.

Seeing that look in his eyes, coupled with the sensations already running through me, I lose it. My orgasm hits me and I *scream*. I've never been a screamer, but the sound tears from my throat before I even realize what's happening.

"Fuck," he groans, pumping into me faster, the veins in his arms and neck standing out. "Fuck," he repeats, and then a soft cry of, "Thea."

And then he finds his own release, his fingers digging into my hips. There will definitely be bruises there in the morning, but I don't care. Not one bit.

His lips find mine and he kisses me greedily as we both come down from our high.

Already I feel exhausted—like I could sleep for five years.

Xander slowly pulls out of me and I flinch.

"Did I hurt you?" he asks worriedly.

I blink up at him. "No, just missing your cock already."

He shakes his head at me. "You and your mouth."

I pout. "You love my mouth."

His eyes zero in on my pursed lips and he mutters, "Hell yes I do."

He goes to clean up, and I lie in the middle of his bed, unable to move.

He returns a few minutes later and moves me so my head is on the pillow and I'm under the covers. He slides in behind me and wraps his arms around my body.

I relax against him as my eyes grow heavier.

Right about now, I should be having regrets and freaking the fuck out, but I'm not.

Instead, I'm the happiest I've ever been and I'm terrified that it's all about to change.

In my experience, when things are too good to be true, it's usually because they are. I just really hope that's not the case here.

thirteen

xander

BEST WEEKEND OF MY LIFE, and as such, it ends too soon.

I slip out of Thea's bed early Monday morning and scribble a note, laying it on the pillow beside her. I have to get out of here and head to practice when I'd much rather stay right here in the peaceful cocoon of her room and pretend the outside world doesn't exist. Rae and Cade came back last night and immediately I felt both Thea and I shift into a different mode. One where we're careful about every movement we make and everything we say.

I fucking hate it.

But I'll do whatever it takes to make her happy, and right now, she's not ready to tell her brother.

I slip my sweatpants on and pick up Prue from the floor. I cut through the bathroom and into my bedroom, just in case someone is in the hall. I doubt Cade or Rae will be up at this hour, but better safe than sorry.

I carry Prue down the steps, clip her leash on, and walk her down the street to do her business. She's been great about not going in the house, but chewing on things is another story all together. She's already chewed holes into three pairs of my socks, ruined a pair of Thea's shoes, and started in on the kitchen table. It's a small miracle she hasn't touched Thea's shark slippers. I'm pretty sure Prue is afraid of the gaping shark mouth.

Prue finishes her business and looks up at me with her tongue hanging out, wagging her tail happily. She seems to be happy with us and I'm more than glad we could give her a forever home. The furball deserves it.

We head back to the house and I remove her leash. Immediately, she runs over to the green tin labeled TREATS and sits, wagging her tail.

"You want a treat?" I ask with a laugh.

She wags her tail harder and it looks like she nods. I remove the lid and give her one.

I head into the kitchen, pour her food into a bowl, and grab a bottle of water.

Heading back upstairs, I change into a pair of gym shorts and shirt—I'll have to change into my gear when I get to the field, but this way, if anyone sees me and asks, I can lie and say I'm going to the gym and it looks legit—and pack my bag with my work clothes.

I still can't believe Thea *knew* and didn't say anything. She surprises me at every turn. It's a relief to have her know, though, and I know I'll feel even better once I tell everyone else. Which will have to be soon. I can't keep doing double-duty. I'm running myself into the ground.

When I have everything I need, I head down to the garage and since it's a nice day, I opt to take my bike instead of the truck.

I get to the field and head into the locker room. Most of my team members are already here—a lot of them live nearby, whereas I'm about an hour away.

I change into my practice gear and head out onto the field.

Coach has us running up and down the field and I quickly lose myself in the steady rhythm.

We move on to working on actual plays and my excitement grows. I love this. I love the strategy and working together with one common goal. To win.

Hours later when I come off the field, the sun is high in the sky and I'm drenched in sweat. I know I'm going to be late for work—like *really* late, and I hope Thea was able to hold down the fort in my absence.

I shower and change into my work clothes—some of the guys look at me with raised brows but say nothing. I'm a newbie and the older guys tend to ignore me. I get it. I have to earn their trust before I can become a part of their inner circle.

Kincaid Architecture isn't too far from practice, but the traffic makes it take twice as long as it should. It's nearing lunchtime, so I say fuck it and stop off at a restaurant and pick up food for Thea and myself.

When I finally walk through the office doors, Thea sighs in relief. "Thank God you're here—answering phones is *so* not my forte. I'm pretty sure I accidentally told your dad to go fuck himself because I got so flustered. He kept asking for these papers and I don't know where they are and he kept asking for you so I told him you had explosive diarrhea."

I look at her in disbelief as I set the to-go boxes on my desk. "You're kidding, right?"

She frowns and mumbles, "No."

I sigh and shake my head. Then I laugh, because it's pretty fucking funny. "I can't believe you told my dad to go fuck himself."

She shrugs. "Might not have been him. He hasn't stormed in here to fire me yet."

"My dad would never fire you," I tell her. "And explosive diarrhea? Really, Thea?"

She shrugs her shoulders innocently. "I was under pressure and I blurted the first thing that came to mind. Nobody questions diarrhea."

I shake my head. "You're probably right about that." I reach for one of the to-go boxes and hand it to her. "Lunch."

"You da best," she chirps, opening the box. "Oh," she moans, "that smells good." She stares lovingly at the seared salmon and vegetables. She grabs the plastic fork and digs in. "Tastes even better. All the blowjobs for you, lover boy."

I snort and am about to retort when Cade pokes his head in. "Something smells good."

Thea squeaks and falls out of her chair, smack dab on her ass.

"Thea?" I ask worriedly. "Are you okay?" I dart over and offer her my hand.

Cade cackles from the doorway. "Didn't mean to scare you, sis."

Thea rolls her eyes and looks at me, shaking her head in disbelief. She places her hand in mine and I help her up. She promptly sits back down and digs into her food.

"Don't even think about trying to steal a bite after that," she tells Cade, pointing her fork at him.

He raises his hands innocently. "Wouldn't dream of it. I was just swinging by to ask you guys if you wanted lunch, but it looks like you beat me to it."

I shrug. "Sorry, man."

He waves away my words. "S'okay. I'm going to head out on my own then. See you later."

With that, he disappears from the office doorway.

"Thank God he didn't hear my blowjob remark," Thea says, her cheeks tinged pink. "I mean, I'm a pretty good liar but I don't think I could bullshit my way out of that one."

I chuckle and shake my head. "Do you remember which file it is that my dad wanted? I'll take it over to him before I eat."

"He was asking about the Ferguson account. I searched all the files on your desk and I couldn't find it on your computer."

"Oh, that one? It's right here." I pick up a folder from the table that sits behind my desk.

Thea's shoulders deflate. "Oh," she says softly. "I didn't look there."

I chuckle and smack the file lightly on top of her head as I pass. "It's okay. You were flustered."

"I still can't believe I told your dad to go fuck himself." She buries her face in her hands. "I'm the literal worst."

"No, you're not—maybe the funniest, but not the worst." I wink and then head down the hall to my dad's office. He's busy on the phone so I lay the folder on his desk and he gives me a thumbs up.

Back in my office, I eat and catch up on emails I missed while I was at practice. It's tedious and annoying, and yet another reminder of why I need to be honest with my parents. The fact that I'm twenty-two and acting like a scared sixteen-year-old kid is kind of hysterical.

I pack up for the day, and Thea does the same. "Can I ride home with you?" she asks.

I raise a brow. "Aren't you worried about raising suspicions?"

She purses her lips. "I suppose I should, but I don't really give a fuck. If I have to ride another hour in the car with Cade when I really want to be with you, I might die."

I don't call her on her melodramatics, frankly because I'm so pleased that she wants to be with me.

I nod. "You can ride with me then."

Her smile is blinding and she runs over planting a kiss on my cheek. "Thank you," she sing-songs, before running out and expecting me to follow.

We pass by Cade's office and she pokes her head in to tell him that she's riding home with me. He's so absorbed in what he's doing that he merely nods and motions us on, mumbling that he's going to be late anyway.

As soon as we enter the elevator and the doors close, she reaches for my hand. My chest fills with happiness at the gesture. It's such a simple thing but I'm so used to being the one that reaches for *her* when we're in public and in the last five minutes she's kissed my cheek and now holds my hand.

It's small, but it's progress, and it gives me hope for what's to come.

"You two look cozy," Rae comments with a raised brow.

Thea and I sit on the couch side by side, under a blanket, watching *Charmed*. Her head is on my shoulder and I suppose we do look "cozy" in the way she implies, but we've always done stuff like this.

Thea glances at her friend with narrowed eyes. "I don't miss your implication, Rae. We're just watching a show, like we always do."

"Mhm," Rae hums, sitting down in the leather chair beside the couch. "I'm onto you." Thea stiffens beside me and I swear she growls like a wolf. Minutes pass and Rae speaks again. "For the record, I've been rooting for you two since the beginning so if you *are* together now, don't think you can't tell me."

With that, she gets up and leaves.

Thea looks at me and sighs and I look down at her with a questioning look.

She shrugs and explains. "Rae picked up on something between us when she first started hanging around us."

I chuckle. "I think most people have. Your brother is the only one who remains oblivious."

"Eh, I don't know if he's as oblivious as he seems. I think he likes to pretend that there's nothing there so he can't feel bad for keeping us apart."

I smile and run my fingers through her hair. "Have I told you lately that you're smart?" She shakes her head. "Well, you are."

She beams up at me. "Have I told you lately that you're my favorite person?" This time, I shake my head. "Well, you are."

I think I like being her favorite person. I think I want to be her *only* person. The one she thinks of first when something good *or* bad happens. The one who's always there no matter what.

fourteen
· · ·

thea

"SHH," I hiss. "We're going to get caught."

"No, it's fine," Xander growls, kissing my neck. "They're not even up yet."

My legs are wrapped around his waist and he holds me up, my back pressed into the shelves of the pantry. I came in here to get oatmeal for breakfast and he followed, shutting the door behind us. I'd be lying if I said the forbidden feeling that clings to this moment didn't turn me on. It's kind of exciting, the thought of getting caught doing something—or in this case some*one*—you shouldn't be.

I lean my head back and his lips descend further toward the open collar of my shirt. My hands delve into his hair and I try not to get *too* lost in the moment, because getting caught making out in the pantry closet would *not* be the best way to tell my brother about us. I haven't told Xander, but I know it's time for us to tell him. It's wrong keeping this a secret, and frankly, he shouldn't give a fuck what we do. And I know, that there's still a chance that we could get divorced at the end of the summer—and that's what I think we *should* do, but continue to date—but tiptoeing around is getting old fast. I mean, we *live* with Rae and Cade. There's only so much we can keep a secret for so long.

Xander's lips move back to mine and his tongue brushes mine. I moan and my arms wrap around his neck. He adjusts his hold on me, his hands on my butt, and something on the pantry shelf falls to the floor.

"I knew it."

So much for not getting caught.

Xander and I jolt apart and he sets me down quickly, while we look into the laughing eyes of Rae.

"You—" she grabs my arm "—are coming with me. And you—" she points at Xander with her other hand "—it's about damn time."

I glance back at Xander over my shoulder, giving him an apologetic smile, and he looks utterly confused as to what just happened.

A quick look around shows me that Cade still hasn't wandered downstairs.

Hallelujah for small miracles.

Rae drags me into the laundry room and shuts the door behind us.

Crossing her arms over her chest, she looks at me sternly. "I can't believe you didn't tell me you were hooking up with Xander." She frowns and the look of hurt on her face makes my stomach hurt. "I've known you guys were perfect for each other for so long. I don't know why you thought you couldn't tell me."

I look away, nibbling on my bottom lip. "You're my best friend," I say, "but you're also dating my brother."

Her shoulders fall. "This is about Cade?" I nod. "You really don't think he'd be happy for you guys? Give him some credit. He's not a douchebag."

I run my fingers through my hair. "It's complicated. He's always warned Xander away from me, and I get it, I'm his little sister, but I'm not that much younger than them. And who knows, maybe he *would* be okay with us dating now, but we're not dating, we're married and that's complicated and—"

"Whoa, whoa, whoa," Rae cuts off my rambling. "Did you just say *married*?"

I smile weakly and nod. "Yeah—we ... um ... kind of got drunk in Vegas and ended up married." I shrug like it's not a big deal and something that happens to everyone.

She gapes at me and then laughs. "Yeah, you're right; Cade would *so* not be okay with that."

I sigh. "I know," I mutter the words and look away.

"So," she hesitates. "Were you guys together before the whole Vegas thing?"

I shake my head. "No, that served as the catalyst. I wanted to get it annulled immediately, but Xander wasn't having it. I promised him the summer to convince me not to get a divorce—and let me tell you, that boy does *not* fight fair."

Rae laughs. "Well, tell Xander that I'm happy for you guys but mad you didn't think you could at least tell me."

"You're not going to tell Cade, are you?"

She snorts and waves her hand dismissively. "Nah, you're on your own for that."

A puff of air leaves my lungs. "Great."

"Oh, and we're having a girls' day today. I'm calling Nova and we're going out to get our nails done or something."

I have to laugh to myself. Rae demanding a girls' day? I'm pretty sure that's one for the record books. I remember how I used to have to *beg* her to go out. She's grown a lot since we've met, and maybe it sounds weird but I'm proud of the person she's become.

"All right," I say. "Girls' day. Woo!" I shake my hands weakly.

Rae laughs at me. "Maybe the guys can do something too."

I force a smile. "That sounds fantastic. Girls' day and guys' day. Fun times."

Not.

xander

I pace restlessly in Thea's room, waiting for her to come up. I'm freaking out about Rae catching us. Not because of her finding out, but because of what her finding out might do to

Thea. I'm terrified it's going to send her back to where she was in the very beginning of this when she was apprehensive and scared and kind of standoffish.

Prue lifts her head from the mess of blankets on the bed and watches me pace. She looks at me quizzically wondering what the fuck is going on, but I don't have it in me to comfort her and tell her I'm okay, because I'm *not* okay.

When the door opens, I immediately ask, "Are you okay?"

Thea looks up at me with wary eyes as the door clicks shut softly behind her. "Fine. Rae was cool with it."

"I know, but are *you* cool with her knowing?"

"Yeah." She shrugs. "She said she wouldn't tell Cade." I nod, waiting for her to say more. "We need to tell him. Soon."

I wet my lips, shocked that she's said this. I expected the whole summer to pass with her still not wanting to tell him. This change is shocking, but I'm okay with it.

"Okay, we'll tell him."

"Maybe we should take him out to dinner. You know, butter him up with a steak and dessert. If we get him full enough he might not chase us if we have to run away."

I snort. "Your brother's in great shape. He could chase us with a gorilla on his back."

She sighs. "True. As much as I don't want him to know, we have to tell him. I can't keep doing this to us. It's not right for us to be a secret." She smiles sadly and closes the distance between us, wrapping her arms around my torso. I hug her back, laying my head on top of hers. "Oh—" She pulls away suddenly. "Rae insists on us having a girls' day and you guys getting together for the day."

I raise a brow. "Sounds delightful."

She laughs and steps out of my arms, heading for the bathroom. "I'm used to being the one that has to drag Rae out. I think this is the first time she's insisted on us hanging out. I think hell might have frozen over." She pauses in the bathroom doorway and I take a moment to look at her. To look at her hair tumbled over her shoulders, and the loose gray t-shirt that falls off her shoulders, to the black shorts that hug the curve of her ass. She's beautiful, inside and out, and she's *mine*. I never thought I'd be able to say that. She smiles at me, knowing I'm looking at her, and braces her hand on the doorway. "Shower?"

I don't hesitate.

"Fuck yes."

The shower was fucking pointless, but I guess it wasn't really about the shower, so *win* for me.

Cade wants to go to the gym, so Jace is meeting us there. Jace has been our friend since high school, and I've been so busy with work, football, and Thea, that I haven't seen him in a month.

Jace is waiting outside the building when we get there. "Fucking slowpokes," he says as we approach, and tosses his cigarette on the ground.

Cade shakes his head. "What an oxymoron. Smoking in front of the gym."

Jace's lips tip up in what someone might call a smile. "I dare to be different, unlike you fuckers."

We head into the building and straight to the free weights.

I don't say much, but none of us really do so no one can comment on my silence.

We stay at the gym for a few hours before showering and heading to a burger joint for lunch. Jace tells us about his music, and some gig he has coming up, so we make a plan to go and support our friend, and, of course, drag the girls along. My chest swells with happiness, because by then Thea and I should be out in the open, and I'll be able to touch and kiss her without worrying about Cade or anyone else.

I take a swig of my beer while Jace and Cade talk. Eventually, their conversation fades and Cade turns to me.

"What's up with you? You're too quiet."

I shrug. "Tired." It's not really a lie. Practice is kicking my ass.

He narrows his eyes. "You've been acting so fucking weird lately—leaving the house way early ..." He pauses. "Are you dating someone?"

I choke on my beer and Jace laughs. "No," I say vehemently. "Not dating anyone."

You know, since technically being married to your sister doesn't count as dating.

"Then what are you doing?"

"Just going to the gym." I shrug, picking at the label on

my beer bottle. "If you get there early enough there's no one around. It's nice."

He grunts. "You need to wake my lazy ass up to go with you then. This morning was the first time I've been all week."

"Mhm," I hum. "Sure." *Not happening.*

"What's up with you?" I ask Jace—hoping to turn the conversation away from myself.

He leans back in his chair and crosses his hands behind his head. "Just working at the bar, same old-same old. Glad to be done with school, though. What a waste of fucking time." He takes a swig of his beer and slams the bottle down on the table. The waitress quickly brings another one over and Jace gives her an appreciative once over. "Hey," he says, giving her a brooding look that I'm sure is meant to be sexy but it looks like he's constipated to me. It must work, though, because she smiles shyly back at him and says hey too. Going places with Jace usually results in him going home with at least three new phone numbers.

The waitress gets called over to another table and the eye-fucking stops. "Have you and Nova been hanging out?" I ask him—referring to Rae and Thea's friend. She and Jace hang out a lot, or at least they did before graduation, but who knows now.

Jace nods and reaches into his pocket for his pack of cigarettes, tapping one out. "Yeah, she's a cool chick."

"Have you ever hooked up?" Cade asks.

Jace shakes his head. "Fuck, no. She's my friend."

Cade snorts. "I didn't know you were capable having a friend that's a girl."

Jace shrugs. "Nova's different. Drop it."

Cade and I exchange surprised glances. Jace isn't normally so testy.

Our food is brought out and I dig into my cheeseburger.

"I wonder what the girls are up to?" Cade muses.

"I don't know," I respond.

But I really fucking hope everything's okay.

thea

I pick out a shimmery orange color for my toes and hand it to the nail technician.

Morticia One and Two—aka Rae and Nova—each pick out dark colors. Rae opts for a maroon red color and Nova chooses a purple so dark it's nearly black. She must really love purple because for the longest time her hair was a violet color. Now it's more of a magenta. It looks cool on her and I give her props for being brave enough to do something different. I'd be too scared to dye my hair a crazy color.

We take our seats side by side and I end up in the middle. This already feels more like an interrogation than a nice day with my friends. Lovely.

"You know," I say, dipping my toes in the hot water, "those aren't very summery colors."

Nova snorts. "Well, I'm not a very summery person," she

counters. "I have to choose a polish that's as dark as my soul to please the beast."

I laugh. "Should've gone with black then." She sticks her tongue out at me. "And what about *you*?" I swing my gaze to Rae.

She shrugs. "I don't really like light colors."

I sigh. "You both suck. I am a unicorn amidst trolls."

I turn on the massage button of the chair and close my eyes. Maybe if I act like I'm asleep they'll leave me alone.

"So, Thea married Xander."

My eyes shoot open and I glare at Rae.

Nova gasps and leans forward in her chair so she can see Rae around me. "Wait, what did you say?"

"Exactly what you think I said." Rae nods and presses her lips together.

"When?" Nova looks at me and even though she's glaring at me I can still see the hurt in her eyes.

"Vegas," I reply. "And *this one*—" I nod at Rae "—only found out this morning by accident, so don't be butt hurt that I didn't tell you."

Nova whistles. "Whoa, this is ... This is crazy."

"I know," I agree. "How do you think I feel? I'm living it."

"I just ... Whoa." She shakes her head back and forth, like she can't seem to wrap her mind around it. It is pretty insane, though. I'd be acting the same way if this situation was reversed.

"Cade doesn't know," I tell her. "So you can't tell Jace."

"I won't," she promises. "The last thing I want to do is get in the middle of *that*." She raises her hands innocently.

I sigh. "He's going to be so pissed."

"It'll be fine," Rae assures me. "Don't worry too much or you'll chicken out."

"So now I understand the need for this emergency girls' day." Nova laughs, wiggling her toes above the bubbles in the water.

Rae nods. "It was of the utmost importance."

"Xander and you are together now, then?" Nova asks.

I fill her in on the details that Rae already knows from when she dragged me into the laundry room. "I really like him, guys," I tell them, biting my lip nervously. "I've loved him forever, and being with him like this … It's everything I always thought it would be, but I'm scared. We're so young and there are a million obstacles in our way."

Rae shakes her head roughly. "No, don't think like that or you'll psyche yourself out. I know being married right now isn't ideal, but maybe that's just the path you guys are meant to take. Let things play out the way they need to and don't overthink it or push it one way or another."

I inhale a lungful of air. I know she's right, but it's scary.

But I guess life would be awfully dull if we weren't afraid.

fifteen
. . .

xander

I DON'T GET the chance to speak to Thea when she gets home, and it's nearing one in the morning now. I slip into her bedroom through the connecting bathroom, careful that the doors don't make noise.

She lies in bed and Prue pads in behind me, going to the corner where there's a bed for her. Thea smiles when she sees me and pats the space beside her. It's become our routine—me showing up, and her welcoming me.

I slip into bed beside her and an infomercial plays on the TV across from her bed. Without me saying anything, she switches it to Netflix and puts *Charmed* on; we're up to season three now.

"How'd your day go?" I ask her.

She shrugs and the blankets ruffle. "We got our nails done, grabbed some lunch, and shopped. The usual. They asked me about us and I told them that we're together." She looks at me with uncertain eyes like she's worried *I'll* be mad they know.

"Good," I say, and relief floods her eyes.

"What'd you guys do?" she asks.

"We met Jace at the gym and had lunch. Cade and I came back here and I mowed the grass. Exciting stuff."

She laughs and snuggles closer to me, entwining our legs together.

"We have to tell Cade tomorrow," I whisper.

There's a long pause before she whispers back, "I know."

I settle my chin on top of her head and we focus on the show. Eventually, we both fall asleep, wrapped around each other like we're terrified we're about to be pulled apart.

Light shines through the blinds when I open my eyes. I glance at Thea's clock beside her bed and see that it says it's a little after eight. She blinks her eyes and yawns, slowly coming awake.

"Hey." I smile down at her.

She smiles back, her eyes still closed as she stretches her arms above her head and nearly punches me in the process. After a moment she says, "Morning," and her voice is thick with sleep.

Prue lifts her head and looks at me with wide begging eyes. I overslept and she's probably desperate to go out.

Before I can move, though, I hear my bedroom door close, and footsteps walking down the hall and stopping in front of Thea's door.

You know that feeling you get before something bad is about to happen? The one where the air around you goes still and your whole body grows cold? Well, I feel that right now times ten.

The door swings open. "Thea, have you seen—" Cade doesn't finish his question as he finds Thea and me in bed together. We could try to play this off innocently, like I fell asleep in here watching the show—which is true—but the way we're tangled together hardly appears innocent.

Thea sits up, panic all over her face. "Cade—"

Cade clenches his jaw, his blue eyes filled with a fiery rage that's directed smack dab at me. "She's my *little sister!*" he yells, shaking his head rapidly back and forth. "How could you do this? I told you to *never* go there and you fucking promised."

His breathing grows rapid and the vein in his forehead looks like it's about to pop. He looks like a red version of the Hulk with the color he's turning.

He looks torn between running the other way and sacking me on the floor. I'm prepared for either option.

"My *sister*," he repeats. "I can't fucking believe you." His hands flex at his sides.

Thea is silent beside me, but I think she's crying.

I push the covers back and stand. "I love her," I say, holding my head high.

Cade snorts. "You think you *love* her?" He shakes his

head rapidly back and forth. "You've never even had a real girlfriend and you think you *love* her?"

I grow angry. "Because it's *always been her!*" I yell back. "Always," I add softly, glancing at Thea. She looks back at me with wide, surprised eyes and parted lips.

Cade's eyes widen in surprise when he hears the truth in my words. He places his hands on his hips and tilts his head to the ceiling, exhaling a heavy breath. When he looks back at us, there's no mistaking the hurt in his eyes. "So, you guys are together?"

Thea looks at me and I look at her, communicating silently. She slips from the bed and goes to her brother. She looks up at him, clasping her hands together with nervousness. "Actually," her voice shakes, and I *know* she's crying this time, "we're married."

It's like all the air has been sucked from the room. We're all eerily quiet, waiting for someone else to say something first. Cade shakes his head and says, "What did you say?"

Thea bites her lip, stifling a sob.

I step up behind her, placing my hand on her hip. "We got married in Vegas."

Cade shoves his fingers through his hair. "I can't fucking believe this. I need to get out of here."

Before we can say anything else, he's pounding down the steps and the door to the garage slams a moment later.

Thea turns her body into mine, sobbing into my chest. Her brother means the world to her, and we were ready to tell him, so having him find out this way isn't good.

The door to Cade and Rae's room down the hall opens

and she pokes her head out, meeting my gaze over Thea's head.

"Well, that went well."

I press my lips together. I don't have a response, and frankly, I don't know how to make this right. If I was in Cade's position, I'd be pissed too. I guess we just have to let things play out. We've fought before and we always work everything out in the end, I'm sure this won't be any different. At least I hope not, because I don't want to lose my best friend.

sixteen

...

thea

I CAN'T BELIEVE that happened.

Hours later I'm still in a state of disbelief. I haven't spoken more than three words since Cade left and I'm pretty sure Xander thinks I'm in some sort of catatonic state. He keeps giving me really worried looks, but I don't have the energy to reassure him that I'm okay, because I honestly don't know if I am.

I'm pissed. Pissed at myself for not manning up—or I guess in this case, *womanning* up—and telling my brother.

In fact, I sort of feel like some divine entity is mocking me. I *finally* decide it's time to tell him, and *bam* he catches us together. Someone, somewhere, is laughing their ass off at me. The fucker.

I flip the pages of the magazine I'm supposedly reading, but I don't even have the energy to look at the pictures.

Xander sits on the stool opposite me at the bar counter and Rae left a while ago to go look for Cade. I made her promise to text me if she found him, but I don't even know where my phone is.

Xander sighs and picks up Prue from the floor, sitting her in his lap.

"Thea," he starts, "talk to me, please. You're scaring me."

I flip another page in the magazine.

"Thea," he says more firmly this time.

I lift my gaze to his. "I don't want him to hate you," I whisper. "You're best friends. I don't want you to fight over me."

Xander's shoulders sag and he lets out a relieved breath. "That's what you're worried about?" I nod and he smiles. "We'll be fine, Thea. Don't worry about us."

"He's really mad." I frown, flipping another page in the magazine.

"Yeah, and I was really mad when we were six and he broke my Nerf gun. I got over it."

I snort. "Yeah, well that was a toy and this is ... This is big."

He shrugs. "We're guys. It's the same difference to us. Things will be fine in no time, you'll see. He just has to work through it in his head."

"I hope you're right." I close the magazine and slide it across the counter.

"Maybe we should take Prue for a walk?" he suggests. "We've been in the house all day. It might do you some good to get out."

I sigh. Going for a walk doesn't sound appealing, but it might help me clear my head so it's worth a shot. "Sure," I say.

He lets out a relieved breath. "Good. I'll get her leash."

He carries Prue out of the room and I stand, stretching my arms above my head. My legs are stiff from sitting in the same position for too long, so I end up stretching them too.

I meet Xander by the front door and Prue wags her tail happily. We head out and down the street, not saying anything for aways, so I'm startled when Xander finally does speak.

"If I give you your ring back, will you wear it?"

I'd been looking at the ground, but my head shoots up at this. He appears nervous and looks away from me, letting the shaggy strands of his hair hide his face from me.

I swallow thickly. There are still lots of people who don't know about this, but I suddenly don't care.

After a lengthy pause, that I'm sure makes him sweat bullets, I say, "I'd love to wear it."

He twists his head my way so quickly I'm surprised he doesn't get whiplash. "Really?" He smiles like a sheepish little boy.

I nod. "Yeah." I smile.

"Seeing a ring on your finger isn't going to give you hives, is it?" he asks seriously, but his eyes sparkle with laughter.

I toss my head back and laugh. "I think I'll survive."

He grins at me and reaches for my hand. He grows quiet again and I think the conversation is done, but then he surprises me yet again. He stops in the middle of the sidewalk and I'm forced to stop too. Prue looks up at us quizzically, wondering why we've stopped, but she promptly shakes her head and starts smelling the ground.

"I wasn't lying," Xander begins, swallowing thickly, "when I told Cade that I love you—but I'm really sorry that's how you heard it. I should've told you first." He lets go of my hand and glides the backs of his fingers over my cheek before tucking a piece of hair behind my ear. "I love you," he says again, more firmly this time. "I always have, and I always will."

My heart pitter-patters in my chest. When your dream guy says he loves you it feels pretty damn good. "I love you too," I whisper and my chin quivers. It's stupid to cry over this, but the love I feel for him honestly scares me. It's intense and all-consuming. The kind of love that has the power to destroy you if things go wrong.

He grasps my chin. "Why are you crying?"

I breathe out. "Because I'm scared."

"Don't be." He presses his lips to mine softly. It's just a simple meeting of lips but it feels like so much more. It feels like the final seal on a deal we didn't have the right to make.

He steps back and calls to Prue who has run as far as her leash will let her.

We start walking again and then circle back to the house.

Rae and Cade's cars are both back in the driveway and I stop. Fear holds me prisoner but it's stupid to be afraid of my own big brother. He's always been my protector. He won't hurt me.

I turn to Xander. "Would you mind walking Prue some more? I want to talk to Cade."

He nods. "Sure thing. I need to run to the store so I'll do that instead."

"Thanks." I smile and stand on my tiptoes to kiss his cheek before dashing in the house.

The house is eerily quiet when I step inside and search around, looking for the two of them. I come across Rae first, sitting in their bedroom fiddling with her camera.

I knock on the open door and she looks up. "Where's Cade?"

"He's out back."

"How was he when you found him?"

She frowns. "In one word?" I nod. "Sad."

My heart breaks and I duck my head, nodding. "I'm going to go talk to him."

I quickly turn away and head downstairs. I open the back door and step out onto the small deck. It boasts a grill and a small table with two chairs. Cade sits in one, a beer bottle dangling loosely from his fingers and he sits, watching the sunset over the trees.

He hears the door open and his shoulders flex, but he doesn't turn to look.

I tiptoe across the small space and pull out the chair across from him. He lifts his eyes to mine and I wave awkwardly. "Hi." I bite my lip. I have no idea what to say.

"Hey," he says gruffly, looking away.

My fingers wring together. This is my chance to speak to him. To pour my heart out and get him to understand. "I'm sorry," I say after a long moment. "I'm sorry for not telling you about Xander and me, but I'm not going to apologize for how I feel about him." His head flicks up at this. "I think you've known for a long time that we've had feelings for each other and it's why you warned him from me, but that wasn't your place." He opens his mouth to speak. "I *know* you're my brother and you're only trying to protect me, but *Cade*," my voice cracks on his name, "you were only hurting us." He looks away and shame flickers across his face. "Xander's a good guy. A great guy, actually. Why wouldn't you want us to be together?"

He sighs. "Xander's like family. I guess I always thought if you guys dated and broke up, I'd be forced to pick sides, and I don't want to do that."

I give him a reassuring smile. "I get that, but now we're both adults who can make our own decisions. If it doesn't work out, those are our consequences to deal with, not yours."

Cade sips his beer and sets the bottle down on the table. "Yeah, I see that now." He sighs heavily and then chuckles, but there's no humor in the tone. "I'm still fucking pissed, though." I open my mouth to protest and he holds up a hand for me to wait. "At myself and Xander. At myself, because I made you guys feel like you couldn't tell me, and at Xander because he's my best fucking friend and he didn't tell me first. Tiptoeing behind my back in my house …" He pauses and shakes his head. "That's fucking low."

I flinch. "I'm the one that made him keep it a secret."

He shakes his head again. "Regardless, he should've told

me. But again, I realize that's my fault." He sighs and scrubs his hands over his face. "It all comes back to me, but I just need time, Thea. I need time to wrap my head around this. Okay?" His blue eyes meet mine, pleading for me to understand.

I nod. "Time," I repeat. "Okay." I stand, hoping he's going to say more, but instead, his gaze returns to the setting sun and I know that I've been dismissed.

I sigh and head inside the house. Xander's not back yet and Rae's still in her room, so I set about making dinner for the four of us. I keep it simple, opting for spaghetti and garlic bread. Hopefully, there won't be any food throwing because it could get messy quick.

Xander comes back just as I'm finishing up and Prue bounds into the house and over to me. She licks my leg and then runs over to her cushion and lies down. Xander smiles when he sees me by the stove and kisses my cheek as he passes.

"I brought you a McFlurry." He holds up the cup and heads to the freezer.

I laugh. "Tonight is definitely ice cream worthy."

He frowns as he closes the refrigerator door. "Did it not go well?"

I sigh and glance toward the deck door. "It went okay, I guess. I think he's more mad at us keeping it a secret than actually being together." I shrug. "I think he realizes that his actions were wrong, but ours were too." My voice grows soft. "It sucks. I don't want him mad at us—at *you*. If he should be mad at anyone, it should be me, but it seems like he's placing all the blame on your shoulders."

Xander smiles but it doesn't quite reach his eyes. "You're his little sister, so it's easier for him to be mad at me than you." He shrugs like it's not a big deal, but it *is*. He comes over to me and wraps his arms around me. "It'll be okay. Just give it time."

I laugh, the sound muffled against his massive chest. "That's what Cade said. That he needs time."

Xander steps back, leaning his hip against the counter. "See, we're all on the same page." He rubs his hand over his stubbled jaw then and I wait for him to speak. "We're having dinner with my family this Friday," he tells me. "Cade and Rae need to come too."

"Oooh, is this the big reveal?" I wag my brows.

He chuckles. "Yeah, I guess so. I want to tell my parents about us too, if that's okay?"

I bite my lip, hating that I hesitate for even a second, but I still have doubts about this actually working. Right now, it's new and exciting and that makes things seem perfect, but what about when summer ends and the real world begins? I'm going to have to go back to school—and I still have no idea what I actually want to major in, so yay me-and Xander's going to be playing for the NFL. His practices are going to get longer and more intense and he's going to be *gone*. Throw in media attention on his end and it's a recipe for disaster.

I swallow thickly and nod. "Yeah, we can tell them." I don't know if that's the right decision, but after keeping it a secret from Cade and having that blow up in our faces, I feel like we have no choice.

Xander smiles. "Great. You know my mom's going to be thrilled."

I laugh. "Your mom's the best." And she is. She's always been like a second mom to me.

I hear footsteps behind us and I turn to see Rae. "I smell food and I'm *starving*."

"It's almost ready. Why don't you grab Cade and we can all sit down and eat together?"

Rae nods and heads out back.

I look up at Xander. "Showtime."

We set about placing the plates and everything on the table and we're almost done when Rae and Cade come inside and sit down. I end up across from Cade with Xander beside me.

We all shovel spaghetti noodles onto our plate in silence. It's weird. I'm used to someone always saying something and not this eerie quiet.

After a few minutes I ask, "So, Rae, photograph anything interesting lately?" It's possibly the worst question I've ever asked, but I don't know what to do to break this awkward tension.

Rae bites her lip to hide her laughter but answers anyway. "Nova's been teaching me how to do more conceptual photos like she does. It's not really my favorite thing to do, but it's interesting and a skill I need to work on."

I nod. I don't understand a word she said. It all sounded like gibberish to me.

More minutes pass and I say, "I think I might join a gym." I *loathe* exercise, but Rae runs every morning, and

Cade usually joins her, and Xander always goes to the gym, so maybe I'm missing out on something.

Xander snorts. "I bet you'll go once and never go again."

I narrow my eyes on him. "Challenge accepted."

He grins back. "We'll go tomorrow."

My stomach sinks and I give a half-hearted, "Yippee."

Xander leans over and presses his lips to the side of my forehead. "Don't dread it too much. I'll be there."

I grin. "Mmm, you shirtless and sweaty. That sounds promising."

A clatter sends me looking in the other direction. Cade's pushed his plate away and shoved away from the table. He doesn't say anything as he stalks out of the room. Rae gives us an apologetic look and shrugs her shoulders.

"He'll get over it."

I sigh. I really hope she's right.

seventeen

. . .

xander

I LOST THE BET. Thea made it to the gym for a second day, but I'm pretty sure she's miserable and questioning her life choices.

"This. Is. Too. Fast," she pants, trying to keep up with the treadmill.

I glance at the number. "You're only going four miles an hour. I think you'll survive."

"Fuck. You." She gives me the middle finger.

I chuckle and cross my fingers over my chest. I've already finished my workout and came over here to cheer—okay, *taunt*—her on.

"If it's any consolation, your ass looks great in those shorts." I bend my head, getting a great look at said ass.

"I'm. Going. To. Punch. You. In. The. Face."

I chuckle. "Just think about all the McFlurrys you can eat now."

"Fuck. You. And. Fuck. McFlurrys." She's growing even shorter of breath now.

"I'm pretty sure you already said that." I lean against the rail of the empty treadmill beside her. "Five more minutes."

"I'm. Going. To. Die."

"You're not going to die." I shake my head. "I kind of like you, so it's insulting that you think I'd let you die," I joke. I'm pretty sure she growls but it might've just been her trying to breathe. Who knows? "Have you talked to Cade about dinner yet?" It's Friday night and we're supposed to be going over to my parents' house for dinner.

"No. You. Do. It."

I shake my head. "I tried. He won't talk to me. He'll barely even look at me." I sigh.

More time. He needs more time.

"I'm. Going. To. Kick. Him. In. The. Balls."

"Settle down, fighter," I tell her. "He's coping. He'll come around."

This time I know for sure that she does growl.

"He's. Being. A. Douchebag."

I can't really argue with her there. I didn't expect Cade to throw us a party for this, sure, but I didn't expect the silent treatment, either. We're not five. But, on the other hand, I suppose the silence is better than him punching me in the face.

"Two minutes."

"Ugh," she groans. "Two. Minutes. Too. Long."

I laugh. "You can do it."

The seconds tick by, and when the two minutes are up, Thea immediately stops the treadmill and hops off, leaning over and pressing a hand to the stitch in her side.

"Coming again tomorrow?"

She gives me the finger and stalks off. I think I have my answer.

I roll our rings around the palm of my hand. I asked Thea if she'd wear it if I gave it back and she said yes, but I've still yet to return it to her. No moment seemed right, not with Cade moping around giving us sour looks. But I want to give it back to her soon. Maybe even tonight after we tell my parents. Fuck, we need to tell her parents too. I'm sure that'll go over about as well as telling Cade.

I sigh and place the rings back in my top dresser drawer. We're supposed to leave for my parents' place in ten minutes. I spoke with Rae and she convinced Cade to come to the dinner.

My palms sweat.

I already pissed my best friend off by not telling him I was with his sister, so I doubt he's going to be pleased I kept this a secret too. I pinch the bridge of my nose. I keep fucking everything up, but I'm not doing it on purpose. I'm doing what I think is right, but it's always wrong in the end.

I force myself to stop thinking about it. I have to let the pieces fall where they may.

I head across my room to the bathroom and make sure my hair is lying flat. My mom hates it when it's all a mess, and if I don't have it fixed she'll start trying to fix it even though I'm twenty-two not twelve. Moms never seem to understand when you've grown up. You're always a baby to them.

When I know that my hair is decent, I open the door that leads to Thea's room. She sits on her bed, slipping her feet into a pair of shoes. She's dressed in a short brightly-colored dress and her hair hangs down in its usual loose waves. Like always, she takes my breath away. More so now that she's actually *mine*. Before, I had to admire her from afar and pretend I wasn't looking when I was. And I *always* was.

She looks up at me and smiles, grabbing her purse from the bed. "Ready to go?" she asks.

I nod. "Are we all going in my truck?" It has a second row, but with the amount of tension that's been rolling off Cade, I think the cab of the truck would feel stifling with all of us.

She shakes her head and frowns. "No, they're meeting us there. I think Cade wants an escape vehicle in case things get ugly."

I clench my jaw and look away. "Right. Of course," I mutter. Prue brushes against my leg and I bend down to pet her. "We'll be home later, girl," I tell her. "We'll miss you."

She tilts her head as she looks at me and I swear she knows every word I've said. She gives my hand a lick and then jumps up on Thea's bed, lying down, and almost completely disappearing in the cloud of pink blankets.

I hold my hand out to Thea. "Should we go then?"

She nods. "Yeah."

We step out into the hall and I call down to the other end. "We'll see you guys there."

"We'll be right behind you," Rae says back. Cade says nothing, but I'm not surprised.

Thea gives me a sad look before we start down the stairs. I know she feels responsible for the strife between her brother and me, but she's not. It is what it is.

Thea and I head out to my truck and I open the door for her, offering her a hand so she can get in the truck.

I close the door and jog around to the other side. I start the truck and sit there for a moment, not moving.

Thea places her hand on my knee in comfort. It's like she's telling me everything will be okay. I want to believe that.

I back out of the driveway and start the twenty-minute drive to my parents' house. They moved out of the house I grew up in—the one across the street from Cade and Thea—a few years ago, into a house my dad designed.

"Are you afraid to tell them?" Thea asks. "About football?"

"Afraid? No. Nervous? Yes."

She wrinkles her nose. "What's the difference?"

"I guess being afraid implies that you're scared, but I'm not scared I'm just ... apprehensive of what their reaction will be."

She nods. "I can understand that, but everything will be fine."

"I hope you're right."

We make it to my parents' house and I park beside my little brother's beat-up Honda Civic.

"Is Alexis coming?" Thea asks, referring to my older sister.

I shake my head. "I don't know. My mom wanted her to, but I'm not sure she could get out of the office in time."

Thea frowns. "I hope she can make it. I was looking forward to seeing everyone. At least Xavier is here. I love him."

I narrow my eyes. "Better not love him more than me."

She laughs and reaches for the door handle. "Of course not."

We get out and head in through the garage. My mom would have a fit if we went to the front door. She's always wanted us kids to feel like we're always welcome at home. I know if she could she'd keep us here forever.

"Sarah," Thea calls when we enter. "We're here!"

My mom comes around the corner and her smile lights up the whole house. Her glossy brown hair is pulled back in a ponytail and her apron is covered in something that makes me think she's baked a cake. She's one of those people that loves to cook and bake but always makes a mess of herself and the kitchen.

"Thea, I'm so happy to see you! It's been too long!" She hurries over to Thea and takes her face between her hands. "My God, you get prettier every time I see you. I keep telling my son he needs to wise up and make a move on you before someone else does."

I snort, pressing my hand against Thea's waist. My mom notices and her eyes flicker from my hand, to my face, to Thea, and back again.

"Wait," she says slowly. "Are you?"

"We're dating, Mom." For some reason, I can't meet her eyes.

She lets out a shriek and hugs us both tight. "Cooper!" she yells to my dad. "Why didn't you tell me Xander and Thea were a couple?"

"What?" he yells back.

"He doesn't know, Mom." I laugh, reaching for Thea's hand.

"Oh." She covers her heart. "I just assumed with you guys working there that he did. My bad."

My brother chooses that moment to walk by, phone glued to his hand as he types furiously. "'Bout damn time."

"Xavier," my mom hisses. "Language."

"About fucking time," Xavier amends with a crooked grin. We look a lot alike. We both have the same messy black hair and are tall, although I'm taller, much to his chagrin.

My mom tosses her hands in the air and mutters. "Why do I bother?"

"I don't know," Xavier says back. "I can't be controlled. You know this."

My mom shakes her head and turns to Thea and me. "Why don't you guys hang out in the kitchen? I need some entertainment that isn't in the form of this doofus." She points a finger at my little brother.

Xavier frowns. "I feel like I should take offense to that, but doofus is a pretty accurate description of me."

"You know what else is?" I ask and before he can respond, I say, "Court Jester." I ruffle his hair as I pass but I don't get far before he tackles me and we tumble to the floor.

"*Boys*," my mom scolds, and I'm sure she's shaking her head at us as we roll around. To Thea, she mutters, "They'll never grow up."

We break apart and laugh, smiling up at our mom. "You love us just the way we are," Xavier says.

She sighs, blowing her bangs away from her eyes. "You're right, I do, but I don't know why." She lifts her hands in the air and then walks down the hall to the kitchen.

Thea stands over us, shaking her head. "Silly boys." Then she passes us by.

"So, you and Thea, huh?" Xavier waggles his brows.

"Shut up." I push his shoulder and stand.

My dad comes down the hall from his office and glances from me to Xavier, who's still sitting on the floor. He shakes his head and mutters, "I don't want to know," before heading into the kitchen.

"Come on, little bro." I hold my hand out to Xavier.

He avoids my hand and stands on his own. "You know I hate it when you say that."

"Which is exactly why I keep saying it."

He sighs. "So, what's up with you?" I ask him. "Ready for Yale?"

Xavier doesn't act like it, and it's not something he likes to talk about, but the kid is practically a genius. Prestigious universities clamored to get him and he's so uninterested in it all. I think all he wants to do is play video games. He finally decided on Yale, but I don't know how excited he actually is to attend.

He shrugs. "Eh, it's just college."

"It's *Yale*. That's a big deal."

"It's still just a school," he counters. He sighs and stuffs his hands in his pockets. "It'll be weird being so far away from home, but I think I need the change."

"I'm going to miss you." It's the truth too. The kid might be annoying as fuck, but I actually kind of like him.

"Don't go getting all sentimental on me, Xander. It's weird."

I shake my head. "Maybe I won't miss you *that* much." I laugh and we finally join everyone else in the kitchen.

The meal is almost done, so my mom has Xavier and me set the table. We only manage to break one plate so I take that as a win. My mom, not so much. When she sees the broken plate, she presses a hand to her chest and mutters, "Not again. So many plates lost over the years."

I make a mental note to buy my mom a new set of plates to make up for all the ones we broke.

"I thought Cade and Rae were coming?" my mom asks as we carry the food to the table.

Right on time, the door opens. "Speak of the devil," my dad says and leaves us to greet them.

I inhale a deep breath. I suddenly don't feel ready for this dinner.

We place the food in the center of the table and take our seats.

Cade and Rae enter the room and stop to say hi to my mom. Cade doesn't even look at me, and maybe it shouldn't, but my blood boils.

Stay calm, Xander. It's one fucking dinner. You can do this.

The problem is it's *not* one fucking dinner. It's so much more.

Thea finds my hand beneath the table and gives it a reassuring squeeze.

Idle conversation is made as we shovel food onto our plates and I contemplate when the best time will be to tell them about football.

I rub my hands on my jeans. My palms are suddenly sweaty.

The door opens again and I hear my sister call, "I'm late, but I'm here!"

She breezes into the room, her dark hair spilling out of the up-do she has it in and her work clothes are ruffled like she's been in a hurry, which I'm sure she has been to get here in time. She taps my head and Xavier's as she passes and then hugs our mom and dad before taking her seat.

Thea glances at me as Alexis piles food on her plate. Her look tells me she thinks it's time to spill the beans. I haven't eaten that much, but what I have sits like a lead weight in the middle of my stomach.

I take another bite of macaroni and cheese but I don't taste it.

Breathe in. Breathe out.

Thea bumps her knee against mine and gives me another look. *Just do it*, this one says.

I clear my throat and shuffle in my seat. I feel like I'm suffocating. Cade gives me a funny look from where he sits across the table from me. He looks almost worried.

"Xander," Thea whispers under her breath.

I scrub my hands over my face. By now, they're starting to notice my odd behavior.

"Xander?" My mom asks hesitantly. "Are you feeling okay? Should you go lie down?"

I smack my hands against the wood table and blurt, "I made the team. I'm on the Colorado Rebels."

Silence. Absolute *silence*.

I'm sweating so bad now that my brow is damp. They all stare at me and I look up at the ceiling. I don't want to see their faces. I don't want to see the hurt there.

"Can you repeat that?" my dad asks.

I breathe out and lower my head, looking directly at him. I'm shocked to see not disgust but ... but *pride* in his gaze.

"I'm playing for the Rebels," I say again, and this time, I meet his eyes and then my mom's, and finally Cade's. Happy tears spring to my mom's eyes and Cade looks—he looks surprised and hurt.

"I didn't even know you tried out," my mom says, clapping her hands together. "Oh, my God, this is great news."

I laugh. "You don't try out—they scout you."

"Oh, right, of course," she mutters, waving a hand through the air. "Oh, my God," she says again. "I'm so proud of you! I have to hug you." She jumps out of her seat and it thumps against the wall as it falls, but she doesn't notice. In no time, she has her arms wrapped around me and she kisses the top of my head the same way she used to when I was a kid.

"Whoa, you're famous now," Xavier comments as my mom releases me.

"I'm not famous." I laugh.

"I'm just so proud of you," my mom says, clapping her hands together and tears now falling freely.

I glance toward my dad. He's been silent and that worries me. "Dad?" I ask hesitantly.

"Wow." He shakes his head. "I'm shocked, that's for sure. I didn't know you wanted to go down that path, but I'm proud of you. I really am."

"You're not mad?" I ask. "I know I kind of led you on with working for you, and I didn't mean to do that, but I didn't want to let you down," I ramble.

He shakes his head rapidly. "Not at all. I mean, I'm certainly surprised, but not mad. This is a great thing for you, and you've always loved football, so if this is the path you want to go down, then that's what you should do. Always follow your dreams."

"Thanks, Dad," I croak, getting choked up.

Finally, I look at Cade, and it's safe to say he's pissed. Can't say I blame him.

"Can we talk outside?" he asks, his voice gruff.

He might not have punched me before, but I have a feeling he's about to now.

"Cade?" Thea says softly.

He doesn't answer her, simply pushes his chair back and stalks from the room.

I stand too, but before I leave Alexis calls out to me, "I'm so happy for you, Xander. You're going to kick ass."

"Thanks." I give her a smile and then head out of the dining room, down the hall, and outside.

I find Cade sitting on the deck steps and I take a seat beside him. I stay quiet, waiting for him to speak first. A full minute ticks by before he speaks.

"What did I do to you?" he finally asks.

My head whips toward him. "Nothing."

He shakes his head, laughing softly but the sound is humorless. "It must've been something, because not only did you think you couldn't tell me you were in love with my sister, but you didn't even tell me you made the fucking team."

I wince. "I didn't mean to piss you off by not telling you. I just ..." I run my fingers through my hair. "It's always been you and me since we were kids. And you were excited for that to continue with us working together for my dad, and I-I don't know, I guess I didn't want to burst your bubble. Stupid, I know." I shake my head.

Cade sighs. "I guess we're not kids anymore, huh?" He glances toward the night sky.

"No." I laugh. "Definitely not."

"Fuck." He chuckles. "We're adults, and it's weird."

I'm surprised to hear him laugh, and I do too. "Yeah, it is," I agree.

"You're married," he says, "playing football for a living, and I'm with the girl of my dreams, doing what I always wanted to do. I guess it was only inevitable that our paths in life divulge, but I wasn't ready for it." He inhales a deep breath. "I don't like change." He laughs loudly.

"It's not changing that much," I tell him. "At the end of the day, we're all the same people."

He laughs, raising a brow. "People that keep secrets?"

"Touché." Silence settles in the air, and after a moment, I say, "I'm sorry. I hope you know that."

"I know," he says, and looks at me. "I'm sorry too, you know."

"Why?" I can't help myself from asking.

He sighs. "It's my fault you didn't tell me. Especially about Thea. I was such a prick about that for years. I used to tell myself the reason I didn't want you guys together was the obvious, she's my sister, and if you guys got together and broke up it could put me in a bad position of having to choose between you. But I think now—" He pauses. "I think there was also a part of me that was scared that you two would run off and leave me behind. I always knew when we were kids that you two had a special bond, and I know it's fucking stupid, but I think I was jealous of that and it's just carried over through the years even as we grew up." He shrugs. "Which is ironic, because I met Rae and fell in love and basically ditched you guys, so it's the same difference."

"You haven't ditched us." He gives me a look and I laugh. "Okay, so maybe you have, but it happens."

Cade stands up and looks down at me. "This thing with Thea and you is going to take some getting used to, but I can't say having you as an official part of the family is the worst thing."

"Thanks." *I think.*

He nods and heads inside. Before I can follow him, Thea bursts outside. She must've been standing just inside the door waiting.

"Did he hurt you?" she asks. "Punch you? Kick you? Slap you like a middle school girl on crack?"

I laugh and shake my head, walking up the deck steps to meet her.

"No, nothing like that. I think we're cool now."

She looks from me and back to the door. "Oh, thank God."

I throw my arm over her shoulder, tucking her into my side, and reach for the door.

She looks up at me and a smile touches her lips. "It looks like everything's going to be okay."

I nod and press my lips to her forehead. "Looks that way."

But I know we have so many more challenges ahead of us, and I can only hope that they don't break us.

eighteen
...

thea

"A BLINDFOLD, really, Xander? If you wanted to get kinky you should've just said something." I twirl the scrap of black fabric around my finger, waiting for his response.

He chuckles. "That wasn't the plan, but now that you mention it..."

Before I can blink, his arm winds around my waist and I'm slammed down on my bed. It jostles from the sudden impact and we bounce up and down. Laughter tears out of our throats. I smile over at him.

"That was completely unnecessary."

He grins back. "You have a flair for the dramatics so I thought I'd give you a taste of your own medicine."

I sit up and brush my hair from my eyes. "Seriously, though, why the blindfold?" I hold it up, dangling it from my finger.

"I have a surprise for you." He smiles shyly and looks away.

I narrow my eyes. "What are you up to?"

"Nothing bad. You're going to love this."

"That's what Cade and you said when I was five and you convinced me to eat that pepper. It burned my nose hairs, Xander. *My nose hairs.*"

He chuckles. "That was hysterical. You were such a gullible kid."

"Hey." I smack my hand against his solid chest and give him a look like *really?*

He raises his hands innocently. "This isn't like that at all."

I huff out a breath. "Do I at least get a hint?"

He narrows his eyes and glances around my room. When he finds what he's looking for, he jumps from my bed and grabs my shark slippers, then proceeds to hold them out to me.

"My shark slippers? That's my hint? Seriously?"

He laughs. "It'll all make sense soon. I promise."

I snort. "It better. But do I *have* to wear this?"

He sighs. "I guess not. I doubt you'll know where we're going anyway."

"Great, now I'm more scared."

I hold out my hand with the blindfold and he takes it from me. He tucks it into his back pocket and mumbles, "Saving that for later."

I snort. "Keep dreaming, buddy, unless *you* want to be blindfolded."

He grins widely. "That has possibilities too."

I choke on my own saliva and he laughs, clearly pleased at having left me speechless for a change.

"What should I wear for this mysterious outing?"

He shrugs. "Casual. I'm changing into jeans and a t-shirt."

"Darn," I say, frowning. "I love those sweatpants." I waggle my brows and eye the noticeable bulge there.

He shakes his head at my antics, but a blush lightly stains his cheeks. I'd think he'd be used to the inappropriate things that come out of my mouth, but I guess I've only very recently been brave enough to say them. The poor guy has *no idea* the kinds of dirty thoughts I've had over the years.

"We're leaving in an hour," he tells me, lingering in the doorway to my bedroom. "Come on, Prue." He whistles and the dog jumps up from the floor and follows him out.

I immediately go into overdrive to get ready. He might've said this is casual, but I hardly think my no makeup, messy bun, pajama-wearing self will be allowed. Heck, I don't even have a bra on. It's been a lazy day, which was *much* appreciated after the craziness of this week and the dinner with Xander's family last night.

Thankfully, they were thrilled for him, and he and Cade made up, but I was so stressed over the whole thing I probably wore a hole through my stomach lining.

With five minutes to spare, I slip my feet into a pair of black flats. I straightened my hair, opting to do something different from my norm, and dressed in a pair of dark wash jeans and a black and white striped top. I added a necklace and a bracelet to dress it up a bit.

I grab my small black cross-body bag and sling it on, then head downstairs. Xander is hanging in the kitchen with Rae and Cade while she cooks dinner.

Xander stands when he sees me. "Ready?" I nod. He tips his head at the other two. "We'll see you guys later."

"Bye." I wave and Rae gives me a look that tells me she's going to expect me to give her a play-by-play of the whole evening. I seriously feel bad for all the times I pestered her like an annoying mosquito. I'm now being punished for that behavior by receiving the same treatment from her.

Xander pauses in the garage and turns around abruptly so I smack into his chest.

"Ow." I rub my forehead. "What are you? Half rock? That hurt."

He chuckles and rubs his thumb over the spot. "You'll live."

"Easy for you to say," I mumble. "You didn't walk head-first into a boulder."

He shakes his head at me. "I wanted to ask—truck or bike?"

"Bike," I answer without a moment's hesitation.

He grins. "I had a feeling you'd say that."

He heads over to his motorcycle and grabs one of the helmets, turning around and placing it on my head. He secures it and does the same with his. Then he hands me a riding jacket of my very own.

I slip my arms through the holes of the jacket. "If I didn't love you before, I love you now," I say.

He laughs. "Wow, all I had to do was buy you a jacket? Noted."

"Well, that," I begin, "and rub my stomach and tell me I'm cute—oh wait, that's Prue."

His laughter echoes through the garage and his eyes twinkle when they meet mine. "I'd like to say I don't do that, but I'd be lying."

"Mhm," I hum, and push the button for the garage door. It whirls and creaks as it goes up.

He rolls the bike out of the garage and I follow him out onto the driveway. It's a little after five and the sun shines down brightly on us.

I look over my shoulder at the house and laugh when I see Prue peering out the window beside the front door.

"Look," I say to Xander. "She's watching us."

He straddles the bike and looks up, letting out a laugh. "Poor girl, she just wants to go with us."dddddddddddddddedddddddffhbyjjjjjjjjjj8opvhy9o9i8

"You'll have to make it up to her later with extra belly rubs," I tell him.

"Enough chit-chat," he says. "Get on."

I don't have to be told twice. I'm insanely curious about what he has planned. The fact that he's obviously put so much thought into something makes me really excited.

He starts out heading for the city, but after about thirty minutes, he changes course and then I have absolutely no idea where he's going so I can't even begin to guess.

He drives for another twenty minutes before we come upon a quaint little town. It's cute with antique and coffee shops on every corner. He comes to a stop outside a movie theater, complete with one of those lit up things that jut out from the roof of the building.

The movie playing today?

Jaws.

The boy is good.

We hop off the bike and remove our helmets.

"Jaws, huh?" I ask.

He nods, grinning from ear to ear. "Yeah. This place shows a different classic movie every week. This week happened to be *Jaws.*"

"Our favorite," I say, and a sudden rush of emotion clenches my chest.

He nods and takes my hand, leading me to the ticket counter. He purchases two tickets and then we get drinks, popcorn, and candy. When we take a seat in the theater there's only one other person—an elderly man that's enjoying his popcorn so much I doubt he'd know if the place burned down around him.

We take our seats in the back—the back is the best, and anyone that says otherwise is a gremlin—and wait for the movie to start.

I munch on a piece of popcorn and Xander fumbles in his pocket. His pack of M&Ms falls to the floor and I reach down to the grab them. "What are you doing?" I ask, sitting back up and dropping the candy pouch in his lap. "Oh," I gasp. "*That's* what you're doing."

He smiles sheepishly, holding my wedding ring out to me. "You said you'd wear it if I gave it back, but it seemed weird to just hand it to you at home."

"So," I draw out the word, "you brought me to a movie theater?"

He winces. "Okay, it sounds really dumb when you say it that way, but it made total sense in my head." He swallows thickly. "There's more, though."

My brows furrow together. Now I'm really confused. "Okay?"

He wets his lips. "I brought you here, because the first time we watched *Jaws* was the moment when I really *knew* you were someone special to me. I remember you getting scared when the shark came out of the water and you whimpered and curled into me and I knew then that I wanted nothing more than to make you feel loved and safe for the rest of your life. So, that's why we're here. For me, this is the start of it all."

Swoon rating? Off the charts, ladies and gentlemen.

I take his face between my hands and kiss him, because I don't have any words that can measure up to that. I hope through the kiss he can feel just a fragment of what I'm feeling.

I pull away, both of us breathless now, and he holds my hand as he guides the simple silver band onto my finger. It rests there, a perfect fit, like it was always meant to be there.

He goes to put his ring on, but I grab it. His dark eyes flick up to meet mine and I think he's afraid I'm about to throw the ring into the depths of the theater, but then I take his hand like he did mine and put the ring on. I struggle to get it passed his knuckle but I manage, and I'm surprised by the happiness it brings me to see it there. The morning we woke up in Vegas I felt anything but happy at the sight of it.

I lay my head on his shoulder as the movie starts.

"Can we do this?" I whisper softly, so as not to disturb the man a few rows down.

I feel Xander nod. "Yeah, I think we can."

I think we can too.

nineteen
...

thea

OUR LAUGHTER ECHOES through the kitchen as Xander spins me around. Turning the radio on while we cooked might not have been our brightest idea, but there are times in life where you have to pause and enjoy the little things.

I wind my arms around his neck, swaying my hips to the beat of the song. His hands rest on my waist and he laughs when I begin to make funny faces.

"Bleck," Cade says, entering the kitchen. "You guys are gross." He picks up an apple from the basket on the table, tosses it in the air, and catches it before taking a bite.

I laugh and step away from Xander, returning to the stove. "You're one to talk," I say to Cade over my shoulder. "You and Rae are the grossest."

"Are not," he argues.

I snort. "We sound like we're six." I throw away the burnt eggs and clean the pan.

Xander takes the pan from me and says, "Maybe I should do this."

"Hey." I pout. "You're the one that started dancing first. It's not my fault the eggs burned in the process."

He shrugs. "I make them better anyway."

I gasp. "Take that back."

"The truth hurts, deal with it."

I narrow my eyes. "Oh, you're in trouble." When he turns around, I jump on his back like a spider monkey. He starts to fall from the impact but quickly recovers.

"Thea," he laughs, "what are you doing?"

"Making it more difficult for you, obviously." Unfortunately, I begin to slide down his body and my butt hits the floor. "Fuck," I curse.

Footsteps pad across the floor and my brother looks down at me. "Forget gross, you guys are just weird."

Xander chuckles and looks down at me, waiting for my response.

"I like weird," I say.

"Me too."

Cade gags. "I'm out of here. I can't take anymore."

I pick myself up off the floor and Cade pauses before leaving. "We're going tubing with Jace and Nova at twelve and Mom and Dad's barbeque is at three," Cade reminds me.

"I know," I laugh. "You told me three times yesterday."

"I don't want you to forget."

"Mhm," I hum as he leaves this time. Before he can make it to the stairs, I call, "The barbeque is at five, right?"

"Three!" he yells back as I cackle. "Dammit," he mutters.

I shake my head. "I love messing with him." I wrap my arms around Xander's body, laying my head against his back. "Well, we've made it to July, one more month to go."

His body stiffens. "Why do you say it like that?"

"Like what?" I step to the side so I can see him.

He flicks his dark hair from his eyes. "*One more month to go*," he mimics. "It sounds like you're getting rid of me after that." Hurt flashes in his gaze.

My heart pangs. "I'm sorry, I didn't mean it like that. It's just that August is technically the end of our agreement." I shrug. "Who knows what'll happen."

He shakes his head. "You're unbelievable."

"What?" My eyes widen in surprise.

"I thought we were doing good and here you are talking about the end of it."

I touch his arm and he *flinches* away from me. "Xander," I say firmly, forcing him to look at me. "That's not what I meant. It was stupid of me to say that. I'm sorry."

He swallows thickly and takes a deep breath. "It bothers me when you talk like that," he says. "We've waited a long time for this and the thought of not having it anymore kills me." He closes his eyes briefly. "I guess when I put that ring back on your finger I thought the agreement didn't exist anymore. I shouldn't have thought that."

"You're right," I say, shaking my head rapidly. "It's pretty much null and void at this point. What I said was stupid. *I'm* stupid—but we know this." He chuckles. "I'm sorry," I say again. "Forgive me?"

He smiles, and it's not quite genuine, but almost. "I forgive you. *But*," he starts, "if you start having doubts about us *tell me*. Don't blindside me."

I shake my head. "I'm not going to have doubts," I tell him.

He stares at me for a moment and then nods. "Good." He kisses me.

The atmosphere in the kitchen returns to more normal, happy levels as the tension from before leaves.

While he makes the eggs, I handle the toast and pouring of the orange juice.

We set everything out and Rae and Cade join us.

I smile at Xander beside me. I hate that we had a tiff, but I guess it's bound to happen now and then. No couple has sunshine and rainbows moments all the time. You have to learn to move past things, and I think for our first kinda-sorta fight, we did pretty good.

Go us.

"This looks dangerous for my boobs," I say, adjusting my bikini top. "If a nip slips out, someone better tell me." I glare around at my group of friends.

Cade pales. "I'm not going to be looking at your boobs, so sorry."

I look up at Xander. "You're in charge of nip duty."

He chokes on a sip of water and spews the liquid all over the ground. "Um, okay," he says, wiping the back of his hand over his mouth.

"Whose idea was it to go tubing again?" I ask, gathering my hair up into a messy ponytail.

"Mine." Jace raises his hand.

I narrow my eyes on him. "If this doesn't end well, I might never speak to you again."

I already saw one girl come back soaking wet and covered in *mud*. I could handle getting wet—you're going to dry off, obviously—but *mud*? That would require at least three hot showers to get all of it off and disinfect my body. I don't have time for that today.

Jace chuckles. "I don't think that would be a bad thing." I glare at him. "What?" He raises his hand innocently. "You talk a lot and I like silence."

"Says the guy who works in a bar," I mutter.

He laughs and counters, "Maybe that's why I appreciate the silence." He claps his hands together loudly and a group of girls looks over. They immediately make googly eyes at him. It's the tattoos all over his arms. Tattoos make girls do stupid things. It's a fact.

One of the girls gives Xander an appreciative look and I bristle, making a hissing sound.

Xander snorts. "Did you just *hiss* at them?"

I hadn't meant to do that. I square my shoulders and lift my chin, owning my moment of jealousy. "Yes," I say. "And I'll piss a circle around you too if I have to," I joke.

He throws his head back and laughs. "You're amazing."

Cade shakes his head. "Are you sure you want to stay married to her? She's kind of weird."

Xander laughs and wraps his arm around me. "Yeah, she's stuck with me."

Jace picks up his black tube. "Can we talk about the fact that I was the *last* person to find out you guys got married? I feel the love, guys."

I laugh. "We haven't told our parents yet, so technically you're not the last one."

He points a finger at us. "You didn't even tell me. I show up here and you're both wearing rings."

"Technicalities." I wave my hand through the air, dismissing his words.

He chuckles. "Are we going or not?"

"I'm so not ready for this," I hiss to Xander.

"You'll be fine."

We pick up our own tubes and follow our little group to where we get in the water.

There's a person there, giving us instructions on what we can and cannot do and which way to go when the river splits.

"I hope you were paying attention to that," I whisper to Xander, plopping my butt in the tube. "Because that went in one ear and out the other for me."

He laughs and gets in his own tube. "You'll be fine," he repeats his words from earlier.

"For some reason, I don't believe you."

He grabs onto the rope attached to my tube and holds on tight. "Feel better now?"

"Somewhat."

We begin to float down the river and I eventually become comfortable enough that I lay my head back and close my eyes. It's a hot day, but the cool river water helps keep me comfortable. I wasn't keen on tubing, but this isn't so bad. It's actually rather relaxing.

Minutes pass, and I eventually open my eyes.

No one is around us.

"Xander?" I ask hesitantly.

"Hmm?" he hums. His head is tilted back and his sunglasses hide his eyes.

"Where is everyone?"

He sits up at that and looks around. "Shit."

Panic rises inside me. "Are we lost?"

"Of course not," he scoffs.

"We're totally lost," I cry. "We're going to get eaten by alligators."

"This is Colorado, not Florida, I think we're safe from alligators."

I look around and around, but everywhere I look, there's only water and trees. The river is too wide and the current is moving too fast for us to get to the bank.

"We're going to die," I mumble. "They're going to write: Here lies Xander and Thea, the idiots who got lost tubing and were never seen from again. We'll become one of those ghost stories they tell kids around a campfire."

"That's not going to happen," he says in a calm, sure tone. "We'll be fine. This probably just brings us out in a different area. We'll meet up with the others in no time. You'll see."

I strain, listening closely. "Do you hear that?"

He listens too. "What is that?"

I look behind me, but it's hard to see. I squint my eyes, trying to piece together what I'm hearing. "Oh, shit."

"What?"

"Waterfall," I say.

Xander's eyes widen, and for the first time, I see him begin to panic. He lets go of my raft and grabs onto my hand. "Whatever you do, don't let go."

I want to argue that I might not have any choice in letting go, but I'd rather pretend everything is going to be okay.

The sound of rushing water grows louder the closer to the waterfall we get. I look again and see that it's about six-foot drop, so thankfully not too steep, but it's going to be a drop nonetheless.

We go over, and I scream as the tube falls out from under me. Xander's hold on my hand tightens to the point of pain, but he still has me so I'm not going to complain. We go underwater and the cold water sears my skin with its iciness. I kick my legs, propelling myself up where much-needed air is. Xander's hand is still in mine and he surfaces a few seconds before I do. Perks of being a giant, I guess.

We look around, but our tubes are long gone.

"Kick as hard as you can," he says. "We're swimming for that rock and then to the grass. Okay?"

I nod, my teeth chattering. It might be early July, but the

water is frigid enough for January. Now I have a new worry to add to my previous ones. Hypothermia.

We swim over to the rock, kicking and using our arms as much as we can without losing our grip on the other. The current is fast and keeps dragging us in the opposite direction which makes it hard to get where we're trying to go.

Finally, after what feels like an hour, we make it to the rock. I'm out of breath and panting like I've lost a lung. Heck, maybe I did and it's now floating down the river.

Come back, I need you.

Xander's out of breath too, which makes me feel a little better since he's an athlete. "Ready?" I shake my head no. "Thea, we have to. We're going to wear out from trying to hold onto the rock."

I whimper and nod. I'm too out of breath to offer him any words.

"Three, two, one." He counts down, and then we're off, swimming for the bank that seems a mile away even though I know it's only fifteen or so feet away.

I kick hard, fighting against the current that seems desperate to send us further away.

"Almost there," Xander says.

When we tumble out of the water onto land, I burst into tears. I don't even know why I'm crying, and it's embarrassing, but I can't stop them.

Xander hovers above me, pushing my wet hair from my eyes. "Are you okay?" He looks at me worriedly. "Why are you crying?"

Anger rushes over me and I push his shoulders, shoving

him away. "You said I'd be fine. This is *not* fine," I practically shriek at him.

"I'm sorry, I guess we sort of dozed off and floated down the wrong path."

I rake my fingers through my hair. "This is a mess. We're soaking wet, lost, and I don't know about you, but I'm currently exhausted." As if to drive home my point, I fall back into the grass, staring up at the sky. "Great, and my sunglasses are gone too. Fucking fantastic."

He laughs. "It could be worse. At least we're alive."

"*At least we're alive*," I mimic. "From the guy who said we weren't going to die." I inhale a deep breath. "How are we ever going to find the others?" I question.

"Well—" he looks back the way we came from "—hiking back that way isn't an option, so we're going to have to go this way and hope for the best."

"Xander," I whine, "there might be bears. And snakes. And I'm in *flip-flops*. I can't outrun a bear in flip-flops." *Wait*. I lift my foot and look. "Fuck, I lost my shoes."

"I'll carry you piggy-back," he says.

I lift a brow. "For how long? We have no idea how far we're going to have to walk." I cover my face in my hands. "This is unbelievable."

Remember when I was worried about mud? Yeah, I'd take the mud over a hike through the woods barefoot with wild animals.

We take a few more minutes to catch our breath before we stand and start making our way down the river. I walk as far as I can, until the ground turns into sharp rocks and twigs and then I hop on Xander's back and he carries me like I'm no lighter than a backpack. Thank God he wore sneakers.

The sun beats down on us, and soon, despite our bath in the frigid water, we're hot and dripping with sweat.

"How long have we been walking?"

"One minute longer since the last time you asked me," he quips.

"Ugh," I groan. "It feels like forever."

I swear time is passing at a snail's pace and the worst part is we don't know if we're even heading in the right direction.

"I kind of want to punch you in the face for this," I tell him. "But I also kind of want to kiss you, because it's very sweet of you to carry my heavy ass."

He chuckles. "I'll take the kiss over the punch any day—and you're not heavy."

"Yeah, you won't be saying that in ten minutes when your arms give out."

We grow quiet and a few minutes pass before I say, "What was that? Was that a bear?" I listen again. "What if it's a werewolf?"

He snorts. "Werewolves are fictional, and I doubt it's a bear."

My voice grows shrill. "But we're near the river, and don't bears love rivers?"

"I don't know," he answers.

"Oh, great. We survived the waterfall and swim just to get mauled by a bear. I did not expect today to turn into an episode of *Survivor*."

"We're going to be fine," he says.

"You don't even know if we're going the right way!"

He grunts. "It's not like there's someone I can ask for directions."

"Yeah, and you're a guy, so even if there was, you wouldn't."

He sighs and mutters, "You're probably right."

Fifteen minutes pass and he sets me down to take a break. I stretch my legs as best I can, but without shoes, I'm scared I'm going to step on a poisonous frog or something.

Are there even poisonous frogs in Colorado?

Xander sits down and leans his back against a tree. He tilts his head toward the sky and breathes out heavily. It's obvious this is wearing on him more than he lets on.

He stands up a few minutes later and motions for me to hop on his back again.

I feel like he walks ten miles more before we start to hear shouts.

"People!" I cry. "I hear people!"

Suddenly, I feel like I'm starring in a survivalist movie and a helicopter is going to swoop down low and a ladder is going to fall from the open door, and then we'll climb up into freedom.

The shouts grow louder and more distinguishable and I pick up on our names.

"Over here!" I yell. "We're over here!"

Footsteps pound toward us and a group of what looks like park rangers emerge through the trees.

"Oh, thank God," I mutter.

Xander sets me down and the park rangers fuss over us,

making sure we're unharmed. When they learn that we're okay they're quick to give us each a bottle of water, which we gulp down gratefully. Unfortunately, they don't have a pair of shoes I can use, so I hop on Xander's back again. One of the rangers offered to carry me but Xander went all alpha and wouldn't let him. I kept expecting him to pound on his chest like Tarzan.

The rangers guide us through the woods and back to where we need to be. It ends up being another twenty-minute walk.

Cade spots us first, where he and the rest of our friends sit at a picnic table, and the idiot starts laughing. Not just a little chuckle, either. Oh no, this is the kind of laughter that keels you over at the stomach and makes tears spring to your eyes.

"Cade Paul!" I yell, using his middle name since I know he hates it. "Stop laughing!"

The idiot only laughs harder. He deserves a swift kick to the shin for that.

Xander sets me down and stretches his arms. They must feel like Jell-O at this point. Poor guy.

"You guys look like you just escaped prison or something," Jace comments.

He's on my shit list now too.

"Hey—" Rae smacks Cade's arm "—this is serious. They could've been hurt."

That sobers my brother up real quick, because it's true.

Xander and I make it to the table and we both sit down,

our bodies seeming to fold in on themselves. One of the rangers that brought us here brings us more water.

"Thanks," I tell her with a grateful smile. If they hadn't found us when they did we'd still be lost in the woods.

"What exactly happened?" Cade asks, now in concerned brother and friend mode.

I shrug, twisting off the cap of the water. "We both kind of zoned out and when we came to everyone was gone. We ended up going over this waterfall—"

"You fell off a waterfall?" Cade looks horrified.

"Like a baby one," I explain. "It was probably six feet."

"Six feet is more than you think," he says.

I shrug. "It wasn't so bad. The swim was worse, and then the walk." Xander grunts. "Okay, so he carried me, so it wasn't so bad for me." I lift my foot in the air. "The river ate my shoes. May they rest in peace." I sigh, brushing my hair over one shoulder. "I could really use a cookie after this. Can we go home now?"

Cade nods. "Yeah, let's go. You guys need to shower."

I mock-gasp. "Are you implying we smell? How rude."

He grins. "You definitely smell, but I'm happy you're alive so I won't complain too much." He reaches over and ruffles my hair.

"Ow," I cry, when his fingers tangle in the strands. Between the beating in the water and the trek through the woods while sweating bullets, my hair is a matted mess.

"Sorry," Cade says sheepishly, untangling his fingers from my hair. I rub the sore spot, glaring at him.

We stand from the table and head for the area where we

parked. It's not really a parking lot, more like a section of dirt and grass that everyone decided to pretend was one.

We say goodbye to Nova and Jace, even though we'll see them later at the barbeque, and get in Cade's Jeep. I'm glad now that he drove and we all rode together, because I feel like collapsing, and I'm sure Xander does too.

I click my seatbelt into place and lay my head on his shoulder. In no time I've fallen asleep and I don't wake up until the car stops in the garage.

I sit up, blinking rapidly as the garage forms around me.

"I'm so tired," I whisper to Xander as we head into the house and then up the steps.

He nods, opening the door to my room, then closing it behind us. "I shouldn't be, but I am," he agrees. "I think now that the adrenaline has worn off I'm exhausted and now it's beginning to set in how bad that could've been." He stares at me seriously. "Come here," he whispers, his voice husky.

My heart stutters. He has that look in his eye—the one that promises so many wicked and delicious things—and suddenly, I'm not so tired anymore.

I take a step, and then another, until his hands grasp my waist and he pulls me flush against his body. My hands land on his chest and I look up at him a moment before his lips descend on mine. He kisses me like he's scared it'll be the last time and I can taste the fear he held at bay while I was the one freaking out.

He suddenly grows frantic, pulling my shirt up and off my body as he backs me into the bed.

"Need you," he whispers in between kisses. "Right now."

He reaches for his belt buckle while I kick off my shorts. In only a few seconds' time, there are no clothes left between us and we fall onto the bed, a tangle of limbs. He separates only long enough to grab a condom and put it on, and then he's inside me and we're both crying out in relief. There is no foreplay, we're both too desperate. I didn't even know I needed this, but I did. I *so* did.

I grip his hair and his fingers dig into my hips hard enough to bruise. We're both frantic, close to losing our grip on reality in a matter of seconds. It's never been like this before—except for maybe Vegas, but I can only remember that in short blips—but I don't mind it. Sometimes you need slow, and other times you need to fuck hard, pure and simple.

My back arches and I come. He pumps into me two more times and then he comes too. We both pant, gasping for air, with our limbs tangled together.

I nuzzle my head into his neck and my eyes flutter closed. I want nothing more than to wrap my body around his and drift off to sleep for the rest of the day. Alas, the real world beckons.

We give ourselves a moment to catch our breath and then we head for the shower.

We're going to be more than a little late to the barbeque, which will probably piss my dad off, but it was unavoidable.

Well, I mean, I guess the sex was technically avoidable, but after our day, I think we deserved a moment to ourselves.

When I get out of the shower, I towel dry my hair and then gather it up in a bun. I don't want to bother taking the time to blow dry it and style it. I change into a pair of high-waisted shorts and a red crop top. I grab my white Converse from my closet and sit down on my bed as I slip my feet into them.

Xander comes into my room at the moment Cade yells up the stairs for us.

"Are you guys ready yet? I mean, seriously, how long does it take to shower? Did you drown in there?"

"We're almost ready," I call back. I snicker as a thought runs through my mind. "You know, when we moved in here I was worried about having to listen to those two have sex all the time. Never thought it would be us."

He places one hand on either side of my hips and leans down so his nose brushes mine. "I don't know about you, but I'm glad."

I laugh. "Oh, I am." I waggle my brows.

He chuckles huskily, and I want nothing more than to pull him down into the bed with me and start all over again, but I know we need to go, so instead, I press a quick kiss to his lips and stand.

I take his hand, and say, "Let's go."

twenty
...

xander

I PARK my truck behind Cade's Jeep—Rae and him went ahead of us since we were taking too long. Music blasts from the backyard and a few neighbors stand in the front yard chatting. The Montgomery's yearly Fourth of July party is always a neighborhood affair.

Thea hops from the truck, and I follow her around the side to the gate that leads into the backyard.

I hear a splash and some yelling when someone jumps into the above-ground pool they always have set up for this occasion.

Thea and I make our way around the yard, saying hi when people greet us, but for the most part we try to keep to ourselves.

"Hey!" her dad yells cheerily from the grill, waving a pair

of tongs back and forth. "Are you hungry? These just came off." He then points to a plate full of hot dogs.

"Starving, actually. Thanks." Everything is laid out like a buffet so you can grab what you want, but before I can head to the table, he grabs my arm.

"Haven't had a chance to congratulate you on making the team. I'm proud of you. Wish I could say the same for my piece of shit son," his voice grows dark.

Mr. Montgomery has always been intensely into football, and followed Cade and me closely, especially Cade since he's his son. I can remember once, when we were little and our team lost, he drove us home and went off about how one loss leads to another and to always, *always* win no matter the cost.

I very carefully maneuver out of his hold. "Thanks," I say, giving him a tight-lipped smile.

He claps his hand on my shoulder. "I'm going to be at every home game. I promise you that."

I nod. "Cool."

This might be the most awkward moment of my life. But if I'm being honest, there's something about Mr. Montgomery that's always been ... *off*. He has this intense, off-putting way about him that instantly puts me on edge. Like he's someone that's dangling precariously from a cliff and one wrong word will send him off. I mean, I've never seen him lose his shit, but there's something in his eyes—something that's not quite right.

I'm finally able to get away from him and I join Thea at the table where she's finishing her plate.

"What was that about?" she asks, her eyes shifting nervously from me to her dad behind me.

I shrug and pick up a plate. "He just wanted to congratulate me on making the team."

"Ah, of course." She rolls her eyes. "Football, the only thing he thinks about." She then gives me a small smile. "Thank God you're not that football obsessed. You love it, but it's not an obsession."

I glance back at her dad. "He's really pissed about Cade not going pro, isn't he?"

She snorts. "Oh, yeah. He would've been thrilled if Cade would've dropped out his junior year and gone pro. Like, I'm not kidding, I'm pretty sure the man would've done a dance and he doesn't dance. Like ever." She sighs and her eyes grow sad. "I wish he could accept Cade for the man he is, and not the man he wants him to be. But he has this idea built up in his head—" she waves her hand near her head to drive home her point "—of what Cade should be and Cade's never going to measure up to that. I don't think anyone can. It's really sad."

I finish fixing my hotdog and the two of us go over to the table Cade and Rae occupy. Cade rubs his hands on his shorts and his eyes shift around uneasily. Something tells me I wasn't the first one to get cornered by his dad.

"We're here," Thea sing-songs unnecessarily since it's pretty obvious that we are, in fact, here.

Cade chuckles and forces a smile. "Glad you could make it and no longer smell like swamp water."

"Hey," Thea scolds. Her anger is short-lived, however,

when she takes a bite of her hotdog and moans. "Oh, that's good. I'm starving." She shoves some chips in her mouth.

I laugh. I love how one minute she can be girly, taking forever to pick out her outfit, and the next she's a total mess and shoving food in her mouth like it's going to disappear from the plate.

Nova and Jace show up a few minutes later and pull over two chairs, making the space at the table tight enough that we all bump elbows. None of us complain, though.

"Is there beer here?" Jace asks. "I need a fucking drink. There are too many happy people and I can't deal."

I snort. "Over there." I point over my shoulder to the coolers.

"You want anything?" he asks Nova.

"Sure, bring me whatever you're having."

"You got it." He drums his hands against the top of the table and then he's gone.

Nova props her head up on her hand. "Is it bad that I'd rather be at home sleeping than here?"

Rae laughs. "I'm with you, girl. Socialization is not my thing. I brought my camera. Did you bring yours?"

Nova nods. "I figured I could get some cool photos of the fireworks. Maybe one of Thea shoving that hotdog in her mouth with ketchup all over her face."

"Huh?" Thea asks, her mouth full. Sure enough, there's a smear of ketchup on her cheek. "Isderketchuponmaface?" she slurs together.

I laugh and nod. "Yeah, right there."

She groans and swipes furiously at her face, only making it worse.

"Stop." I grab her flailing arm. "Let me get it." I grab a napkin off the table and wipe her face clean. "There, all better."

She gulps down her food and pants, "Thanks."

Jace returns to the table and drops down into the chair with a loud groan. He holds a beer bottle out to Nova and she takes it gladly. Jace tips his back and takes a long drink.

"Ah," he breathes out, "that's better."

"If you get drunk, you're sleeping in the yard. I'm not driving you home," Cade warns.

Jace winks. "I don't want you to take me home anyway, sweetheart." He then makes kissing lips and leans across the table toward Cade.

Cade mutters, "What? No." And leans back in his chair trying to get away from Jace. Apparently, he leans too far because the chair falls back and he goes with it, dropping onto the ground. I'm pretty sure one of the plastic legs snap, but I can't be sure because it's hard to hear anything over the sound of Jace laughing his ass off. Okay, I'm laughing too.

Cade hops up and looks around. "No one saw, right?" he asks. I clutch my stomach, doubled over with laughter. He glares at Jace and me. "Fuck you and fuck you." He kicks his broken chair aside and grabs one from another table. Rae sits with her hand covering her mouth, trying to hide her laughter.

When Cade plops down in his seat, mumbling under his

breath, she loses it and starts laughing like us, which leads Thea and Nova to join.

Cade's lips thin in irritation. "Ha-ha," he mocks. "I get it. It's so hilarious."

We manage to sober after another minute, but it takes some effort. I see Cade crack a grin that he quickly tries to hide.

My parents and brother arrive and make a beeline right for us.

My mom wraps Thea in a tight hug before moving to me. I reach out for her and she gasps, grabbing my forearm. "Mom?" I ask, wondering what she's doing.

"Is that a wedding *ring?*" she practically shrieks, not in happiness but in pure disgust and irritation. Thea very slyly tries to move her left hand under the table, but my mom catches the movement and turns to look. "I think I'm going to pass out," she mutters and her hand flutters to her chest.

She lets go of my arm and rocks back a few steps.

I stand. "Mom, I can explain—"

"Explain?" she spits the word like it's a curse word. "You're my *son* and you got married and didn't tell *me?* I'm your mom, I deserve to know something like that, Xander. First you didn't tell us about football, and now this? I could understand the football thing, but *this?*" She looks from me to Thea. "You're like a daughter to me, Thea, but right now I feel very betrayed by both of you." She begins to cry and I reach for her.

"Mom, please—"

"No!" she shouts—and I mean *shouts*. Everyone at the

party stops what they're doing and the small show we were putting on suddenly becomes a much larger one. "Do not touch me," she says coldly. "I'm leaving. I can't be here."

"Mom—" I call after her, starting to follow.

My dad catches my shoulder and stops me. My eyes meet Xavier's and even he looks hurt and pissed off. Great, just great.

"No, just don't," my dad says, shaking his head firmly. He lets me go and heads in the same direction my mom left.

Xavier gives me one last disgusted look, shoves his hands in his pockets, and then he too is gone.

Unfortunately, the worst isn't over.

Mr. Montgomery stands in front of the grill, pieces of burning meat smoking the air, and points those fucking tongs at me again. His normally calm, cool, and collected demeanor has been stripped bare and pure rage has settled on his face.

"Married. You two are fucking married?" The tongs swing from me to Thea and back again.

Thea's mom stands by his side with a bowl of macaroni salad in her hands and she looks shocked and maybe a little wary.

Mr. Montgomery's face grows red and a vein in his forehead throbs. The tongs swing again and this time land on Cade. "*You*," he spits. "How could you let this happen?" Cade blinks, looking almost ... scared? "Come here," Mr. Montgomery yells, not at me, but at Cade.

I watch as Cade stands, head bowed like a scolded child, and he stalks through the grass and toward his father.

"This way," he hisses, and like an obedient soldier Cade follows.

I stand there, wondering what the fuck is happening. I look back at the table and Rae looks worried. Thea does too.

Thea pushes back her chair and makes her way over to me. "This is so bad," she whisper-hisses, glancing around at everyone who still stares at the soap opera playing out in front of them. "Come on." She takes my hand and drags me up the deck steps and into the house.

Immediately, the sounds of her father shouting can be heard and she flinches. I can't make out what he's saying, but the gist of it is he thinks Cade should have stopped us.

Thea lets go of my hand, and I follow her through the house and down into the basement, which is her dad's space. As kids we always knew not to go down there.

"You worthless piece of shit!" he yells. "You couldn't even play football like you were supposed to and then you let this happen!" We round the corner and see Cade standing there, not saying a word in defense of himself and it's obvious this isn't the first time he's been dragged off and yelled at like this. "Say something!" he yells in Cade's face, but Cade continues to stand there doing nothing. It's obvious Mr. Montgomery hasn't heard us enter the room, and it's made even more obvious when he cocks his arm back to punch Cade in the face.

I stare, frozen in horror.

But not Thea.

"No!" she screams and darts in-between the two,

colliding with her father's fist. Blood spurts onto the floor, *Thea's* blood, and I see red.

My feet unfreeze and I barrel forward into a crouched position and tackle Mr. Montgomery to the floor. He's not expecting it and goes down easily, his head colliding with the floor. That'll leave a nasty bump, but he fucking deserves it. He *punched* Thea, and he was going to punch Cade, and it was obvious it wasn't the first time.

I quickly roll off of him and stumble over to Thea. Cade has his hands on her shoulders, helping her to sit up and she clutches her nose, blood gushing between her fingers. Tears fill her eyes when she looks at me.

I move her hands aside and assess the damage.

"It doesn't look broken to me, but I'm not a doctor," I say, smoothing her hair away from her forehead and trying to comfort her as much as possible. Unfortunately, I only manage to get blood in her hair. Great.

Mr. Montgomery starts to stand and I whip around, pointing a threatening finger at him. "If you ever come near either of them again ..." I let my threat hang in the air. I don't know what exactly I'd do, but it would be bad.

A squeak by the stairs has us all turning and I see a kid there, maybe ten years old, and I vaguely remember her being a cousin of theirs.

"Bella, sweetie, don't tell your mom," Mr. Montgomery says in a sickeningly sweet voice.

I growl and turn to the kid. "Don't listen to him. Tell everyone what a monster he is. He's a bad man."

The kid nods, but I don't know whether she's nodding at

me or him, and suddenly she turns tail and runs up the stairs like her ass is on fire and she can't get away fast enough.

Almost immediately, we hear the girl yell, "Thea's dad hit her and she's bleeding!"

I start to help Thea up, but Mr. Montgomery spits, "You fucker, you've ruined everything!" Suddenly *I'm* the one being tackled and since I wasn't expecting it, I go down easily.

Luckily, I'm a lot younger than him and in much better shape, so it doesn't take me long to gain the upper hand. Not before he slams his fist into my cheek, though. Pain blossoms across my face, throbbing in time with my heartbeat, and I hear Thea cry out.

I flip to the side and end up on top. I grab his flailing arms and stop his fists from flying.

I give him a nasty smile. "I want nothing more than to punch you in your too-smug face, but that's too good for you. Much worse is coming for you. I promise you that." I shove his arms back and stand.

Cade has Thea up now, her arms wrapped limply around his torso. Blood is smeared on his shirt where she leans her head against him, but for the most part the bleeding has subsided.

"Come here." I take her from him, lifting her into my arms. She wraps her arms around my neck and leans her head against my chest, letting out a contented sigh.

When we reach the top of the stairs, I stop, surprised to find half the people from the party standing there. They take one look at Thea and gasp in horror.

I find Thea's mom in the crowd and anger surges inside me. "Did you know?" I spit at her. "Did you know what a monster you married? Someone that hurt your kids and continues to do so?"

Tears spring into her eyes and she turns away, grief overtaking her face.

"We're leaving," I say, like it isn't obvious already. "I'm taking her to the hospital."

"Cade?" Rae calls out, pushing her way through the people. She appears a moment later. "Are you okay?" Before he can respond, she gasps and slaps a hand to her mouth. "Thea? No."

Cade grabs my shoulder and I look over at him. "Get to the hospital. We'll be right behind you."

I nod. "Whatever you do, don't cover for that bastard. He deserves to pay for this." I look down at Thea, and her eyes are closed, but I know she's not asleep.

Sweet Thea. The girl that always goes out of her way to make someone's day better and put a smile on their face. She doesn't deserve this. No one does.

Cade gives me a tight-lipped smile and nods.

I move through the crowd of people, down the hall, and out the front door. Thankfully, my truck hasn't been blocked in and I'm glad we didn't take the motorcycle because there's no way Thea could ride on it now.

I manage to get the door open without dropping her and then set her inside. She buckles her seatbelt and looks at me sadly and a single tear slides down her cheek. I reach up and wipe it away as she gives me a sad smile.

"I couldn't let him hit Cade again," she whispers.

I swallow thickly. When I walked in on the scene, I suspected that their dad had been using Cade for a human punching bag. "How long has this been happening?"

"I didn't know until I was in eighth grade," she whispers softly, like she's never spoken the words aloud and it hurts to do so. "I came home early from a friend's house and they didn't know I was home. I heard shouting and then I saw him hit Cade. It stuck with me, and then I started remembering all the times I'd seen bruises on Cade and it was easy to figure out it had been happening for a long time."

I shake my head, horrified. I can't imagine growing up in a household with a father like that. My dad was the kind who worked all day but couldn't wait to get home and hang out with us. I even remember him playing dolls with Alexis. It was important to him to do things we liked.

I close her door and head for the driver's side. I start the truck and get out of there as fast as I can. I can't take being in the shadow of that house a second longer and I'm sure Thea feels that way more than I do.

After a few minutes of silence, Thea begins to speak again. "I always knew as a little girl that my dad had a quick temper. I remember once when I was about five, I dropped a glass of orange juice in the kitchen and he just went off, like a switch had been flipped. My mom said to him, 'It's just a little juice.'" She shakes her head, sadness clinging to her. "That pissed him off more. She was already down on her hands and knees, cleaning up the mess while I cried, and he grabbed her by the hair and shoved her head down and said if it was just a little juice then she could lick it clean." I glance at her, horrified, and she wipes her tears away. "He's never hit me before today, and we all know he was aiming for Cade, but that doesn't mean he didn't hurt me too. Words and actions are just as powerful as fists, if not more so. *This* will heal—" she points to her face "—but *this*—" now she points to her heart "—will always bear those scars."

"Thea," I say softly. I'm at a loss for words and I don't know what to say to make it better. I don't think there's anything I *can* say.

So, instead, I hold her hand and give it a small squeeze, silently reminding her that I'm here.

We arrive at the emergency room a few minutes later, and as per usual, it's a major clusterfuck. The place is full of people in all different states—sick, bleeding, crying. You name it, someone's doing it. There's even a guy peeing in one of those potted plants.

Thea gives the woman at the front desk her name and insurance information and then is handed a stack of papers to fill out. Thea sighs heavily and we maneuver our way around, looking for a place to sit. We finally find two seats together near the back beside a woman with a crying infant.

Thea goes to work on filling out the information but I notice a slight shake to her hand and she keeps quietly crying. After another minute of this, I take the clipboard from her and fill it out myself. I know practically everything so it's not a big deal, but she looks up at me with these big shining eyes like I've just done the greatest thing ever. It's such a simple thing, but those things mean the most to someone.

I finish filling out the paperwork and return it to the front desk. I'm starting back to our seats when Cade, Rae, Jace, and Nova come in. I wasn't expecting all of them, and I hope Thea won't feel overwhelmed.

"Hey, guys," I say. "She's over here waiting."

I lead them over to our chairs and sit down beside Thea. She forces a small smile for everyone.

"Whoa, you look like a star in a horror movie," Jace says. Nova glares at him and gives his arm a smack. "Ow, I was trying to be funny. Lighten the mood."

Nova rolls her eyes. "You're such a guy. Keep your mouth shut, how about that."

Jace's lips thin and he looks to the ceiling. Nova is the only girl I've ever met that can shut him up.

Before much else can be said, they call for Thea and we follow someone down a long hall while the others stay behind.

She gets put in a room with three cinderblock walls and one all glass with a clear view of the information desk.

"Put on the gown and someone will be in to see you shortly." The door closes behind us.

Thea hops onto the bed, kicking her legs back and forth. "I'm not putting that gown on," she warns me. "I will fight someone if they try to get me to wear that."

I pull up a chair and sit down beside her. "I don't think they'll care. You're here for your nose."

She turns to the side. "Do you still think it's not broken?"

I stand and assess the damage again. I broke my nose once

in middle school and there was an immediate bump in the bridge. Even once they set it the bump never quite went away. But Thea's nose is still perfectly straight. "I think you're good, but it's still best to get it checked out."

She nods, still swinging her legs. She shivers and rubs her hands up and down her arms. It is freezing in here, but since it's hot as balls outside I don't have a jacket to offer her. There is a blanket sitting on another chair and I grab it and drape it around her shoulders.

"Thanks." She gives me a grateful smile.

There's a knock on the door and I turn around to see our friends.

Rae pokes her head in. "They said we could come back."

I nod and motion them inside.

With the four of them there's not much room left in the small space, but I can see Thea relax, happy that they're here.

"So," Jace begins, "would anyone care to tell me what the fuck is going on?"

I look at Cade and see his shoulders tense. Rae wraps her arms around him and whispers something in his ear.

Cade takes a deep breath and the room fills with tension. "My father abused me as a child, but the abuse never really stopped. It's continued even now. He was aiming for me today and got Thea instead." He sweeps his fingers toward his little sister and winces. "You shouldn't have gotten in the way, Thea."

She raises her chin defiantly. "He shouldn't have been hitting you in the first place."

Cade sighs. "True, but it is what it is."

Thea snaps. "No, no, *no*. Don't say that. It's not, 'it is what it is'. Don't excuse his actions. He doesn't deserve that. He's not a good dad. He's a bad person and he should've never laid a hand on you." She begins to cry anew. "It should have never been *normal* for you."

Cade wets his lips. "How'd you know? You had to know or you wouldn't have followed us."

Thea swallows thickly and tells him the same thing she told me in the car about coming home early and witnessing Cade getting hit by their father.

Everyone in the room grows solemn. Abuse is one of those things you *know* about, but don't really think about until you're confronted face to face with it and it's scary to think that someone that should protect them, their *father*, hurt them both so deeply. Cade with fists, Thea with words. I can't imagine having a child and ever hurting him or her. It seems impossible to feel so darkly toward a child.

"I didn't want him to hurt you *again*." Thea's voice cracks. "I wanted this to be the last time."

My gaze swings to Cade, standing at the foot of the bed with his back against the wall, and I watch as he breaks down. He covers his face and a sound escapes his throat that's half-tortured, half-relieved. Rae rubs his back as he cries, hiding his face from us. I don't think I've seen Cade cry *ever*, and it's weird to see him breaking down to this degree, but we all know he needs it so we say nothing and give him this moment.

I feel Thea's hand on my stomach and I reach down,

placing my hand on hers. She looks at me with sad but hopeful eyes.

"Fuck," Jace says after a while and once Cade has composed himself. "I never even imagined." He presses his lips together and then asks the question I think we've all been wondering. "Why didn't you hit him back? At least, once you got older? I mean, you're a big guy, you could've taken him."

Cade looks to the ceiling and Rae squeezes his hand. He sighs heavily and says, "I'd come to expect it and feel like I deserved it, and then, in recent years, I've ..." He paused. "Hitting him back felt like stooping to his level and I didn't want to do that."

Rae leans her head against his arm and whispers something.

Cade whispers to Thea, "I can't believe you knew. I thought I was protecting you by not saying anything. I never wanted him to go after you."

She gives him a sad smile. "He might not have gone after me with fists but he went after me in other ways. I hope Mom will finally leave him," she whispers the last part. "We've all spent too much of our lives being scared of him and he shouldn't get to rob the rest of our years. I want to wash my hands of him and pretend he doesn't exist."

"Me too," Cade echoes. "I'll tell Mom if she needs a place to stay she can crash with us. It's not like this one sleeps in his bed anymore." He points at me. I laugh and lower my head to Thea's, hiding my smile behind her hair.

Another knock sounds on the door and it opens, revealing the doctor and a nurse.

"Oh," the doctor says, reeling back in shock at the amount of people. "Um ..."

"We'll be in the waiting room," Cade says, leading Rae out.

Jace and Nova follow, both giving Thea reassuring smiles.

Once the door closes behind them, the doctor introduces himself and looks Thea over. Like I thought, her nose isn't broken, but it's going to be sore and she's going to have one wicked bruise on her face.

Before we leave the room, Thea heads down the hall to wash her face and I wait in the room for her.

Today has been insane, which feels like the understatement of the century.

Between the tubing thing, my mom going ape-shit about the marriage, and then this with Thea's dad, I'm exhausted.

But I know the battle is only beginning.

We've opened up a massive black hole where everything's being sucked inside, and I really fucking hope we're not next.

twenty-one
...

thea

I WAKE up the next morning with Xander's arms wrapped around me and Prue by my legs. It might be a sweet moment if it weren't for the throbbing of my face. I feel like shit.

I maneuver my way out of his hold and manage to get by Prue without kicking her.

I stumble into the bathroom, the throbbing in my head making the short walk seem impossible.

I get into the bathroom and grasp the counter, holding myself steady as my head spins. It's so bad I think I might throw up. I reach for the switch and turn the light on. I slowly lift my head and get a look at my reflection.

I squeak in fright. "Oh, my God what is that?"

Me. It's me.

My hair is a mess, basically a wild and untamable beast, but my face? It looks I stuck it in a blender and tried to puree it. The skin around my nose and left cheek is a mixture of red, purple, green, and yellow, and if I stare closely enough I can see where it looks like blood vessels have popped. I look like a cartoonish monster from a kid's book.

I take a deep breath and turn the faucet, running warm water. I splash some on my face, wishing it would wipe away the disgusting swirl of colors there, but unfortunately, they stay.

Ugh.

Shower. A shower is a must if I'm going to at least have my hair under control.

I turn the water on and make sure it's steaming hot. I plan on staying in there as long as I can.

After my shower, I wrap a towel around my body and blow-dry my hair, then slather the makeup on to hide the hideous bruise. I pad into my room and over to the closet. I grab a pair of black scallop shorts with a gray t-shirt.

I drop my towel in the hamper and Xander gives a sleepy yawn. "Hey," he says, his voice thick.

"Morning." I walk over to the bed and sit down, stretching my legs out.

He leans over and presses a quick kiss to my lips. He smiles crookedly but quickly sobers. "How are you feeling?"

"My face feels like I took a meat mallet to it, but other than that, I'm fantastic." I smile.

He chuckles. "You're hysterical."

"I try." I laugh and he grabs my hips, pulling me closer. My laughter intensifies and I end up in his lap, straddling him. I place my hands on his firm chest, and his skin is so warm it nearly burns my palm.

"I'm sorry you're hurt," he whispers, touching his fingers delicately to my tender skin. I did a good job of covering it up with foundation and concealer but some spots were impossible to hide completely.

"It'll heal," I whisper back, entwining my fingers behind his neck and leaning my forehead against his.

He presses his palm to my chest, right over my heart. "Will *this* heal?"

I nod. "Eventually." I press my lips together and then admit, "I hope I never have to see him again. I know it's wrong to say this, but I hate him. I hate him for what he did to Cade, to me, to my mom, and I hate him even more for the act he put on to everyone else like he was this great guy when it was nothing but a lie. He was a monster hiding in plain sight, and it's scary to think about how many others are out there like that."

Xander nods, rubbing his hands up and down my arms. "Yeah, it is scary," he agrees.

I have had enough serious talk so I press a kiss to his lips and slip from the bed. "I'm going to grab some coffee. You want any?"

He shakes his head. "Not right now."

I nod and head downstairs, fixing the coffee since no one else is up yet.

Prue comes down and gives a little whine so I put her leash on and take her down the street. On the way back, I grab the newspaper from the box and take a look at it as I walk back up the driveway. One article causes me to pause.

Local Football Hero Victim of Years of Physical Abuse

"Oh, shit," I whisper. Then think to myself, *how?* How does the news know about this already? Then it clicks. "Stan," I hiss.

Stanley Berk went to high school with Cade and then went off to college for journalism. I remember him working for the high school newspaper and he was always doing these revealing articles on his fellow classmates. The guy was a leach.

Sure enough, I search for the author of the article, and the name **Stanley T. Berk** stares back at me.

I head inside with Prue and let her off her leash, then sit down at the table so I can read the article.

Yesterday, on a beautiful July Fourth evening, it came to light that our local football hero, Cade Montgomery, has been living a secret hell. His father, a man we always assumed was a kind and supportive man, physically abuses him. On this night, his sister, Thea Montgomery, stepped in the way and got hurt, and was subsequently taken to the hospital. At this time, we do not have an update on her injury, but as I was a witness, I can attest to the fact that it was a bloody scene. After his sister was carried off, Cade Montgomery revealed to the group of us that his father has abused him since he was very young. For all of you that have wondered why Cade Montgomery didn't go pro and follow the path we all thought was destined for him, I think we finally have our answer. I'm hoping to acquire an interview with Cade and his sister to follow up this article.

I sigh heavily. Fucking Stan.

If this is already in the newspaper it will soon be online everywhere and it *will* be a big deal with the star power Cade had on his college team. He only recently graduated. He still matters to so many people and they'll be heartbroken and livid to find out their star player has been subjected to abuse his whole life.

I push the newspaper away. I can't think about it right now.

I pour myself the cup of coffee I originally came down for and add enough cream and sugar to put an elephant in a coma.

I head upstairs and back into my room.

Prue is already on the bed again and Xander is sitting up, his hair a mess.

"I think we should stay in bed and watch TV all day," he declares.

"Sounds good to me," I agree, climbing in bed.

I giggle as he pulls me over and in-between his legs. "*Charmed?*" he asks. "We have one season left."

I nod. "Let's do it. Rip it off like a Band-Aid." He chuckles. "Hey," I defend, "it's always sad ending a show we love."

"Yeah, but we get to start a new one."

"True," I agree, and then laugh when Prue licks my toes. "That tickles."

Xander grabs the remote and starts the show and soon I'm sucked into the mysterious world of the Halliwell sisters.

We're halfway thru the second episode when Cade barges into the room. I'm not surprised to see the newspaper dangling from his fingertips.

"Did you see this?" He tosses the newspaper on the bed and Xander grabs it. "This is unbelievable." Xander scans the article and hisses between his teeth. "An interview?" He puts his hands on his hips and paces my room. "Is he out of his mind? Like I'm going to talk to him?"

"Cade," I say hesitantly, "I think you *should* talk. Maybe not to Stan, but to a journalist you respect. You speaking out could help a lot of kids."

Cade winces. "Talking about it is difficult."

"I know," I say softly. "But think about when you were younger. If someone you had respected had come out that they were abused, maybe it would've helped."

He pinches the bridge of his nose and mutters. "Fuck."

I know I've finally gotten to him, so I continue. "I think you should see a therapist too."

"Thea, I don't need a fucking shrink. I'm not a crazy person. I'm not Dad."

"I know that, but sometimes you need someone who's not family or a friend to talk to. Someone with an unbiased opinion on the situation. Think about it," I plead.

Cade sighs, his jaw clenched tight. "Yeah, I'll think about it," he agrees reluctantly. He claps his hands together and says, "Let's go out for breakfast."

I lift my head and look at Xander. "We're having a lazy day," I say.

Cade snorts. "Every day is a lazy day for you two. You're couch potatoes."

"Hey," I defend. "I went to the gym twice this summer."

He gives me a look. "Yeah, *twice*."

"I go every day." Xander raises his hand. "Plus, practice."

I glare at him. "Yeah, well, you're an overachiever."

"Breakfast," Cade says again. "Let's go. We all have to eat and you can have your lazy day later."

"Ugh," I groan. "You're so annoying. Go pester your girlfriend."

He heads for the door and hollers, "Breakfast!" before he closes the door.

"We need to move," I tell Xander. "Stat."

He chuckles. "About that ..."

"What?" I look over my shoulder at him.

He brushes my hair over my shoulder. "With my paycheck I can afford for us to have our own place. I didn't want to say anything, because I didn't want to push you, but it's a possibility. Think about it."

I swallow thickly and push down the panic. I know what I just said, but I meant it jokingly.

"What about when I go back to school?" I ask.

"We can get something close to there."

"But then you'll have to commute," I remind him.

He laughs. "If we get something in the city *you'll* have to commute."

I press my lips together. "I don't even want to go back to school," I admit. "I feel so lost there, like I don't belong. I hate being this clueless on what I want to do." I take a sip of coffee, irritated by how cold it already is.

"You'll figure it out," Xander assures me.

I sigh. "I hope so."

It sucks not having any idea what I want to do with my life. Nothing makes me feel excited or warm and fuzzy inside. I don't want to pick something and settle, and end up unhappy for the rest of my life. I want to do something I love and ultimately make a change in the world.

"Breakfast!" we hear yelled again.

I laugh and slide my legs to the side and off the bed. "Man, he's determined."

Xander shrugs and stretches his arms above his head. I might ogle his chest shamelessly as he does that, but with the show his muscles put on how can you blame me?

"He's worried about you," he says, standing and oh Lord, the way his sweatpants sit low on his hips ... Mmm, it's safe to say I'm thinking *all* the dirty thoughts.

"Yeah, well he can just unworry," I counter.

Xander snorts. "I don't think *unworry* is a word, but nice try."

"I like it," I defend. "It makes it sound like there's a switch you can flip on and off. Worry and unworry."

He shakes his head at my antics. "I'm going to shower. Why don't you head downstairs before your brother loses his mind?"

I sigh. "Sure thing, Captain." He chuckles and closes the bathroom door behind him. "Come on, Prue." I pat my hip, and she obediently jumps off the bed and follows me out of the room.

I find Cade in the family room, watching TV.

Before I can say anything, he yells, "Breakfast!" again.

I slap my hands over my ears. "Dude, chill out," I groan. "I'm here and Xander will be down in a minute."

Cade glances behind him, over the back of the couch, and grins sheepishly. "Sorry, I didn't hear you come down."

"Obviously." I rub my ear to try to stop the ringing. "Why is this *breakfast* so important?" I mimic his tone.

He shrugs and I take a seat beside him, drawing my legs up criss-cross.

"I don't know," he answers. "After yesterday, I think we should all be together."

"That was insane," I agree.

"Has Xander heard from his mom or dad?" he asks.

"Huh?" My brows furrow in confusion.

"You know, since his mom was so pissed." He looks at me like I've completely lost my mind for not remembering, and I guess I have. In the aftermath, it slipped my mind.

"Shit," I mutter, shoving my fingers through my hair roughly. "I forgot."

The look on his mom's face, that had hurt. I completely understand where she's coming from, but that doesn't make it suck any less. Especially for Xander.

"Maybe we should send her a gift basket of wines and cheese. Everyone loves wine, right?" I reason.

"Yeah, and maybe while you're at it you could send her a singing telegram."

"Oooh!" I snap my fingers. "A stripper. We'll send her a stripper." Sobering, I say, "I don't know what we can do beyond talking to them and hoping for the best."

He shakes his head. "That's one conversation I wouldn't want to make."

I glare at my brother. "Thanks for the vote of confidence."

"Just being honest," he defends.

Rae comes in the front door, her body drenched with sweat from her morning run. Her earbuds dangle from her iPhone as she winds them up.

"Hey," she says rather breathlessly.

"We're going to breakfast," Cade tells her.

She nods and starts for the stairs. "I'll take a quick shower. Promise."

An hour later, we all pile into Cade's Jeep and head down the road to a local place.

The floors are always sticky and the air smells like syrup, but the food is the best so I don't complain.

I slide across the plastic booth and Xander sits beside me, resting his elbows on the table.

Cade slides in across from me and his legs bump mine in the narrow space.

Menus are already on the table and we each pick it up, scanning it even though that's really unnecessary.

Our usual waitress comes over and flashes a smile before sitting our drinks on the table. We didn't order them yet, but she knew what we'd get regardless.

"The usual?" she asks, tucking her tray under her arm.

We all nod and shuffle the menus to the end of the table. "I'll have that right out for you." She smiles again and heads off to another table.

Cade's phone starts going off and he looks at the screen before clicking ignore. Before I can ask who it is, it goes off again. He answers this time.

"Stan, I don't know who the fuck gave you this number, but if you call one more time—" He rolls his eyes and taps his fingers against the table impatiently. "I'm not doing an interview for you. Why not? Because you're a dick." He laughs but there's no humor in the tone and I can hear Stan grow irritated on the other end. "Mhm," he hums. "Fuck you too." He hangs up and drops his phone on the table before covering his face with his hands. "I'm going to strangle Stan," he mutters from between his fingers. His phone starts ringing again and he groans, "Going to have to change my number." He looks at it anyway and his eyes widen in surprise. "Mom?" he answers. He listens for a few beats, nodding his head. "Yeah, of course that's fine. Head on over whenever."

He hangs up and looks across the table at me. "Looks like Mom's had enough of his bullshit and she wants to leave him."

I breathe out a sigh of relief—one I think I've been holding for years.

"It's about damn time."

twenty-two
...

xander

"WE NEED to talk to your mom," Thea announces from the bathroom.

I sigh heavily. "I know."

"We can't keep putting it off," she continues.

"I know," I say again.

It's been three days since the Fourth of July party, and I'm still puzzling out what to say. Nothing I come up with sounds any good, but I guess I just have to be honest.

Right now, though, I have to head to practice, and I've managed to get my coach to agree to let Thea and Cade come watch. I think the only reason he agreed was because of Cade. They really wanted him for their team and were saddened when he didn't opt to go pro. I think my coach is hoping if Cade sees a practice that he can sway him and pull some strings to get him on the team.

But I know Cade doesn't want that. His dad pushed football onto him, and instead of being something he loved, it became something he hated.

"We should get her flowers," Thea says, peeking around the bathroom doorway. "Do you know her favorite?" I shake my head and she curses. "Okay, I'll guess then. Where's her favorite restaurant? We could ask her to meet us there."

"That place in the city." I snap my fingers together, thinking.

"Xander, think," she says, exasperated. "There are a million places in the city."

"Gregory's? Does that sound right?"

"Sure." She waves her hand dismissively. "You let her know, and after you're done with practice I'll make reservations and grab some flowers."

I nod. "Okay. Sounds like a plan." I try to sound optimistic but my voice falls flat.

I've called my mom a few times in the last three days, and she's only answered once and promptly hung up after only a minute of conversation.

"Call her." Thea glares. "*Now*."

"You're bossy today," I mutter, but do as she says because there's no point in putting it off.

I call her twice and she doesn't answer either time. My mom's been mad at me plenty of times over the years but never to this degree. Her coldness is off-putting, to say the least.

Since I can't get her, I suck it up and call my dad. *He*

answers, but instead of his usual cheery hello I get a gruff, "What?" instead.

I sit up and scratch the back of my head, awkwardness overtaking my body. "Um," I hesitate, "Thea and I would like to take you and Mom to dinner tonight. To ... uh ... talk?" I say it like a question, then promptly wince. I'm going about this all wrong and I sound like an idiot.

He sighs on the other end and I can hear the sound of shuffling papers and I imagine him in his office working. "When and where?"

"Eight o' clock at Gregory's?"

I then hear a squeak as he presumably leans back in his chair. "We'll be there."

"Thank you," I say.

He clears his throat. "Your mom loves you, and she'll forgive you, but don't forget that she's allowed to feel hurt. Don't belittle her feelings."

"I won't," I vow.

"Good. See you then."

The line clicks off, and I drop my phone on the bed.

Thea pops back through the door. "Did you get her?"

"No, my dad."

She frowns. "I still feel bad for quitting, but without you there, I didn't see the point in staying. No offense, but I don't find architecture all that stimulating."

I crack a grin and she walks toward me. I place my hands on her waist and then move them down, over her ass, to settle on her legs. "But me, you find stimulating?"

She places her hands around my neck and then climbs

onto my lap, grinding her hips into mine. "Oh, yeah," she sighs breathily.

She bites her bottom lip, drawing it slowly between her teeth, and her eyes flick down to my lips.

We need to leave in a short time, but fuck it.

I close the space between us, wrapping my fingers in the strands of her hair and drawing her mouth to mine.

She lets out the softest little sound that's half-moan and half-purr.

I flip her onto the bed and cover her body with mine. She's so small beneath me and I love that my body shields her so easily. I smooth my hands down her sides and then grab the bottom of her shirt, quickly removing it. Her eyes watch me, warm with pleasure, and she licks her lips. I love that she gets turned on so easily—that she truly wants to be with me. It's something I thought might never happen.

She sits up and I reach for her bra strap, popping the clasp so the black scrap of fabric falls down her arms. My eyes rake her in and my blood heats. I've never felt possessive before, and I'm not sure what I feel now can even be described as that, but there's this primal need to mark her some way as mine.

She pushes my sweatpants and boxer-briefs off my hips and takes me in her hand. My breath catches and my eyes close as I fall to the bed. A moment later, her mouth joins her hand and I lose all sense of reality.

"Fuck, Thea." I wrap my fingers around her silky hair, and watch her work her mouth up and down.

My heart bangs like a drum inside my chest, so loud that I can't even hear my thoughts.

I push her shoulders gently and she releases me, giving me a lazy smile with her eyes half-mast.

I grab a condom and rip it open. She watches me as I roll it on and then I grasp her hips, pulling her toward me and sliding inside her. She lets out a small gasp and her fingernails dig into my arms. Her hands move to the center of my chest and I grab them, pinning them above her head. Her eyes darken.

I press my lips to her neck and then move down between her breasts.

Her hands grow restless between mine, desperate to touch me, and I can't help but smile against her skin when I kiss the underside of her breast.

"Xander," she pleads, fingers wiggling. "I need to touch you."

"Not this time." It's not often that I take complete control, and this is the only time I've refused to let her touch me.

She whimpers as the heat of my body leaves her and then I flip her over, grab her ass between my hands, and slam back inside her with a groan.

I lean over her, pressing my front to her back, and whisper in her ear, "I fucking love you."

She doesn't respond with words, just the smallest fucking whimpers as her fingers dig into the sheets. She comes, her body shaking, and I hold her steady so she doesn't fall to the bed, and then I'm right behind her finding my own release.

She sits up on her knees and I hold her against me, my breath coming out in pants against her back.

After a moment we both collapse onto the bed, and she sprawls across me, burrowing her head against my neck.

"That was intense." She laughs.

I nod. My brain's turned to mush, and there are no words.

"Now I'm all sweaty and I smell like you." She laughs again, heartier this time. "Think about *that* while you practice."

Fuck.

"So, what'd you think?" I ask Thea as we head out to the parking lot. My hair is still damp from my after-practice shower and my gym bag thumps against my leg. "Was it everything you thought it would be?"

She clasps her hands together and does a little spin. "It was spectacular, and so intense. I can't wait to see you play in a real game, because fuck, if I'm this turned on after a practice I'm going to jump you after a game. You've been warned."

I laugh, shaking my head at her. "You realize I'll be dead tired after a game, right?" Even now, my legs hurt and my arms are protesting every time I lift them even slightly. I never complain, though, because I'm living my dream.

She waves her hand dismissively. "I can fantasize about

some dirty against the locker sex, okay? Give me a break." She spins again and then stops. "Oh, I made the reservations for eight like you asked, but we still have several hours to kill so what do you want to do?"

I shrug. "What do you want to do?"

"Hmm." She stops by the truck and presses her fingers to her lips. "We could go to Larimer Square?" she suggests.

I nod. "Sounds good to me."

We head over that way and roam the streets for a while. When we pass a flower cart, Thea stops and insists we pick out some flowers for my mom.

"Which one do you think she'd like?"

I rack my brain, trying to remember if I've seen any of these around the house before. After a minute, I point to one. "Those, I think."

She nods and grabs them. "Lilies, good choice."

I buy the flowers and we continue down the street, ducking into the shops now and then. There's a pet store and we pick up some things for Prue that we know she'll love.

Eventually, we stop at a café, and grab some coffee, taking a seat at one of their outdoor tables since it's not blistering hot.

"Oh, this is good," Thea croons, sipping on her blended coffee drink.

I set the flowers on the table and stretch out my legs. Tonight's dinner isn't far from my mind, and I'm trying not to overthink it.

"Hey," Thea says softly, trying to get my attention. I swivel my head toward her. "Are you okay?"

I nod, tapping my finger on the lid of my coffee. I don't know why I even got it, I don't want any. "I'm worried about tonight," I admit.

"Oh." She frowns, and looks away.

I clasp my hands together and rest them on the table. "She has every right to be mad, my dad too, for that matter. First I don't tell them about football, and then this." I wave my hand at her. "If I was in their shoes I'd be pretty fucking pissed too." I cover my face and let out a groan. "I don't know how to make it okay again, and you *know* me, I hate conflict. I want everyone to be happy, but all I keep doing is making everyone miserable."

Thea reaches across the table and takes my hand. "We all make choices that we think are the best at the time, and sometimes hindsight shows that we were wrong, but we can't go back in time and change it so we have to follow the course and let things play out. It'll be okay, I believe that, and you should too."

I sigh. "Between this, and your mom and dad, and Cade …" I pause. "It's a lot going on."

She nods, her eyes growing misty. Her mom's staying with us now, in my room, so I moved all my crap—at least, most of it—to Thea's room. Her mom has been quiet and distant with all of us, staying mostly in her room out of sight. No word has come from Thea's dad and I'm really fucking glad, because I don't know if I could stop myself from hitting the guy this time.

"Yeah, it is," she agrees. "Hopefully, it'll all be over soon," she whispers.

"Yeah, I hope so too," I echo.

Thea and I are the first to arrive at the restaurant and we're led to a secluded table in the back, and I wonder if Thea requested that we be seated away from everyone else.

"Thank you." She flashes a smile when the host pulls out her chair and hands her a menu.

I take my seat and a menu from him and he tells us that someone will be by with water.

I clear my throat and wiggle restlessly in my seat.

"Stop," Thea hisses. "You're acting like a five-year-old who can't sit still. Everything will be *fine*."

I mess with the collar on my shirt, trying to loosen it. "Is it hot in here?"

"No, you're just a hot mess," she groans. "Calm down. You're going to have a heart attack before they get here."

"What if they don't come at all?"

She gives me a look. "They'll come."

Someone comes by and fills up our glasses with water and I slurp mine down like I haven't had any water all day.

"Whoa, slow down," Thea warns, placing her hand on my arm.

"I'm nervous," I hiss under my breath.

She snorts. "I hadn't noticed."

I see my parents and glance at Thea in panic. "Am I sweating?"

"No, you're fine. Take a deep breath."

I take her advice, but then I forget to breathe out so by the time my parents are taking their seats I exhale heavily, sounding like a whale, and everyone stares at me.

Fucking great. This is already fantastic.

Thea's hand touches my knee. "Are you okay?"

"Fine," I squeak, and take a sip of water. It's empty.

This gets better and better.

I was less nervous telling them that I made the football team and wasn't going to work for Dad than I am now, and I thought I was pretty nervous at the time.

I clear my throat. "I got you some flowers," I tell my mom. I notice she chose the seat across from Thea.

Her head is behind the menu when she says, "I saw."

I sigh. Her coldness is expected, and warranted, but it hurts anyway.

"How was work?" I ask my dad.

Small talk is good, right?

"Good," he says, picking up his water. "We closed the Holtzman account today, so you know how glad I am to get that account."

"Oh, wow, congrats, Dad. That's fantastic."

It really is. He's been working for months to get that account. It's a huge deal for designing a building downtown and three more over the next ten years.

"Yes," he says, setting his glass down, "so this is like our celebration dinner."

My mom sets down her menu and crosses her fingers.

"Really? I thought this dinner was for my *son* to explain to me why he got *married* and didn't tell me?"

I need a drink. Or ten.

"Mom—" I start, but she promptly holds up her hand.

"I need my food and a glass of wine before I hear anything you have to say."

I glance at Thea and she's holding in a snicker.

I'm glad she's amused by this.

Our waiter stops by the table with a basket of bread and a bottle of wine.

"Can I interest you in a glass of our house wine. It's—"

My mom holds up her glass. "We'll take the whole bottle since my son's paying."

Thea smacks her hand over her mouth, but not quick enough to hide her snort.

"Oh, okay." The waiter pours her glass then reaches for another empty one.

"Oh, no, that won't be necessary," my mom says, grabbing the bottle from him. "This is just for me."

This time Thea's laugher escapes and she does nothing to stop it. Instead, she sits there cackling, entirely amused by this situation.

"I'll give you another minute to decide what you want and I'll be back soon."

"Thanks," I mumble. I'm pretty sure my cheeks are red with embarrassment right now and Thea's *still* laughing.

I slide my menu to the edge of the table. I've already picked out my meal, but it hardly matters because I doubt I'll be able to eat it.

"So," Thea says cheerily, "marvelous weather we're having."

I pinch the bridge of my nose. The *weather*, that's what she goes with?

"This wine is fantastic." My mom points to her glass. "I'd offer you all some, but it's mine." She cradles the bottle like a baby.

I cover my face with my hands.

Please, tell me this is a nightmare?

I open my eyes and she's drinking straight from the bottle.

I think I might die.

"All right, that's enough. You've embarrassed him sufficiently." My dad grabs her arm and forces the bottle from her mouth.

She sets the bottle on the table and gives us all a big grin. "I think so too. That was good, right?" she asks my dad.

"What?" I say, exchanging a look with Thea.

"After this little stunt, you deserve to be embarrassed a lot worse than this, so hold your tongue, Xander." I press my lips together. "And start talking. I thought you guys were dating, when did you get married?"

I glance at Thea with a *what the fuck* expression. I feel like I've slipped into a parallel universe or something. But it looks like my mom has just been fucking with me, because she can.

"Vegas," I answer. "We got married in Vegas."

Fuck, it sounds stupid when I say it, and I guess it is. It took getting drunk in Vegas for me to finally get the girl. Where was my game at?

My mom glares at my dad. "At that stupid convention you sent them to?"

Dad raises his hands innocently. "Don't look at me. Getting married wasn't on the to-do list there. These two went off and did that all on their own."

"But you told me you guys were *dating* when you came to dinner. Can you see how I feel a little hurt?" She frowns, picking up a piece of bread and slathering it with butter. "God, bread makes everything better," she says after taking a bite.

"I know, right." Thea laughs in agreement.

I clear my throat. "We figured that was easier than coming out and saying we were married—and I guess, we worried it might fizzle out and wanted to spare everyone the heartache of knowing." I look at Thea and the love I feel for her, there's no way that's ever going away. I take her hand beneath the table. "But I think we're in it for the long haul. I have faith in us and I hope you do too." I look at my parents, waiting and hoping for their approval.

My mom sniffles, tearing up a bit. "Of course we do, but you got married without us," she cries. "You're my oldest baby, don't you think I wanted to be there?"

"It was kind of a spur of the moment decision," I mutter. My voice growing in volume, I add, "I don't take it back, either, because if we hadn't done it we wouldn't be together today and I wouldn't give this up for anything."

Thea lets out an audible exhale of, "Aww," beside me.

"You guys will have a real wedding, though? Right?" my

mom asks, her eyes pleading. "Renew your vows or something, so we can all be there?"

I shrug. "Maybe, in time, if Thea wants."

My mom zeroes in on Thea like a vulture. "*Thea?*"

Thea nearly chokes on her water. "Um, I wouldn't be opposed to it, but right now my primary focus is what happens once I start college again and Xander's gone all the time."

My mom presses her lips into a thin line and exhales heavily. "Think about it, please. It's something that would mean a lot to us, and I think, down the road, it would mean a lot to you both to have a real wedding."

I glance at Thea. "We'll think about it."

I wish she'd shut up about this before she sends Thea into a panic. Thankfully, Thea doesn't seem to care, or if she does then she's not showing it.

The waiter comes back and takes our order, giving us funny looks, probably because of the bottle of wine my mom still has beside her. He's probably worried we're all a bunch of crazies and are going to bail on the crazily expensive meal.

Luckily, the rest of the dinner goes smooth, and I'm glad to have worked things out with my mom. I can tell she's still slightly hurt by the situation, but she's not pissed anymore, so I'll take that as a win. I'll make sure to stop by the house with lunch one day this week so we can chat just the two of us.

We leave the restaurant and part ways, with hugs and goodbyes.

Thea takes my hand and we start down the street. Jars filled with lights hang from the trees.

She tilts her head back, smiling up at them, and the light dances across her face making her look almost angelic.

She grabs onto my arm, leaning her head against my shoulder as we stroll down the street.

Her happiness radiates off of her like a physical energy and I feel bowed by it. Her vibrancy and zest is contagious.

Things aren't perfect, not by a long shot, but right now, in this moment, it almost feels like it is. So I take that small victory and make it mine, smiling like I own the whole world as I walk beside the girl I love.

twenty-three
• • •

thea

"YOU TALK TO HER."

"No, *you*," I argue with my brother.

He clenches his jaw and glares, looking from me to the closed door that once led to Xander's room, but now has been taken over by my mom.

"You're the girl," he reasons.

I snort. "*So*? You're the favorite."

"Am not."

"Are too."

Rae shakes her head as she walks by. "You guys sound like you're five."

"Stay out of this!" we yell simultaneously.

"Whoa." Her eyes widen. "All right then."

"You talk to her," I hiss to Cade. "You're older. More worldly."

He sighs and crosses his arms over his chest. "We'll *both* talk to her."

I lift my chin. "That is a reasonable compromise, but *you* go in first."

"Fine," he huffs. "We'll shake on it."

"Deal." I spit in my hand and hold it out. "Put it there, partner."

Cade spits in his hand and we shake on it the way we used to as kids. When I look behind him Rae is watching us with a horrified expression. She raises her hands, shaking her head.

"I'm going to pretend I didn't watch that." She disappears into their room.

"You first." I nod my head at the door that separates us from our mom.

Cade sighs heavily and wraps his hand around the knob, turning it. The room is dark, like a dungeon, and I see that Xander's black curtains are pulled over the window allowing no afternoon sunlight to slip through. One lone light on the dresser is all that's on, providing a measly amount of light for the room.

"What's that smell?" I pinch my nose.

Cade tilts his head this way and that trying to make heads and tails of the form buried under a mountain of blankets. "Mom?" he says hesitantly. "Are you okay?"

There's a distant groan that I think is meant to be *yes*.

Cade and I exchange a look. It's worse than we thought.

Since I'm more brazen than Cade, I stride forward and

yank the covers off my mom. She cowers away like the minimal light in the room sears her skin.

"Get up. Shower. And put some clean clothes on." I glance back at Cade and mouth *tough love.*

She doesn't move and she looks up at us with bleary, tear-filled eyes. "I couldn't protect Gabe and I couldn't protect you two. I'm a horrible mom and I don't deserve you."

I wince like I've been shot.

Gabe.

My little brother. I never think about him. It's too difficult to think about that big gaping hole in our life. A hole that's my fault. All because I wanted to go horseback riding on that *stupid* vacation. If I'd never begged and pleaded to go, he wouldn't have died. He'd still be here and we'd still be a family. A whole family and not a fractured one built up with hate, hurt, and lies.

My heart stutters inside my chest as I think about the little boy we lost before we even got to know him. He was only eight.

"Mom," my voice cracks. "There was nothing you could do. It was my fault."

"Thea," Cade says softly, resting his hand on my shoulder. I shake it off. "It was a freak accident."

"If I hadn't begged for us to go horseback riding it wouldn't have happened!" I shout. "He wouldn't have fallen off his horse," I say softer, losing steam, "and he'd still be here with us."

Tears prick my eyes.

If I think back on it, that's the day when things changed for good.

My dad was already an asshole, but after that he had an even bigger reason to be a jerk, and my mom? That day *broke* her, and she hasn't been the same since. She became overbearing, and uber critical and turned a blind eye to everything Dad did.

"My fault," my mom says from the bed, her body shaking. "No, it was my fault. It was all my fault." Her eyes grow clearer and she grabs my hand with surprising strength. It's then that I notice how thin she's become. This isn't sudden thinness, either, it's obvious this has been happening for a while, and I wonder what her life has been like left alone with Dad the last year. "I should've left him a long time ago. If I'd left him when I should have Gabe would still be here."

Cade steps forward, his presence crowding behind me.

"It's *neither* of your faults and you have to let it go. Gabe wouldn't want you blaming yourselves."

Tears burst from my eyes when I think of Gabe's sweet cherubic face and his wide round eyes. I know Cade's right. That kid ... He was a goofball and the sweetest thing ever and he wouldn't want us blaming ourselves. That's why I never try to think about him, because when I do, guilt floods me and nearly drowns me in its depths.

"And Mom," Cade says, "you've left him now, that's what matters. Just please, *please* don't go back to him."

She doesn't respond, but I hope that his words have gotten to her.

I wipe my tears off my cheeks, sniffling. I hadn't been expecting a cry fest when I came in here.

"I think we should get her in the bath," I tell Cade. "She smells like a rotting carcass."

Cade gives me a horrified look. "You're on your own with that."

I glare at him. "At least help me get her into the bathroom, and I'll do the rest."

He sighs. "I can do that." He picks her up easily and she looks so small in his arms and I realize now that she's even smaller than she looked in the bed and it's *scary*. She's no more than skin and bones.

Cade gets her into the bathroom and promptly leaves.

I sigh. It isn't going to be fun, but I have to do what I have to do.

An hour later, she's clean and dressed in real clothes with her hair brushed. She looks human and not like a sewer rat, so I take that as a win.

"Come downstairs and have something to eat."

"I'm not really hungry," she replies, shuffling for the bed.

"Oh, no you don't." I grab her hand and halt her progress. She gives me an indignant look. "You need to eat," I argue. "No offense, but you look like shit."

She sighs. "Always so eloquent, Thea."

"I try." I give her a little nudge toward the door and she reluctantly goes.

Downstairs, we pass Cade and Rae in the family room. Cade gives me an encouraging smile and I give him one back that's the equivalent of *bite me* since he abandoned me.

I pull out a chair at the kitchen table and guide my mom into it.

Once seated she covers her face with her hands, her fingers sealed tight, letting no light penetrate her eyes.

I opt to get her some toast with butter. She hasn't been eating properly so I figure it's best to start light.

I fix it and set the plate in front of her.

She doesn't move her hands.

"Please, for the love of God feed yourself. I already had to bathe you today."

She drops her hands and gives me a look that says I'm three seconds away from being in trouble, which must mean she's feeling more like herself.

She picks up the piece of toast and takes the smallest bite imaginable. Seriously, a bird would've nibbled more off.

"*Mom,*" I groan.

"I'm just not very hungry," she defends with a shrug.

I throw my hands up in exasperation.

There is only so much you can do to help a person and the rest is up to them.

"Your dad used to be a good man," she says suddenly. "Before."

"Before what?" I snap, my patience at a whopping zero.

"Before I married him." She looks forlornly at the table.

"I thought when I got pregnant with Cade that would fix him." She snorts. "How naïve is that? But the anger ..." She trails off, her eyes distant. "It stayed. He could hide it, most of the time, but it would flare up every now and then and once Gabe died ... Well, I think after that he didn't see the point in pretending."

"That's when he started hitting me all the time," Cade pipes up, standing in the doorway of the kitchen. Rae stands beside him with her hand resting reassuringly on his forearm as she looks up at him lovingly. "Before then it would be a shove here and there, maybe yelling in my face, but when Gabe died ..." He looks away. "I think it made him feel better to hit someone and I was the easiest target."

"I don't know why we pretended for so long, that his evil didn't exist," I whisper.

"Because," Cade starts, "we had no choice. We couldn't get away from him and we had to deal any way we could."

My mom sniffles and rubs her eyes. "I'm going to get a divorce. I'm going to make this right for you," she vows.

"No," Cade says firmly. "You make it right for *you*. You deserve to be free, Mom."

She sniffles again and then tears pour from her eyes.

"I'm scared," she admits between sobs.

"Don't be," Cade tells her, coming to wrap his arms around her. "We're here for you."

"Malcolm Montgomery is a dangerous man," she warns. "He won't let us go easily."

Cade looks at me over the top of her head, his blue eyes like steel. "Then we'll make him.

twenty-four

...

thea

I GLARE at my email and shudder, slamming my laptop closed.

"What is it?" Xander asks, chuckling at me.

"Email from the university, welcoming me back. School doesn't start for another three weeks. You'd think they could hold up until the day before to ruin my life."

"Don't go back then."

I wrinkle my nose. "And what? Stay home and *knit*? I don't think so."

He chuckles. "Not what I had in mind." He reaches over and tickles me. I try to swipe his hand away, but he's stronger than me. My laughter fills the room and tears fall from my eyes.

"Okay, okay," I breathe between laughing fits. "Stop, please," I beg.

He gives me another tickle and then stops, smirking at me. I clutch a pillow over my stomach in case he gets any wild ideas.

A lot has changed in the last few weeks since that conversation with my mom.

She, Cade, and I all talked it over and agreed to see a therapist. We each have one appointment a week on our own and one with all three of us.

We've only been to one collective appointment together and today's our second. The first was helpful, and I'm expecting today's to be even more so. Like I told Cade, sometimes you need an unbiased person to talk things over with to put things into perspective.

"When do you have to leave for your appointment?" Xander asks, and I swear it's like the boy can read my mind.

I glance at the clock. "Two hours."

He grins. "Plenty of time to start a new show."

We've long ago finished *Charmed* and plowed through *Prison Break*.

I stretch out on my stomach, stuffing the pillow under my chin. "What do you have in mind?"

"*Supernatural?*" he suggests.

"Ooh, I've heard great things about those Winchester brothers." I waggle my brows and lick my lips.

His lips curl in disgust. "Maybe not then."

"Too late." I snatch the remote from the bed and switch to Netflix, finding *Supernatural* easily. He quits his pouting pretty quickly when the show proves to be fantastic.

"Thea!" Cade calls a while later. "Time to go."

"Ugh," I groan, and point at Xander. "Don't even *think* about finishing this episode without me. I'll cut you."

He laughs and raises his hands innocently. "I won't. I need to go to the gym anyway." He wets his lips then and shuffles nervously.

"What?" I prompt.

"I scheduled for us to meet with a relator tomorrow to see some places."

My mouth pops open. "And you're just now telling me this?"

He shrugs, smiling sheepishly. "I figured you'd freak out if I gave you too much notice."

"Yeah, well…" I touch my hand to my chest, where I can feel it constricting and cutting off my air supply. "I'm definitely freaking out."

"Hey," he says. "We're just *looking*. That's all this is."

I nod. "Just looking," I repeat.

I know moving in together wouldn't be the worst thing in the world. We already do live together but with other people. I guess, it all feels so fast to me. I'm still getting used to us being together and *married*. Living on our own? I don't know if I'm ready for that, especially with still being in college. I'm probably being stupid. We get along great, so it's not like I have to worry about him irritating the crap out of me. If anything, *I* would be the one irritating him.

"I want us to explore our options," he says.

"Okay," I agree. "And then we'll talk about it, together, right?"

He gives me a funny look. "Yeah, of course. I'm not going

to buy us a place and not ask you first. It's *ours* not *mine*." He pinches my side slightly and jumps out of the way before I can swat him. "You better go."

"Oh, right."

After he brought up the relator I totally forgot that Cade had called for me.

When I get downstairs I find that my mom and he are already outside waiting in the Jeep.

I pet Prue on her head and she licks my leg before I dart out the door.

My mom's sitting in the back, so I end up sitting in the front with Cade.

None of us speak on the way and the silence is deafening. In fact, I'm convinced that silence is the loudest sound in the world. An oxymoron, perhaps, but true.

Cade pulls into the lot of the building and I stare at the white stone building. It's clean, modern, almost clinical. When you walk inside it feels like you're about to be operated on, and maybe you are. It sure feels like they're poking around in your head and pulling out the important bits and pieces, laying them out on a table and deciphering what the hidden parts of your mind mean.

Cade turns off the Jeep, lays his palms on his knees, and breathes out heavily.

None of us move.

None of us are ready.

But in order to heal, you have to make that step and do the hard thing, instead of letting the pain beat you.

I put my hand on the door handle and push it open. "Come on," I say, coaxing them out of the car.

Cade follows first, then my mom.

We all say nothing as we head inside the building, check-in, and take our seats in the waiting area.

Little time passes before we're being called back into Dr. Long's office. He's an older man, about fifty or sixty, with gray hair and a heavy beard. He's kind and patient, though, and as far as therapists go, I don't think he's that bad.

Cade and I sit on the couch and my mom takes the chair.

Dr. Long sits in his chair, his legs crossed, and smiles kindly.

"I'm glad to see you all back today," he says. "I know this is only your second visit together, but consistency is progress, and I think these meetings together, as well as your separate appointments, are key in healing." He claps his hands together and appraises us. "What would you all like to talk about today?"

I bite my lip. So many thoughts are running through my mind because there's an endless list of things we need to talk about.

Cade surprises me by speaking first. "Gabe. I want to talk about Gabe."

My head swivels toward him, and like always, whenever I hear Gabe's name a pang pierces my chest.

Cade swallows thickly and looks at me and then Dr. Long. "Thea blames herself, and I want her to know that it wasn't her fault. It was *no one's* fault. It was a freak accident."

I exhale a shaky breath and my eyes dart to the ceiling. "Is that true, Thea? Do you think it's your fault?"

I press my hands over my eyes. In the last month I've thought more about Gabe than I have in the eight years since he died. It's too painful, and every time I think of him, it's like someone's stuck a knife in my chest and torn open the muscle and bone, splitting me in half.

"I know it's my fault," I mumble.

"Why is that?" Dr. Long asks. "Why do you *know* it's your fault? Tell me what happened."

I take a deep breath as flashes of that day flit through my mind.

"We were on vacation," I start. "I wanted to go horseback riding so we all went. Gabe didn't really like it, and he kept saying he wanted to get off and not do it. I called him a baby." I press my lips together, fighting the rush of emotions. "His horse got spooked and reared back, and he fell off. He hit his head and bled out. God, there was so much blood." When I close my eyes, it's like I'm back at that day, watching him bleed, and there's nothing I can do and the last thing I ever said to him was that he was a baby and he needed to suck it up.

Dr. Long presses his finger to his lips. "I don't see how this is your fault, Thea. You didn't push him off the horse. It sounds to me like a freak accident."

"If I hadn't begged for us to go, we wouldn't have been there." I pause, gathering my breath. "And you know how they say horses can sense your emotions? I think that horse knew Gabe was scared and it made it antsy, and then ... who knows." I shrug. "All I know is that it was my choice that led us there."

Dr. Long sits back in his chair. "Hmm."

"What?" I ask. "Say it."

"It seems like this could have easily happened some other way. For instance, what if Cade had suggested you go zip-lining, and the gear had failed and something had happened to Gabe that way. Would you expect Cade to blame himself for that?"

"No," I whisper.

"And if Gabe had suggested horseback riding himself and something happened, would you have then blamed Gabe for his own death?"

"No," I whisper again. "I would have said it was an accident."

"Exactly." Dr. Long smiles. "It *was* an accident. Nothing could have prevented it."

"I feel so guilty," I sob.

The warmth of Cade's arms wrap around me. "Please, don't feel guilty," he begs.

"Do you have anything you'd like to say, Lauren?" Dr. Long asks my mom.

My mom wipes a tear from her eye. "I think we've all been carrying a lot of guilt about Gabe. I blamed myself, thinking if I'd left Malcolm we wouldn't have even been there. I hadn't even wanted to go on that vacation, but I had to do whatever he said." She laughs humorlessly. "God," she groans. "I was so stupid to stay with him."

"Stupid," Dr. Long repeats. "Why did you stay with him then?"

She presses her lips together and then sighs. "Fear. I was afraid he'd hurt me if I left. Or hurt the kids more than he already had. I was scared I'd have to share custody and I wouldn't be able to protect them. But as it is, I wasn't able to protect them even when I was there. Again, I was too scared to even stick up for my children, and that makes me as much of a monster as him."

Dr. Long steeples his fingers together. "I'm not saying what you did was right, because there is no right or wrong in your situation, but you did what you had to do to *survive*. All of you have."

"I want him gone from our lives for good," I whisper. I look my mom straight in the eye and say, "I don't want any of us to ever speak to him again. He doesn't deserve the right to be our dad."

She nods. "I'm not going *back*," her voice cracks.

"Promise me," I beg. "*Promise*."

"I promise," she whispers.

This time, when I breathe out, my chest feels lighter than it has in years.

twenty-five
...

xander

THEA and I walk the streets of downtown Denver, hurrying to keep up with the realtor.

Anna Walker might be five foot two and wearing six-inch heels, but the woman mows through the people on the street, leaving Thea and me in her dust.

"How does she move her little legs so fast?" Thea hisses under her breath.

"I have no idea."

Anna stops in front of shiny steel doors. "The first place is on the top floor of this building."

I grab the door and let her and Thea in first.

"Whoa," Thea gasps. "This lobby is gorgeous."

Everything is shiny black and chrome, giving it a modern industrial vibe.

Anna heads straight for the elevators. There are four total, two on each side.

The doors on one slide open and we step inside. Anna swipes a card and then pushes the floor button.

"You have to have a card to operate the elevators," she explains. "So no one from the streets can wander up to your door. Several players on your team live here as well, if you choose this place," she tells me with a smile. "It's one of the more popular buildings. It's central to everything downtown and has excellent views."

She continues to rattle off various facts about the building, but I'm only half listening. Instead, I'm watching Thea for any signs that she's uncomfortable. After her reaction yesterday when I told her about the realtor, I worried I'd pushed her too far. It's not that I'm desperate to move out, but with the added addition of her mom, it has grown crowded in the house. If she doesn't want to move, I'm cool with that, but I do think we need to see what's out there and talk about it.

There's a lot we need to talk about. There are only a few weeks left until Thea's back in school and then my game season is going to start.

The summer's been well and good, but adulthood is about to smack us square in the face and we have a lot to figure out.

The elevator doors slide open and we enter into a long hall.

Anna leads us to the last door on the right. "This is a corner space, so *lots* of windows and natural light."

She unlocks the door and it swings open into a small foyer.

"Door to your left leads to a powder room," she explains, opening that door and turning on the light so we can see. "And this door is a closet." She points to the one on the right.

Thea opens that door and pokes her head inside.

Anna leads us through the archway and it opens into a large living space.

"This would be your family room and dining area, and the kitchen is there to your right, open to this space. It's an excellent place for parties," she says exuberantly like this is a major selling point.

"I like the floors," Thea comments, pointing at the shiny black wood floors. "And the view is nice."

It certainly is. The whole left and back wall are solid windows, overlooking the city and mountains in the distance.

I head to the window and nod. "Yeah, the view is amazing," I agree.

"Bedrooms are this way." Anna claps her hands together to get our attention.

Thea and I follow her down the hall and see another bathroom, guestroom, and master bedroom.

"What do you think?" Anna asks us, leading us back through to the front door.

I shrug and look at Thea, waiting for her to speak first.

"It's nice," Thea hedges, and Anna beams. "But cold. It doesn't feel like a home."

Anna's smile falls but then she quickly goes into sales mode. "You can make it a home, though. *Your* home."

She shrugs and looks at me. "This doesn't feel like our home to me, does it to you?"

I shake my head. "No, it doesn't."

Anna's shoulders slump, but she puts on a winning smile. "That's okay. That's why you have me. We'll keep looking."

We see three more places after that, each one worse than the last.

We part ways with Anna and it's easy to see she's feeling a bit frazzled that we haven't liked anything. But they were all too modern and not us.

Thea and I start down the street, back toward where I parked my truck, but I spot an ice cream shop and pull her inside.

She smiles widely. "Ooh, ice cream."

We each order a cone; I get mint and she gets cookie dough.

There are tables and chairs outside the shop and we take a seat so we can eat our ice cream in peace instead of walking down the street with it.

I lick my ice cream and then ask her, "How'd it go yesterday with the therapist?"

"Good, I think." She shrugs. "We still have lots to talk about, but I think we've made a lot of progress in a short amount of time, so that's good. I think Mom's feeling a lot better. She's looking and acting more like a human being."

I nod and grab a napkin, wiping melted ice cream off my fingers. "Any word from your dad?"

She nods. "He keeps calling my mom, non-stop, apparently. She never answers, but that doesn't stop him from leaving nasty messages. I keep telling her she needs to change her number." She shakes her head. "Cade's caught him driving by the house twice, looking for her, I guess."

My eyes widen in surprise. "Has Cade confronted him?"

She shakes her head. "He never stops. Only gives dirty looks."

"We should get a security system installed."

She nods in agreement. "Yeah, we definitely should. He might be my dad, but I don't trust him. At all." Fear flashes in her eyes.

I don't like seeing that she's afraid. Especially of someone she should be able to love completely. It's a shame she's been robbed of that.

"We talked about Gabe too, at therapy, I mean," she adds.

I nearly fall out of my chair. I can't even remember the last time I've heard someone utter Gabe's name. After he died it became this unwritten rule that we never speak his name.

"Gabe?" I repeat, hating how squeaky my voice sounds, but she's completely surprised me. "How'd that go?"

"Good." She licks her ice cream, her brows furrowed so I know she's thinking deeply about something. "I feel better, since we talked about him yesterday. Like a weight has been lifted from my shoulders. I've blamed myself for what happened for a long time, and Dr. Long is showing me that it isn't my fault. Accidents *do* happen."

I frown. "I didn't know that."

"Know what?" She bites into her cone.

"That you blamed yourself. You never talk about it."

"Exactly. I don't talk about it, because it hurts too much, and I felt like for a long time I could've prevented his death. So, I guess, it became easier to pretend he doesn't exist, which was wrong of me. I don't want to erase his existence from my life." She presses her lips together, staring off into the distance. "I want to go visit his grave. I haven't been in years."

"We can go. Just say when."

"When." She smiles, but it's a little bit sad.

"Right now?" I confirm.

"Well, after we finish our ice cream. We should probably get some flowers too. Aren't you supposed to take flowers to a grave? Maybe a toy too? Gabe loved trains."

"Whatever you want."

"Thank you," she whispers.

"Don't thank me."

"You deserve to be thanked," she argues. "You're pretty awesome."

I chuckle. "No, I just love you."

She grins. "Same difference."

We finish our ice cream, and since we're already downtown, it doesn't take us long to get flowers and a toy train.

We head back to my truck and get in, then drive back toward home, and to the cemetery.

I reach the cemetery gates and park on the street.

I can feel Thea shudder beside me and her hands flex in her lap. Eventually she takes a breath and gets out of the car. I reach into the back and grab the flowers and train before joining her.

She stares at the wrought-iron gates with fear in her eyes. She steels her shoulders, though, and lifts her chin defiantly, refusing to be bowed.

Thea takes a deep, shaky breath and her hand finds mine. I squeeze hers in reassurance.

"When you're ready," I tell her.

She nods and gives me a small smile in thanks for not pushing her.

This is a big deal for her, and she has to go at her own pace.

A few minutes pass, and then she finally takes the first step forward, letting go of my hand.

She's slow at first, but then picks up speed, until she wraps her hands around the gate and pushes it open. I follow behind, so that I don't crowd her. If she needs a moment alone I want her to have it.

Eventually, she stops and turns around, looking at me with panic in her eyes. "I can't remember where it is. *Xander*," her voice cracks on my name, "it's been so long that I don't know where my own brother is buried. How wrong is that?"

"It's okay," I assure her. "We'll find it." I scan the area and point. "I think it might be that way. I remember it being near a big tree."

"Right, right," she chants. "That sounds right."

She heads off the way I pointed. I scan every marker we pass, and up ahead, Thea gasps, dropping to her knees.

"This is it," she breathes.

I hand her the flowers and toys and start to back away, but her hand quickly darts up and grabs onto my jeans. "Stay," she pleads, looking up at me with wide eyes. "I don't want to be alone."

"Are you sure?" I ask.

She nods. "Please." Her voice is no more than a whisper, the pain evident in the way she can barely speak.

"Okay." I clear my throat and sink down onto my knees beside her.

She takes my hand, wrapping her fingers firmly around mine.

I look at her, but she keeps her gaze pinned on the gravestone. It's just a simple stone marker, spelling out Gabe's name, birthday, and the day he died.

"Hi, Gabe," Thea says softly. "I'm sorry I haven't come to visit you in a while. I'm a shitty sister." She wipes a tear away. "I'll be honest, I've tried hard to forget you. It was easier to pretend you didn't exist, but that was wrong of me. *So wrong*. And I'm sorry. I hope you can forgive me. I promise I'm done being that selfish now, and I want to celebrate you in any way I can, every day, so that you're always here with us." She traces her finger over his name. "You were a cool kid, even if you irritated the crap out of me. I really do love you, so much, more than you'll ever know, and I'm sorry I never got to show you. I'm sorry your life was cut short." She begins to sob, and I place my hand on her back, trying to offer her any comfort that I possibly can. "I hope wherever you are up there, that it's beautiful, and that you're always smiling."

She wipes her eyes and places the flowers the way she wants them and then puts the train above his name.

She turns to me, mascara smudged beneath her eyes. "Look at me." She laughs. "I'm a mess."

I chuckle and grasp her neck, pulling her toward me so I can kiss her forehead.

"You're *my* mess."

twenty-six
...

thea

"THE DIVORCE PAPERS ARE HERE," I announce with glee.

Xander's head snaps up from the kitchen table, where he was eating his breakfast, and says, "What?" His eyes are wide with horror and he looks torn between pissed off and hurt. He starts to slide the chair out from the table, no doubt ready to confront me.

I smack him on the head with the padded envelope. "Not for us, you dipshit. For my mom."

"Oh." His body sags with relief and he gives me a boyish smile. "My mistake."

"Now that you mention it, though ..." I start, tossing the envelope on the kitchen counter. I saunter over to him and sink into his lap, straddling him. His hands fall to my thighs.

"The summer is *dangerously* close to over. So, what do you say, Kincaid? You wanna be stuck with me forever? Sure you don't want to take one of those pretty cheerleaders for a ride?"

He shakes his head, his brown eyes darkening. "You. I only want you." He licks his lips. "How about you? You want to explore the party college life? A new guy every weekend?"

"Eh, I did that last year." I wave a hand dismissively. He gives me a look of horror. "The *parties*, not the guys."

He chuckles and leans his forehead against mine so our noses touch. "So, we're going to make this work?"

"Yep." I pop the "p" driving home my point. Growing serious, I add, "I don't want anyone else, and this may not be how I imagined us getting together, but I don't regret it. It's part of our story and that's a beautiful thing."

He cracks a grin and leans back. "Look at you being all poetic."

I shrug and wrinkle my nose. "It happens every once in a blue moon."

Cade's footsteps sound into the room—I know it's him, because he walks like an ogre—and he makes a gagging sound. "Do you guys have to be so lovey-dovey all the time? You're making me sick with all this sweetness."

I stick my tongue out at him. "It's about time you got a taste of your own medicine. Deal with it."

He shudders and opens the refrigerator, scanning the items inside. He grabs the orange juice and pulls it out, taking a swig straight from the bottle.

I give Xander a horrified look. "Remind me to never *ever* drink the orange juice under any circumstances."

Cade closes the bottle and wipes the back of his hand over his mouth. "You might want to avoid the milk too." He winks before heading from the room.

"Ew," I groan, and reach for the only thing on the table that's acceptable for throwing; I toss the orange at him and it hits him square in the back.

He doesn't even flinch.

"I'm going to pretend you didn't do that," he calls back.

I shake my head, laughing under my breath. "Maybe our own place wouldn't be so bad."

Xander smiles. "All you have to do is say the word."

"Are you always going to put the ball in my court?" I ask him.

"Well, yeah, you're the bossy one in the relationship."

I bust out laughing. "Is that so?" He nods, tucking a piece of hair behind my ear. "Eh, I guess you're right," I say after a moment.

He chuckles. "I like that you know what you want. It makes things easier for me. There are no guessing games with you."

I slide off his lap and pick up the envelope. "I better give this to her and make sure it gets signed and sent back. The sooner this divorce is final, the better off we'll all be."

My dad has been driving by more and more frequently, and he hasn't even gotten the divorce papers yet. He'll probably go ape-shit when that happens.

I head upstairs with the envelope, surprised by how heavy

and thick it is. Apparently, you need a lot of big fancy words to end a marriage. I always imagined it would simply read:

THE END

I knock on her bedroom door and she calls out for me to come in.

I hold up the envelope. "They're here." I watch surprise, pain, and finally happiness flicker in her eyes. "All you have to do is sign your name and then you'll be free."

"Free," she repeats, padding across the room and taking the envelope from me. "I'd resigned myself to being stuck in my own personal hell for the rest of my life, it's strange to realize I'm coming out of the hole on the other side."

"Believe it." I give her an encouraging smile. "Now, sign these papers and end it." She opens the package and pulls out the papers. I grab a pen off the desk and hand it to her. "I feel like I should take a picture," I joke. "This feels like a very important moment."

She laughs, signing her name in the designated spots marked off with brightly colored sticky flags. "Maybe we should."

"Hang on," I tell her, and pull my phone from my pocket. "Smile," I tell her.

She does, and then I take another with her holding up the papers proudly.

I think this is the happiest I've ever seen her. In fact, I can't recall a time when I've seen a smile this genuine on her face, and maybe it's strange to say, but I'm proud of her. She left a bad situation and she's gaining back her life. Some might argue that she should've done it sooner, but I don't see it that way. She *did* it and that's what matters, not the when.

"Well," she says once she's done signing everything, "this will all be over soon."

I hug her. "And your life can finally begin."

She hugs me back. "It already began, it just took a detour and I hit a few pot holes along the way, but I'm finally on the right route again." She lets go and holds me by my shoulders, looking me over. "I don't tell you enough, but I'm proud of the woman you've become. You're strong and caring and funny and *amazing*. I'm lucky to be your mom."

I sniffle. "Don't make me cry."

It's too late, though. The tears begin to fall and I'm helpless to stop them, but instead of sad tears, these are happy ones, and they cleanse my soul.

twenty-seven
. . .

xander

PRACTICE KICKED MY ASS. Each one gets more and more intense as we grow closer to the game season. I feel ready to fall over as I head to my truck. All I want to do is get home and fall into bed.

"See you tomorrow," one of the guys calls after me.

I stifle a yawn. "Yeah, see you," I say back, not even paying attention to whom I'm speaking too.

It's late, we practiced all day, and the sun has almost completely set.

I reach my truck and climb inside the cab. I pull my phone from my pocket and check for messages. I smile when I see a text from Thea. I open it and laugh. She sent a picture of herself holding Prue. I text back: **Cute** and seconds later my phone rings, and it's Thea calling. "Are you on your way home?"

"Yeah," I answer, stifling another yawn. "I'm really tired so I think I'm going to head straight to bed."

"Okay ..." There's a long pause on her end, and then, "Are you fucking kidding me?"

"What?" I ask, starting the truck and heading toward the exit.

"My stupid dad is parked out front. Can't he catch a hint and disappear? No one wants him around."

I instantly tense. "Is Cade home?"

"No," she answers. "He took Rae out to dinner. It's just Mom and me."

Should've gotten that security system.

"Whatever you do, don't let him in."

I instinctively know, rather than see, that she rolls her eyes. "Yeah, he might be my sperm donor but I'm not letting him in the house. He can rot and die for all I care. Don't worry, okay? When it comes down to it, the man's a big chicken. He won't do anything."

"Thea—" I warn.

"Iloveyoubye," she slurs and hangs up.

I sigh. "I love you too," I say to the empty line, and toss my now silent phone on the passenger seat.

I try not to worry on my drive home, but it's hard not to. Thea might not think that her father's capable of anything, but I saw the look in his eye that night in the basement, and the man is unstable.

A person who has lost it all is the scariest kind out there, because they have nothing left to lose. There's nothing holding them back from going off the deep end.

When I'm about twenty minutes from the house, I call Cade.

"What? This better be important?" he says when he answers.

"Are you home?"

"*No*, I'm out with Rae. We'll be home soon."

"How soon?"

"What the fuck is going on, Xander? You sound weird."

I'm sweating now. It's like a sixth sense has come over me that something bad has happened or is going to happen, and I'm powerless to stop it.

"Thea called me when I was leaving practice and she said your dad was parked out front. I have a bad feeling about this."

Cade grows silent on the other end. "Shit," he breathes out after a moment. "I'll be home as soon as I can, but I don't think I'll be there for at least thirty minutes."

"Fuck," I curse. "I'll be there before you. Hopefully, I'm freaking out for no reason."

But my gut says I'm not.

"Drive faster," Cade says and hangs up.

His parting words are enough to tell me he doesn't think I'm crazy.

I just have to hope I can get there in time.

twenty-eight
...

thea

"SORRY, Prue, but you're going to have to wait until Daddy gets home to go for your walk. He might be tired, but I'm not going out there with that psycho sitting in his car."

I peer out the window for the hundredth time and sure enough my dad's car is still parked by the curb right by our mailbox. I called the cops, but they were extremely unhelpful and said that as long as he was parked there and not disturbing anything then they couldn't help me. If that isn't insane then I don't know what is.

My mom's footsteps sound on the steps behind me, and I immediately turn away from the window. Too late, though.

"What were you looking at?" she asks, trying to see behind me and out the window.

She looks better than she has in a long time. Her hair is

fuller and bouncy, her face isn't so sallow, and her eyes have a brightness in them now. She looks *happy*.

"Nothing," I say quickly. She gives me a look, so I quickly lie. "The woman across the street is watering her plants."

Apparently, this explanation still isn't good enough, because she pushes around me and moves the curtain to peer out. She immediately hisses and rears back like she's been burned.

"What's he doing here?" she seethes. "Why can't he leave me alone?"

I snort. "Probably because he likes control and he's lost all of it, so he's trying to gain it back."

She lifts her chin defiantly. "I'm going to talk to him."

"No, Mom, please don't." I grab her arm, but she shakes out of my hold. "He's not worth it."

"I want him to sign the damn papers so I can be done with this." She makes a cutting motion through the air with her arms

"That's probably why he's here. I'm sure getting those didn't go over well."

"He needs to let this go." She reaches for the door.

"Mom," I plead again. "Don't."

She doesn't listen, and I let out an exasperated breath.

I step out on the front steps and watch her head to his car. When he sees her, he steps out and stalks forward, looming above her. I always thought he used his height to his advantage in trying to make us feel afraid. It's funny, because

Xander's tall, but he's never made me feel anything but protected.

"I want to talk to you about these. This is fucking bullshit," he spits, holding out the stack of papers. "A *divorce*? We're not getting a divorce. You've made your point, now come back home."

"I'm not coming back home, Malcolm," she says softly, crossing her arms over her chest.

Anger flares in his eyes. Beside me, Prue slips out the half open door and sits next to me.

"Get in the car," he snaps. "We're going *home*." He grabs her arm, his fingers digging into her skin.

"No," she argues. "I told you, I'm not going back. Sign the damn papers," she snaps, fighting back as she tries to wiggle out of his hold.

I move down another step, edging closer and closer.

"Stupid, bitch, you—"

I've heard enough and I stalk over to where they argue by his car.

"Let her go," I say coldly.

His head whips toward me and his nostrils flare. "*You*," he hisses. "You caused this. You ruined everything."

Before I see it coming, he backhands me across the face. My jaw throbs and my skin stings as my eyes water.

My mom lets out a squeak. "Go in the house," she tells me.

"Not without you." I grab her hand. To my dad, I say, "You need to leave."

"Like hell."

Mom and I start back for the house, our feet moving quick enough that we're practically sprinting.

We're not fast enough.

Before we can close the door he's *there*, pushing his way through. I scream when he forces the door open and it rams into my back, shoving me into a wall. I fall to the floor, my head banging against the wall as I go down, and my mom looks at me with a horrified expression.

"Run!" I yell at her. He wants her, not me.

Thankfully, she does, taking off through the kitchen and around the corner. I pray that she can get into a room and barricade herself from him.

He spares me a glance as he takes off after her and that look? It promises a hell of a lot of hurt and pain.

I hear my mom scream, and I wince, but I have to pick myself up off the floor. This isn't the best place to be.

I need to hide.

My whole body hurts from the fall, though, and now there's a ringing in my ears from where he hit me.

My heart pounds like a vicious drum, like it's counting down how many beats I have left and that *terrifies* me. This can't be the end.

I crawl up the steps and drag my body into my bedroom.

"Phone," I mutter. "Where's my phone?"

Downstairs. It's downstairs on the couch.

"No, no, no, no," I chant.

I pick my body up off the floor and lock my door.

From somewhere in the house, I hear a scream again, and a bang that sounds all too much like a gun shot.

I drop to the floor and everything disappears.

xander

Fear holds me prisoner the whole drive and my knuckles are white where I grasp the wheel. When I reach the house, I park half on the driveway and half on the street and immediately jump out of the truck. I was exhausted only an hour ago, but now my body is hard-wired with adrenaline, and I feel like I could take on anything.

It's obvious that my gut instinct of something being wrong was, in fact, right.

Malcolm's car is still here, but he's not.

The tinkling of a dog collar has me looking down and I find Prue staring up at me, and that's *definitely* not normal.

I take off running for the front door, which is *open*.

Each of my heartbeats seems to be chanting *Thea, Thea, Thea* and I know I have to get to her.

I pause, listening to the soft sounds of the house. Everything is eerily silent and that's the scariest part and I hope to God I'm not too late.

I head down the hall and glance in the kitchen. A bowl is knocked on the floor and fruit is scattered around, but other than that, it seems undisturbed.

Further down the hall I go, my steps as quiet as possible.

I poke my head into the bathroom.

Empty.

The wave of panic grows even bigger inside me.

There's only one room left.

The laundry room.

The door is cracked open slightly and I place my hand on the cool wood and push.

It swings open.

I brace myself for what I might find.

Malcolm Montgomery lies on the floor in a pool of blood and Lauren stands above him, the gun shaking in her hands. She raises it, pointing it at me, and I lift my hands in surrender.

"Lauren, it's me, Xander," I say softly. Her face is wet with tears, her hair matted from struggle, and there's blood coming from her arm. I can't tell whether it's a cut or she was shot too.

"Is he dead?" she asks, her voice wobbling.

I bend down and the blood makes a squishing sound when I step in it. I've never been one to be queasy but my stomach is rolling.

I bend down and press my fingers to his neck, feeling for a pulse. "He's still alive for now." I stand back up again and hold my hand out to Lauren. "Give me the gun."

"I'm not going to go to jail, am I?" she sobs. "H-He came after *me*. I-I did what I had to do."

"You're not going to jail," I tell her, even though I have no idea when it comes to this kind of thing. "Did he shoot you?" I point to her bleeding arm.

"I-I don't remember," she sniffles, and finally, *thankfully*, gives me the gun.

"Come on," I tell her, trying to take her hand. "You don't need to stay in here."

"I shouldn't have gone outside," she mumbles, chin shaking as she holds back tears. "He hurt Thea."

My body goes cold. "Where is Thea?"

After walking in on this bloody mess I completely forgot that I haven't found Thea.

"I don't know," she sobs. "She told me to run, so I did. I messed up again. I'm a bad mom. I never do the right thing. I should've protected her. I should've—" She buries her face in her hands and sobs and anything said after that becomes gibberish.

I give up trying to get Lauren out of the laundry room and my sole mission becomes finding Thea.

I drop the gun on the kitchen table and head upstairs, straight to her room.

The door is locked.

"Thea?" I bang on it, shaking the knob.

No sound.

Oh, God.

I feel like I might be sick, but I have to keep my head on straight. I go to my room, and the door is open, so is the one to the bathroom. I head straight through and grab the knob of the one leading into Thea's room. If she was smart she locked this one too.

But the knob twists beneath my hand and I open the door to find Thea lying on the floor.

I rush to her, expecting to find her covered in blood, but she's surprisingly unscathed.

I shake her slightly and her eyes flutter open. She doesn't realize it's me at first and screams, trying to get away from me.

"Thea," I whisper her name, and she recognizes my voice. "Everything's okay."

All the fight goes out of her and she breaks down crying, crawling into my arms and wrapping her arms around me.

"I thought I was going to die," she confesses against my neck and my heart stops.

Hearing the person you love say they thought they were going to die feels like a kick to the gut, coupled with the fact that she could have. I hope she knows I'm not letting her leave my sight ever again.

I wrap my arms around her and inhale the scent of her shampoo.

"I almost lost you," I mumble. Tears burn my eyes. I can't even remember the last time I cried, but if there was any moment that warranted tears it's this one.

"I heard a gunshot," she says. "And I thought this was it. I thought he was coming for me next and I was going to die and kept thinking about how much I love you and how this wasn't enough time and how I do want to have your baby."

I laugh and pull her back so I can see her face. "Faced with death, you think about a baby?"

"Well, yeah. I might not want one now, but someday, and I thought I was going to be robbed of that experience. What happened?"

I shake my head. "All I know is your mom shot your dad, but I don't know the details."

"Wow," she whispers. "I didn't know she had it in her."

"Me either," I agree, brushing my fingers through her hair. I don't want to stop looking at her or touching her. It reminds me that she's here and she's safe.

"I love you," I tell her.

"I love you too." Her eyes fill with tears and she kisses me. Our tears mingle together, but neither of us mind. She's okay —she's *safe*, and that's all that matters.

Downstairs, I hear Cade and I call to him that we're up here.

His feet pound loudly on the steps and then he curses when he tries to open the door and can't.

"Open the door," he yells.

"Go through my room."

I can hear him hurry to my door and I see him through the open bathroom doors.

"Is she okay?" he calls, looking us over for any signs of harm.

I nod. "She's fine."

Thea lifts her head from my shoulder and looks at her brother. "I'm okay, promise. Just shaken. It all happened so fast, but it felt like forever," she mumbles.

"Where's mom?" Cade asks. "Did you check downstairs? Is he still in here?" He suddenly crouches down like he thinks his dad is going to come flying out from somewhere at him.

"Your mom's downstairs. She's pretty frightened. She ... she shot him. I don't know anything other than that."

Cade's lips part with shock. "She *shot* him? My scared, meek little mother *shot* him?"

"Hey, just telling you what I saw."

Cade shakes his head, baffled. "How'd she even get a gun?"

"Dude, I don't know. And we need to call the cops."

"Right." He nods. "I'll do that and I'll check things out with Mom. Was ... was he dead?"

I shake my head. "Not while I was there. There was a lot of blood, so that might've changed."

Cade swallows thickly and nods. "I can't believe this happened," he whispers.

"Believe it," I say. "Men like your dad are capable of anything. Breaking into a house and terrorizing people is nothing to someone like him."

"Yeah, I guess you're right." He shakes his head again and unlocks her door. His boots pound against the stairs as he runs down.

Thea's hands are ice cold where they touch my skin and she begins to shake uncontrollably. I'm pretty sure she's going into shock.

"Thea?" I rub my hands up and down her arms, trying to create some friction. "Are you okay?" She nods woodenly. "You're scaring me," I tell her.

"My head," she mumbles. "My head hurts."

I pull her back and look into her eyes, finding them dilated more than they were a few moments ago.

Sirens sound in the distance.

"The police are coming and paramedics should be with

them. They need to check you out and make sure you're okay."

"I'm just happy you're here," she whispers, trying to burrow into my arms again. I can see her eyes fighting to fall closed.

I take her and push her slightly. "Thea, I need you to stay alert. Okay?"

"I'm trying, but I'm so tired after everything."

"I know you are," I tell her. "But there will be time for sleep later."

I stand up with her in my arms and carry her out of the room as the amount of voices in the house grows. The cops are definitely here and all I can hope is that Malcolm's still alive because he deserves to go to jail and be punished in some way for everything he has done to his family. He shouldn't get to take the easy way out.

A cop stops me when I reach the bottom step. "Is she injured?" he asks.

"She was fine a few minutes ago, but now she's acting funny and says her head hurts."

"There's an ambulance out on the street with a medic. He'll see her."

"Thank you."

I carry her outside and I'm met with several cop cars, two ambulances, a firetruck, and every neighbor on the street.

They all watch the house with looks of shock and horror, as they try to see what I'm doing so they can piece everything together.

Rae comes tumbling out of Cade's Jeep and running over to me, where I stand in shock, unable to take a step.

"Is she okay?" she asks, panic written all over her face.

"I don't know. I need to get her to the paramedics." Suddenly, my feet seem to remember what I'm supposed to be doing and I carry Thea over to one of the ambulances. Rae walks beside me, trying to get a good look at Thea.

"She was fine a few minutes ago, but now she's saying her head hurts and acting funny," I tell the paramedic the same thing I told the cop.

He goes into action, quickly taking her from me and laying her on a stretcher. Her eyes are still open, but she only responds to his questions with one word answers.

Rae's hand touches my arm and I look down at her. "Breathe," she coaxes. "She'll be fine."

We hear the sound of wheels on another stretcher then and both turn to look.

Malcolm is being carted out, and not in a body bag, so I take that as a good sign. They put him in the other ambulance and drive away with a cop car following.

Lauren and two cops come out next, and they steer her over to the ambulance we stand by. Her arm is bleeding worse than it was before and when she sits down and pulls her sleeve up, it looks like she got hit by a bullet.

"We're going to take these two to the hospital for further evaluation," the paramedic tells me. "You all are welcome to follow us after you finish up with the cops."

"I can't leave her," I plead, trying to get around the guy and into the ambulance with Thea.

"I'm sorry, sir," he says. "But you can't go. You need to stay here, but you can come later."

"She's my *wife*," I say like that will make some sort of difference. I'm beginning to panic now, that something is seriously wrong with her and they're not telling me. "Please, you have to let me go. *Please*."

He shakes his head. "I can't. I'm sorry."

"Come on, Xander." Rae tugs on my arm. "Let's finish this up as fast as we can so we can go to the hospital."

I run my fingers through my hair and tug while he closes the doors to the ambulance and I can no longer see Thea.

I watch it pull away, sirens blaring, and I feel sick to my stomach.

The cops ask us to speak to them in the house, away from the prying eyes of the neighbors, and Cade, Rae, and I each give our statements. We explain the whole situation with Malcolm and how he's been lurking around the house in recent weeks.

The cops don't say anything, but based on the looks they exchange, I assume we have a good case against Malcolm. It's about time the man was punished.

We finally finish up with them an hour later and can finally head to the hospital.

Cade insists on driving, since apparently he doesn't trust me to get there and not crash on the way.

Only a month ago we were here when Malcolm hit Thea, and now we're here again because of him. This better be the last fucking time.

Before Cade can park his Jeep, I hop out and run inside. I can't get to Thea fast enough.

I stop in front of the information desk. "Thea Kincaid's room, please," I say, tapping my fingers impatiently on the counter.

"Sorry, there's no one here by that name."

I growl. "Try Thea Montgomery."

She gives me an irritated scowl and types something into the computer. "Room four-twelve." She hands me a badge. "Go through those doors there and take the elevator up to level four."

"Thanks," I mumble, taking off down the hall as Cade and Rae finally make it into the building.

I don't stop to wait for them to get their own badges.

I'm so preoccupied by my thoughts that I run right past the elevators and have to go back. I press the button impatiently, willing the elevators to go faster.

Finally, the doors slide open and I step inside. I press the 4 button and the doors slide closed.

When the elevator stops on the second floor to get people, I nearly lose my mind. I'm wasting precious seconds getting to Thea, and that's not okay with me. I have no idea what's going on and it's coming up on two hours since I've seen her. *Anything* could've happened.

Thankfully, we don't stop again until we reach the fourth floor and we all get out. I turn to my right, scanning the room number directions that hang from the ceiling. I follow them until I find the right room and then I burst inside.

Thea lies in the hospital bed, hooked up to several monitors, and from her eyes I can tell she's been crying. I rush to her side and take her hand, bending to kiss her forehead, each of her cheeks, and finally her lips.

"Are you okay?" I ask, brushing her hair off her forehead so I can see her better.

"They made me wear the stupid gown." She pouts.

Despite my worry, I laugh. "*That's* the first thing you have to say?"

"It's really ugly," she reasons. "And itchy."

I chuckle. "I don't care about the gown, I care about *you*, what did the doctor say? Have you seen one yet? Do I need to get one?" I ramble.

She presses her hand over my mouth, shutting me up.

"They've looked me over thoroughly, I promise." She forces a smile. "I have a minor concussion from the fall, and they said he fractured a bone in my cheek when he slapped me. Didn't even know that was possible," she mutters the last part.

Anger simmers beneath my skin. "How do they fix a bone in your face?"

"They don't," she sighs. "It has to heal on its own. They said they'd give me pain medicine and something for the swelling." She shrugs and her hand flexes around mine.

"I should've been there," I whisper.

"You *were* there," she counters.

I shake my head. "Too late to protect you, though."

"You're not Superman, despite what you seem to think, and from where I'm sitting, I'm *okay*. Beaten and bruised, sure, but I'm alive and that's what matters. You risked your life by coming into the house. You didn't know what was happening and you could've been hurt too." She moves her hand up my chest, brushing her fingers over my cheek. "You're still my hero, though. You always have been, and you always will be."

I close my eyes and grab her fingers that linger by my cheek and bring them to my lips, kissing each of her fingers.

"All of this is so crazy," I tell her. "I feel like none of it would have happened if we hadn't gotten married. You wouldn't be lying right here, right now, hurt."

She shakes her head. "That might be true, but I don't regret it."

"You don't?"

"No." She smiles. "Sure, things didn't go perfectly, but life never is perfect. Don't get me wrong, I was completely against this whole marriage thing, but not anymore. Having you as my husband isn't so bad. In fact, it's pretty great. You bring me McFlurrys. What's not to love?"

I laugh heartily. "McFlurrys, huh? That's all you love me for?"

"I love you for a million reasons, that's just one."

I grin. "Does this mean you'll marry me for real? In front of all our friends and family?"

She smiles back, her eyes shining with happiness and not tears this time. "Yeah, I'm game for that."

I don't know what the future holds for us, and knowing us, the road is bound to be rocky, but with my partner in crime by my side, something tells me it's going to be the best time of my life.

epilogue

...

thea

ONE MONTH *Later*

Something I've learned in the last four months is how quickly things can change. At the start of the summer, I believed it would be like any other summer. Boring and over all too soon.

Well, it certainly did end too soon, but it was anything but boring.

I thought my accidental Vegas marriage would be the craziest thing to happen. Little did I know that it would be the catalyst for much bigger things, like the implosion of my parent's marriage, and finally bringing justice to our family.

The break-in and attempted murder—since it turns out my dad was the one with the gun and my mom managed to wrestle it away from him after he grazed her with a bullet—ended up on almost every news station. It was weird seeing us on TV for something like that and the attention has been too much to bear at times, but it's finally dying down, at least for most of us. Not Cade, though. After the news that broke earlier in the summer, coupled with this, he's been roped into interview after interview to speak about the abuse. He doesn't like it, and he could say no, but he knows that his voice could help someone else out there and so he's finally willing to talk about it. He won't admit it, but I think it's helping him heal to put it out there.

Now that all the darkness is behind us, I can finally focus on the good in my life.

Like, for starters, I finally figured out what I want to do with my life.

I want to help kids like Cade and me and women like my mom. I want to help someone in a way we didn't have. I want to make a difference.

When I told Xander he grinned from ear to ear, kissed me, and told me he couldn't have thought of anything more perfect for me to do.

I feel good now, finally having a purpose.

We talked some more about moving out, especially with some of the unpleasant memories that house now holds, but in the end we decided to stay for the time being while I finish school and since Xander will be gone a lot. It'll be nice to not be alone and have my brother, mom, and Rae around. There's already been a lot of change lately, and for now, letting this stay the same, sounds pretty good to the both of us.

Xander's first NFL game is at the end of the month, and it's out of town, but we're all going to surprise him and fly out there. I know he's going to do amazing. He's been working hard, giving it his all, and all the while being there for me while I dealt with everything.

Now, it's time for me to make good on my promise and marry the boy for real.

No seedy wedding chapel.

No half-drunken slurred vows.

No wedding night I can't remember.

We're doing this right this time, with our friends and family, a dress, and the whole shebang.

I stare at my reflection in the mirror. My hair curls halfway down my back in soft waves and my makeup is light, and simple. But my dress?

That's anything but simple.

I wanted something unique and different. Something daring and *me*.

I was lucky to find something off the rack on short notice and it was like it was made especially for me.

The color is a creamy off-white with a floral lace design. It has spaghetti straps and the bodice is fitted before flaring out at the hips. The back of the dress boasts scallop detailing as does the front where the dress cups my breasts. My mom and Xander's mom tried to talk me into something more traditional—you know, *white*—but it isn't me, and this is, so I ignored their pleas for me to change my mind.

"Ready?" Rae asks.

I turn away from the mirror and smile at her. She looks gorgeous in her turquoise bridesmaid dress with her dark brown hair braided to the side.

I nod. "Yeah, I'm ready."

Never thought I'd be saying those words in regard to marriage.

But technically, I'm already married, and it's actually pretty great.

Rae hands me my bouquet of pink peonies and loops her arm through mine.

Out in the hall we meet Cade. His lips part when he sees me and he clears his throat, clearly overcome with emotion.

"You look beautiful," he tells me.

"Thanks." I smile up at my big brother. He offers me his elbow and I grab onto it.

Since my dad obviously won't be walking me down the aisle—you know, since he's rotting away in prison and attempted to kill us—I asked Cade.

"All right, that's my cue." Rae smiles and kisses my cheek and then Cade's before running off to where she'll exit into the Kincaid's backyard.

We could've gotten re-married at any number of places, but it only made sense to do it here. The Kincaid's might live in a different house now, but so many of our adventures took place in their backyard growing up, so it only made sense to start this adventure here.

"I'm proud of you," Cade says, as we start walking toward the open French doors.

"For what?" I look up at him.

He shrugs. "For never giving up on what you believe in and always fighting."

I laugh. "Funny, you used to tell me I was too stubborn for my own good."

He chuckles. "Yeah, well, we all grow up and see things differently."

"That we do," I agree.

The music changes and I hear the shuffling of everyone standing and my heart skips a beat.

This is happening.

This is really happening.

Cade leads me out the door and my breath catches. It's the first time I'm seeing the backyard. I handed over the reins on decorating to our moms—all I cared about was my dress—and they did a beautiful job.

The aisle is covered in white petals and above us is a canopy with more flowers hanging down and little lights twinkling. It looks like a magical fairy wonderland.

At the end of the aisle is a whole wall of flowers in all shades of pale pink and white and in front of them stands Xander with Prue by his side.

He stands with his hands clasped in front of him and he looks like a model in his fitted navy suit and tie. His eyes rake over my body and then stop when they meet mine. I see tears shimmer in his eyes, and he smiles widely as we stop in front of him. Xander takes my hand. Cade kisses my cheek, claps Xander on the shoulder, and then stands to the side of him.

Rae is to the side of me and I hand her my bouquet so I can give Xander both my hands.

I don't know why I feel nervous, but I'm suddenly sweating bullets.

We repeat our vows one after the other and I manage not to stumble over my own name, so *score*.

Then I hear the words, "You may kiss your bride."

Xander mutters, "It's about damn time."

I laugh as he takes my face between his large hands and kisses me. His hands descend to my back and he dips me down, deepening the kiss, as our family and friends whistle and catcall.

I smile against his lips as he pulls away. "We did it for real."

"It was always real," he says with a smile, touching his fingers tenderly to my cheek. He pulls me against him so my body is flush with his despite my poofy dress. He lowers his head, pressing his forehead to mine. "Ready?" he asks.

"Ready," I concur.

Life can throw whatever it wants at us, but we'll be ready, and we'll handle it together, because we're more than husband and wife, we're best friends, and that's everything.

www.ingramcontent.com/pod-product-compliance
Lightning Source LLC
LaVergne TN
LVHW030313070526
838199LV00069B/6465